Dust Spells

Dust Spells

ANDREA LYNN

CamCat Publishing, LLC
Fort Collins, Colorado 80524
camcatpublishing.com

Hardcover ISBN 9780744308464
Paperback ISBN 9780744308488
Large-Print Paperback ISBN 9780744308532
eBook ISBN 9780744308518
Audiobook ISBN 9780744308556

Library of Congress Control Number: 2023945537

Book and cover design by Maryann Appel
Interior artwork by Sage Vandenberg, Sylverarts

5 3 1 2 4

To my cheerleader, hero, and forever friend–my sister.

CHAPTER

Stella would have thought the sky was a harbinger of the apocalypse if her world hadn't already ended. The early morning light was sickly yellow and filthy as always. The clear, blue skies and lush, green fields of five years ago seemed a dream. It was hard to imagine her home had ever been anything but diseased and covered in dust, though she knew it had. She knew a lot of things she didn't want to know, like how the entire world could be upended overnight, forever changing not only her life but the lives of millions, and none of them had the power to change it back again. Not ever.

Stella pulled her family's Chevrolet pickup into Jane's driveway and put it in park. When she cut the ignition, the engine sighed, as if as tired as she was.

Don't you die on me now, she thought. *You're the last luxury we have.*

A harsh, discordant clanging met her ears when she stepped outside. Jane's neighbor, a widow named Mrs. Woodrow, had an ungodly number of wind chimes on her already cluttered porch. Stella cursed her silently as she hurried up Jane's drive. Why have even *one* wind chime in a place where the grimy, choking wind never let up? Where dust storms called Black Blizzards rose up and blotted out the sky, raining debris on cars and buildings, tearing through the cracks in the most well-sealed homes, and mutilating the Great Plains as thoroughly as they had mutilated Stella's life forever.

Stella opened Jane's back door and let herself in. She closed it behind her, muting the chimes, but then heard the equally irritating sound of a baby's cry.

"Morning, Stella," Jane called, rushing into the kitchen with Jasper in her arms. She sat down at the table and opened her blouse, baring her right breast. "Sorry. I meant to feed him before you got here, but he wasn't hungry."

"Not a problem," Stella replied, grateful no writhing parasite depended on her for its sustenance. She had too many people dependent on her as it was. "Is everything ready?"

"Yes," Jane said as Jasper found her nipple and quieted. "I filled the jars last night."

Grateful that part was already done, Stella turned and crept down the rickety stairs to Jane's basement. When she passed the large copper still, she fought the urge to blow it a kiss.

When Jane's parents died, they left her two blessings: a house with a paid-off mortgage and her father's old moonshine still. President Roosevelt had repealed prohibition the previous year, but that didn't matter in Kansas, which had been dry since the last century, and Stella—who almost never prayed—prayed it would stay that way. With liquor outlawed, she and Jane could make fifty cents a pint.

The idea had been Stella's. Though Jane was four years older, the two of them had been friends since childhood. Jane married right out of high school, but her dirtbag husband abandoned her and Jasper after losing his job last winter. Jane made ends meet by taking in laundry, but when Stella remembered Jane's father's old still, she suggested they go into business. Jane brewed the moonshine, and Stella delivered it, hidden among the laundry. Her heart thumped as she crouched down and picked up the crate. Sixteen beautiful jars. She held the equivalent of eight dollars in her hands. After three months, she and Jane had twelve consistent clients. And the demand was growing. Their only competition was the local drug store where the owner sold malt whiskey smuggled in from Colorado, but most people couldn't afford it. Jane's moonshine wasn't cheap, but it wasn't so expensive it would break the average person. If they had a bigger still, or more people to help, Stella knew they could make their little sideline a real business.

But they didn't. And Stella knew enough to be grateful for what she did have. She started up the stairs, holding the crate that would bring her the only thing in the world that was hers alone. The thing that, once a week, brought her closer to her dreams.

Jane had finished feeding Jasper by the time Stella finished loading the crate and laundry into her truck. When Stella walked back inside, Jane was burping him over her shoulder.

"Do you ever want to murder Mrs. Woodrow?" Stella asked, closing the door behind her.

Jane laughed. "I hardly notice those wind chimes anymore."

"How? They're maddening."

"She thinks they ward off evil spirits."

"They're about to ward off my sanity."

Jane laughed again, and Stella wiped her brow.

"How are you on ingredients?" Stella asked.

"I have plenty of corn and yeast, but I'm running low on sugar."

"I'll pick some up." She smoothed her hair and checked to make sure the patches she'd sewn beneath the worn spots on her dress were well-concealed. "How do I look?"

Jane smiled, her dimples showing. "Like a sweet eighteen-year-old girl."

"Wash your mouth out with soap. There is nothing sweet about me."

The last thing Stella wanted to be was sweet. Greta Garbo and Jean Harlow weren't sweet. They were vixens wrapped in diamonds and furs who consumed men like champagne. Jane was a sweet girl.

Sweet girls ended up alone with a baby.

"But sweet girls aren't bootleggers," Jane countered. "They'll never suspect."

"True," Stella agreed. "I'll be back with some sweet, sweet dough."

THE SUN HAD BARELY RISEN, but the inside of the truck already felt like an oven by the time Stella reached her first stop. She dabbed at her forehead with a handkerchief and checked her lipstick in the rearview mirror. Just because she lived in a dusty, prairie town didn't mean she had to look like it. The money she would earn today could buy her powder, blush, mascara, and maybe even a new dress, but it was going straight into her Folger's can in the attic, so lipstick alone had to do. The crimson stain was perfect, so she stepped out of the truck.

Her first client was a man named Lewis Johnston, who lived with his mother and preferred to take his deliveries at work. Stella always made his stop first because he worked at the train station, and the train-hopping bums who littered the place were mostly asleep in the morning. They camped in the hobo "jungle" in the nearby woods, and some of them liked to whistle and yell at the women who walked by.

That morning, the coast seemed clear as Stella clipped up the drive to the station, holding Lewis's shirts with the mason jar between the folds. But then she heard shouts, and two men tumbled out from between the trees. The first one fell onto his back, and the second leapt on top of him and punched him square in the face. Stella shrieked and jumped back. With a savage groan, the first man shoved the other man off and scrambled back to his feet. Then, he gripped the man's shoulder and swung his fist deep into his stomach. The second man doubled over, and the first seized his head and drove it down into his knee. Blood burst from his nose and splattered the pavement as well as the first man's pants. He crumpled to the ground, and the first man spat on him.

"You bastards always make the same mistake," he sneered. "You go for the face."

"What's going on here?"

Both men looked in Stella's direction. She blinked and spun around. A police officer was jogging up the drive. She heard a scuffle and turned back around to see both men bolting toward the trees; the first moving like lightning, and the second stumbling and clutching his stomach.

"That's right, get out of here," the cop yelled, and Stella turned back to face him. He nodded and tipped his hat. "You okay, Miss?"

Stella stared at him, suddenly very aware of the mason jar in her arms.

"Oh, yes. They didn't hurt me. They were fighting each other."

"Dirty bums," the cop grumbled. "Why can't they kill each other out in that jungle, away from decent folks?"

Stella nodded and started back toward the station.

"What's a young lady like you doing here so early anyway?"

She stopped. After closing her eyes and taking a deep breath, she turned back around.

"I'm delivering laundry. To a man who works at the station."

The cop stepped closer, glancing down at the shirts. "He doesn't want it delivered to his house?"

He looked back up, but before he met her gaze, his eyes lingered on a few other places. Her crimson lips, her dark curls, the swell of her breasts beneath her dress.

Men.

"I guess not," Stella said with a laugh. She stepped closer, glad she'd taken the time to dab on a bit of her dwindling reserve of perfume. "You men can be so silly sometimes. I never know what you're thinking."

He smiled sheepishly and blushed. "I suppose we can be. Well, go ahead. I'll make sure no more of these hobos get in your way."

"Thank you, so much," Stella said, flashing a smile. Then she turned and walked up the drive, thinking Jean Harlow couldn't have done any better.

OVER THE NEXT HOUR, Stella made the rest of her deliveries. Not all were for moonshine; some were just laundry. When she finished, however, she cursed herself. She needed to get more sugar for Jane, but the general store was all the way by the train station. She should have gotten it after her first delivery. Now, she would have to go all the way back and risk arriving home late, running behind on her chores, and disappointing her Aunt Elsa. She sped to the store and used two of the eight dollars she'd made to buy fifty pounds of sugar. Then, she hoisted the two twenty-five-pound sacks over each of her shoulders and trudged out into the heat.

"That's a mighty amount of sugar."

She turned around and stifled a gasp. The man who'd beaten up and spit on the other man at the train station was leaning against the wall. He was more of a boy than a man, she now saw. Just a year or two older than she was. His lower lip had been split by the blow he'd taken to the face, and he was picking small chunks from a stale loaf of bread, eating carefully. There was a bakery next door, and Stella guessed the loaf had been thrown out with last night's trash. Her stomach turned, and she flopped the sacks onto the bed of her truck.

"What's it to you?"

"Just wondering if you might have the same amount of yeast and corn somewhere."

She froze and then spun back to face him. He read the guilty look on her face and grinned.

"That's what I thought."

She stared at him. Besides the split lip, he had a yellowing bruise beneath one eye and a scar through his other eyebrow. His skin and clothes were filthy, and his hair was a rumpled mess beneath his flat cap. Her gaze slid down to the knee of his pants, stained with the other man's blood. He followed her gaze, popped a piece of bread into his mouth, and looked back up.

"Don't worry," he said as he chewed, "I'd never hit a woman. You could come at me with a knife, and I'd just let you stab me, sugar."

She flushed, determined not to let him know she was afraid. "How thoughtful. If you'll excuse me."

"Hold on." He stood up from the wall and stepped into the sunlight. "I'm interested in becoming a customer."

He had a backwoods, southern accent. Maybe Texas or Louisiana. Some desolate, nothing place even dustier than Kansas.

"I don't know what you're talking about."

"Come on, now. No girl in worn-out out heels is gonna spend that much money on sugar unless she expects some kind of return. And I watched you work that lawman this morning. Saw the fear on your face when he looked at those shirts. Saw the way you turned on the charm to fool him. Pretty impressive."

Stella's lips parted. Even the man who'd sold her the sugar hadn't questioned why she'd bought it. He was just happy to make the sale. This boy talked like a hick, but he was smart. She studied his face. It was pleasant. Beneath the dirt and scars anyway.

But then she remembered his rude remark about her shoes.

"You couldn't afford it."

She purposefully raked her eyes over his filthy clothes as she said it. But his grin only curled, and he stepped closer.

"Ain't you heard, sugar? We got a depression on. People trade and barter for things all the time."

"Stop calling me that. And you have nothing I want."

He placed another chunk of bread in his mouth and looked her over. "We've only just met." He lifted his gaze. "You don't know what I got to offer."

She flushed again. "You're disgusting."

"Disgusting?" He cocked his head to the side. "My, what dirty thoughts you've got in that pretty head of yours."

Feeling a sudden kinship with the man who'd punched him in the face, she spat, "Don't flatter yourself," and turned away, tossing her curls.

"I see those patches in your skirt, sugar," he called. "Don't pretend you're better than me."

"At least I've taken a bath this century."

She didn't look back when she said it, but she caught sight of his face in her peripheral vision when she opened the door to the truck. His smile was gone. Guilt rose in her throat, but she swallowed it, got in her truck, and drove away.

She sped toward Jane's house, now certain she would be facing Aunt Elsa's wrath when she arrived home. There were six dollars in her pocket, three of which were hers, but she found herself too shaken to enjoy their comforting presence.

Because, the boy had been right. Her family was barely hanging on by a thread, and though they weren't sleeping in hobo jungles and fishing stale bread out of the garbage, that could change at any moment.

Nothing was certain. No one was safe.

CHAPTER 2

Stella parked outside her family's three-story Victorian house, its former cheerful robin's egg blue exterior now gray and peeling. She'd taken its luxury for granted until four years ago, because—while she still lived there—it wasn't *her* house anymore.

For the first few months following the stock market crash, Stella's family remained one of the most comfortable in Dodge City. But as fewer and fewer people could afford cars, her father's dealership suffered, especially when the dust storms arrived to terrorize the farmland. It was 1930 when Stella's world imploded.

The dealership went bankrupt, her mother died, her father left to search for work in Wichita, her Aunt Elsa turned their home into a boarding house to make ends meet, and Stella and her sisters moved into the attic to help her run it. The creaking of the old walls against the wind was the only sound Stella heard when she crept inside which told her the boarders had already left for work.

Dammit.

She trudged to the kitchen. When she stepped inside, her older sister, Lavinia, spoke without looking up from the dishes.

"Aunt Elsa's stripping the beds. And yes, she's mad."

Stella groaned, pulled an apron from one of the pegs near the door, and joined her at the sink.

"I would have made it back in time, but I was accosted by a vagrant."

Lavinia's head shot up, her coffee brown eyes bulging. "What?"

"Well, not exactly *accosted*," Stella clarified. "He tried to get me to sell him some moonshine. I did see him beat up another bum by the station earlier, though."

Lavinia let out a breath and returned to the dishes. "You shouldn't go down there alone. It isn't safe."

"Don't worry. There was a cop who put a stop to it before anyone got killed."

Lavinia's head shot up again, which, this time, had been Stella's intention.

"It was fine," Stella assured her, laughing as she took the dripping bowl from her hands and dried it off with a towel. "He didn't suspect a thing."

"You take too many risks," Lavinia scolded her, picking up the next bowl.

And you don't take enough, Stella thought as she watched her scrape the oatmeal out from the bowl. Lavinia's hair was as curly as Stella's, but instead of a black so black it was almost blue, her hair was a vibrant, apple red. She wore it the same way as Stella, but for a different reason. Stella cut her curls in a chin-length bob because that's how Myrna Loy wore her hair in *Penthouse*, but Lavinia did it so she could hide her face more easily.

Over the last three years, Stella had grown used to the jagged scars that covered the left side of Lavinia's face: a patchwork of puckered, white gashes that clawed their way from beneath her left eye to the hinge of her jaw, as if she were a porcelain doll whose left side had been smashed and pasted back together by a hasty, trembling hand. Lavinia had always been the most reserved of the Fischer girls, but since receiving the scars, she'd withdrawn even more, rarely leaving the house or looking strangers in the eye.

Stella wasn't sure how she would have reacted if it had happened to her, which it could have just as easily. Perhaps, she would have withdrawn as well, but she still wished her sister wouldn't act as if her life was over at twenty-two, resigned to working at the Fischer boarding house the rest of her life, the husband and children she desperately longed for forever out of reach. To Stella, Lavinia was still beautiful, as well as good, loyal, and hardworking. She was nearly as bright as their younger sister, Mattie, and as nurturing and resilient as their mother had been. Not what Stella sometimes suspected she thought she was.

Which was worthless.

"Jane says, 'hello,'" Stella said as Lavinia handed her the next bowl. Jane hadn't, but she would have if they'd had more time to talk. She and Lavinia were the same age and had been good friends in school. "You should visit her sometime."

Lavinia looked away. "I know. It's just hard to find the time. Things being the way they are . . ." She paused, glanced up from the sink, and lowered her voice. "And I think things are even worse than Aunt Elsa is letting on. I saw the water bill in her room this morning. It's due tomorrow, and I don't think we have enough. Daddy hasn't sent money in over a month. And I know Aunt Elsa paid for Mrs. Kelly's last doctor visit."

Stella gaped at her. Mrs. Kelly, one of their boarders, was an older woman with lung trouble, exacerbated by the dust. Dust pneumonia, they called it. Mrs. Kelly slept in a gas mask at night, and her room, which used to be Stella's, always smelled of Vicks VapoRub. Stella pitied the woman, but still wished Aunt Elsa would control her damn bleeding heart.

"You don't think they'll turn off our water?" Stella whispered. "The boarders—they'd leave, and we'd—"

"Stella Marie Fischer."

Stella looked up to see Aunt Elsa hurrying in with a basket of sheets. She plopped it on the floor and slammed her hands on her hips.

"Aunt Elsa, I'm sorry—"

"When I said you could help Jane with her laundry business, you promised it wouldn't interfere with your duties here. Mattie had to help Lavinia and I make breakfast this morning, and now she's behind on weeding the garden, and I'm behind on the laundry."

"I know. I'm sorry."

"I don't understand why Jane needs the laundry delivered anyway," Aunt Elsa went on. "Why can't her clients come to her place and pick it up themselves?"

Lavinia met Stella's gaze and then turned to the sink to hide her face. At least she was aware of how bad she was at concealing things.

"She can charge more money if she delivers," Stella replied calmly. "But of course, she can't do it herself. Not with Jasper."

As she'd expected, mentioning the baby deflated Aunt Elsa's anger. Her face lit up, and she pressed her hand to her heart. She looked more like her brother, Stella's father, when she smiled, her emerald green eyes crinkling at the corners.

"How is Jasper? He must be getting so big."

"He's got more hair," Stella said with a smile. "Silvery blond, like Jane's. Not dirty blond like that low-life Jacob Ryan's."

The three of them instantly spat at the mention of Jane's husband, a habit they'd picked up from Stella's late grandmother, Aunt Elsa's mother.

"Well, don't be late again," Aunt Elsa said, retrieving the basket of sheets. "Lavinia can finish the dishes. You do the dusting, then beat out the front rug. Oh, and feed the chickens. I don't think Mattie has done that yet."

Stella dried her hands on her apron and hung it back up on the wall. She left the kitchen, walked up the stairs to the third floor, wrenched down the attic ladder, and climbed.

The stuffy, cramped space was hers and her sisters' bedroom now. They shared a single mattress in the middle, but each of them had a section along the wall that was their own. In one corner, Mattie stored her books, their father's Kodak camera, and a framed picture of their late grandmother. Lavinia's romance novels, old porcelain doll, and empty jewelry box sat nearby. Stella walked to her own corner, which contained her lipstick, magazine cutouts of her favorite movie stars, and her precious Folger's can. She took the three dollars from her pocket and slid them reverently inside, gazing up at Greta Garbo like she was the Virgin Mary.

One day soon she would have enough money to get her to Hollywood and out of this dusty town. Her sisters knew of her plan—as well as the sideline she'd created to make it happen—but not her father or Aunt Elsa. It would break their hearts, she knew, but she had no choice. Lavinia had no desire to leave, and Mattie was smart enough to get a scholarship to Kansas University or Kansas State, which both accepted women, but there was nothing for Stella in Kansas. All she had was her looks, and they would get her nothing in Dodge but marriage, children, and an endless cycle of hard work and misery. Here, she would always remain as she was—a poor, powerless girl who could be blown away and forgotten. But in a big city, or up on the silver screen, she could be someone. Someone high above the chaotic struggle of poverty. Someone respected, admired, and in control of her destiny. Money could make her matter, could make people see her as someone *worth* something, and every dollar she made brought her closer to that dream.

She slid off her dress and put on a white, cotton shirt and overalls, trading her heels for a pair of old, leather boots. Running a boarding house was just like running a hotel. Everything had to be cleaned while the tenants were out, and the constant filth in the air made dusting a daily activity. Stella ran wet rags over the bannisters, stairs, and floors. Then, she made her way through the boarders' rooms, dusting their shelves. First, her parents' former room, where Aunt Elsa now slept, then Lavinia's, where an old nurse and a young hairdresser now lived, Stella's, where Mrs. Kelly and a railroad telegrapher resided, and Mattie's, which now housed a hardware store clerk and a musician.

Once Stella finished dusting, she grabbed the bucket of chicken feed and trudged to the backyard. After feeding the squawking creatures, she started back inside the house, but then she caught sight of Mattie, kneeling in the vegetable garden. She was picking tomatoes, but as she plucked them, she was bent down over the vines and bowing her head, murmuring something.

"Are you kidding me?" Stella asked, approaching her younger sister. "Please, tell me you didn't take that bunk seriously."

Mattie barely spared her a glance. "You know what Puri Daj would say if she heard you call it bunk."

"How does someone who reads the books you read and gets the grades you get still believe in her grandmother's fairy tales?"

"Stories aren't just stories," Mattie replied. "They contain wisdom gleaned by our ancestors over the ages. That's why they endure." She looked up at Stella, smirking and tossing her braid back over her shoulder. "If *you* read a book every now and then, you'd know that."

"I don't have time for books. Or for talking to plants to make them grow."

"You get out what you put in," Mattie said. "It makes perfect, logical sense. This garden gives because it was given to. Because it was treated with respect. You can't deny that."

Of all of them, Mattie took after their late grandmother the most. She was small with Stella's black hair and Lavinia's coffee brown eyes. She was only sixteen but had acted like an adult since infancy. Partly because of her intellect—she'd learned to read by the time she was three—but partly because of their grandmother's insistence she was "blessed." Supposedly, she possessed a "second sight," but Stella knew it was nothing more than superstitious garbage. Mattie hadn't foreseen the Depression, their mother's death, Lavinia's accident, or anything else that mattered.

Still, Mattie did sometimes seem to know what other people were thinking. And the garden she tended was the only one on the block that consistently thrived, as if it were immune to dust and drought.

But Stella wouldn't give her the satisfaction of agreeing.

"You're a nut, you know that?"

"Sticks and stones."

Stella started back toward the house, but then paused. "Did Lavinia tell you about the water bill?"

Mattie looked up, her smirk gone. "Yes."

"How short do you think we are?"

"Stella, I told you to beat the front rug," Aunt Elsa called as she and Lavinia emerged with a basket of clean, wet sheets and walked to the clothesline.

"I'll get it now."

She walked back inside, set the chicken feed down, and plodded to the front hall. Before she bent down and rolled up the rug, however, she glanced at the coatrack.

Her father's nicest hat was still there, as if waiting for him. She stood up, picked it up from the rack, and sniffed it. It smelled like his hair: a hint of sweat and the pomade he'd used, back when they could afford it. An ache spread through her chest, and she placed the hat back on the rack.

Her hand drifted up, grasping the ghost of a necklace that wasn't there. When she and her sisters played dress-up as children or wanted to look like grown-ups at the square dances, county fairs, and town festivals that had blown away with the rest of their former lives four years ago, their mother would let them each wear a piece of her jewelry. They'd felt like princesses in the gifts their father had given their mother on their first, fifth, and tenth anniversaries—Lavinia in the pearl earrings that gleamed like her hair, Stella in the emerald necklace that matched her eyes, and Mattie in the opal ring she wore on her thumb so it wouldn't fall off her tiny fingers.

Perhaps, after the world changed, her mother would have been forced to sell the treasures, but she never had the chance. Stella could smell her father's scent on his hat every day, and—God willing—in the flesh when he came home, but she would never smell her mother's lavender-powdered skin again, never hear her chirping laughter, never see her eyes well up with love, never taste her strawberry icebox cake, never touch her silky manicured hand, and she and her sisters would never wear her jewelry again, because it was gone forever, just like her.

Stella blinked back tears and bent down to roll up the rug. There was no use in dwelling on her mother or any part of her old, irretrievable life. Only the future remained, and she would flee this barren wasteland and make her dreams come true or die trying.

She heaved the rug up over her shoulder, grabbed a broom from against the wall, and headed back to the porch. But as she neared the door, she heard a man's voice.

"You see, I saw the cat on your mailbox."

Stella groaned. That damned cat. A hobo had drawn it on their mailbox earlier that spring. Apparently, it was a symbol that a kind woman lived in the house, and Aunt Elsa often traded work for food with those in need. Stella admired Aunt Elsa's kindness but couldn't help the panicked feeling that rose every time a tramp came by to deplete her family of their limited resources.

"Goodness, honey," said Aunt Elsa. "What happened to your face?"

Stella stiffened. It couldn't be. She wasn't *that* unlucky. Gripping the rug, she pushed open the screen door and stepped onto the porch.

He was standing just beyond the faded, white picket fence, his cap in his hands. When the screen door slammed shut behind her, he looked up, and his eyes widened.

Then he smiled, as though stifling a laugh.

"Just a little jungle disagreement, ma'am," he said, turning back to Aunt Elsa and touching his lip.

"You poor thing," Aunt Elsa said. "What's your name?"

"Lloyd, ma'am. Lloyd McCormick. You got a nice crop of tomatoes there. And I noticed your string beans are ready to be picked as well. I'd be happy to help you out in exchange for a bite to eat."

"Of course. Come on in."

He slid his cap back on and stepped through the fence's swinging door. As he passed, he tipped his hat toward Stella. "Pleasure to see you again."

Stella's blood froze in the heat. Lavinia's head shot up from behind the sheet she was pinning to the clothesline. Mattie looked up from the plants, her eyes darting between the two of them. Aunt Elsa, who had started up the stairs, glanced back and then turned to Stella.

"You two have met?"

"This morning," Stella said quickly. "When I was delivering Jane's laundry."

She met Lloyd's gaze, her eyes pleading. Aunt Elsa didn't know, *couldn't* know, about the moonshine. If she did, she'd put a stop to it, and Stella's dreams would be crushed.

"That's right, ma'am," he replied with a smile, holding Stella's gaze. "Your daughter here was kind enough to welcome me to town."

"These are my nieces," Aunt Elsa corrected him. She looked less offended that he'd assumed she was old enough to be Lavinia's mother—though at thirty-eight, she technically was—and more stunned that Stella had welcomed anyone anywhere. She turned to Stella, gaping but pleased. "It's nice to know you're finally learning to show some charity, Stella." She continued up the steps, past Stella, and opened the screen door. "I'm going to start the next load of laundry. Lavinia, come down and help me once you've finished pinning the sheets. Lloyd, just the tomatoes and string beans. Nothing else is ready to be picked. And

Stella—" She met Stella's gaze, silently telling her to keep an eye on the stranger. Stella nodded, though annoyed at yet another chore heaped onto her plate. Once Aunt Elsa hurried into the house, Stella looked at Lloyd. She knew she should thank him for keeping her secret, so she opened her mouth to do so.

"Those are some high-class overalls, sugar."

She snapped her mouth shut again, glared at him, and stomped to the opposite clothesline.

"Stella, is this— Is he the—"

Lavinia closed her mouth as well when Lloyd turned to look her way. She flushed and bent down over the sheets, shielding her scars with her hair.

"Yes," Stella replied, flopping the rug over the clothesline adjacent to Lavinia's. "He's the one who made me late."

Mattie stood up, brushed the dirt off her hands, and stuck one out toward Lloyd. "I'm Mattie, and that's Lavinia." She grinned. "And I would love to hear how you really met Stella."

"I saw her buying a heap of sugar," he replied, returning the smile and shaking her hand. "I guessed what it was for. But your sister was less than interested in selling me her product."

"The key word is 'selling,'" Stella said, smacking the broom against the rug. A bigger cloud of dust than she had anticipated erupted, and she coughed. Mattie laughed, and Lloyd smirked.

"I told you, sugar. The barter system is how it's done nowadays."

He and Mattie sat down a few feet away from the clotheslines, and he tugged a string bean from its stalk.

"I figured there must be some reason you called her 'sugar,'" Mattie said. "Lord knows she isn't sweet."

That's right, Stella thought, thinking of Jane's words earlier that morning.

"Mattie—" Lavinia began but stopped and hid her face again when Lloyd glanced up at her.

"I think it fits," Lloyd said, returning to the string beans. "More and more, things like sugar are becomin' a luxury, and your sister seems like someone who fancies classy, luxurious things."

"You're not wrong about that," Mattie said, not bothering to hide how much she enjoyed seeing Stella fume. "So, where are you from?"

"Texas."

"Where in Texas?"

"Pampa."

"Where is that?"

"Pretty much nowhere." He nodded up at the house. "Nice place you got here."

"It used to be our place, but now it's a boarding house we run. Lavinia, Stella, and I sleep in the attic."

"Mattie," Stella snapped, glaring at her. "He doesn't care about our—" She caught his gaze and then looked away, reddening. "—sleeping arrangements."

She pounded the rug again, unsure if she could actually sense his smile or if she was only imagining it.

"So what's your story?" Mattie asked as she plucked a tomato. "You riding the rails?"

"Yep."

"Why'd you leave Texas?"

Stella saw him pause for one, infinitesimal second, his tan, calloused thumb and forefinger stiffening on a string bean.

"My parents died soon after our farm did," he said, picking the bean and plopping it into the pot. "Nothin' left for me there." He reached over and picked a ripe tomato from Mattie's plant, but instead of dropping it into her pot, he placed it beneath his nose and inhaled deeply. "There's nothin' like the smell of a fresh tomato. That and the smell of the earth when it's wet with rain. Those are my favorites." He put the tomato into the pot and glanced up at Lavinia. "What about you? What are some of your favorite smells?"

It took Lavinia a moment to realize he was speaking to her. Her hands froze on the clothespin, the white sheets flapping around her like wings.

"Me?"

Stella lowered the broom, watching her sister. She couldn't remember the last time Lavinia had been addressed by anyone other than their family or the boarders. Not only because she rarely left the house but because strangers avoided her has much as she avoided them, as if her disfigurement was contagious.

"Yeah," Lloyd confirmed, snapping more beans. "What are your favorite smells?"

Lavinia smoothed her hair over her cheek. For a moment, Stella thought she might bolt inside the house, but then she said, "Honeysuckle. And Aunt Elsa's chicken and noodles."

"Mmm. I'll bet that's delicious," Lloyd said with a smile. "And I agree with you about honeysuckle. Folks always talk about the smell of roses, but they ain't got nothin' on honeysuckle."

"I like the smell of books," Mattie chimed in. "Especially old ones. And mint and wild thyme."

Lloyd looked up at Stella. "How about you?"

Stella glanced at him and then returned her attention to the rug, thinking of her father's hat and her mother's lavender powder. "A fresh tube of lipstick. A new magazine. The smell of a still when the mash turns and the liquor is ready to run."

Lloyd raised an eyebrow. "You partial to moonshine?"

"I'm partial to money."

She met his gaze, unashamed, and he smiled.

"So, I've gathered."

"Lavinia," Aunt Elsa called from beyond the screen door. "Are you finished pinning the sheets?"

"Yes. I'm coming," Lavinia called. She snapped the last clothespin in place and picked up the empty laundry basket.

Then, after a smile and nod at Lloyd, she hurried inside.

"That was nice of you," Mattie said to Lloyd when she'd gone. "Not to say anything about her scars. You didn't even stare at them the way most people do when they meet her."

"Was it broken glass?" Lloyd asked. "An accident with a mirror or window or somethin'?"

"Yes. A car window. Three years ago. She was driving to a farm south of town to trade our eggs for soap the farmer's wife made—"

"It doesn't matter why, Mattie," Stella snapped, though she didn't know why she felt particularly protective of the story. Lavinia would be glad they had explained it so she wouldn't have to. Maybe Stella just didn't want to think about that day, about the joy she felt when Lavinia arrived home, the suffocating fear of losing her—like they'd lost their mother—releasing its hold on her lungs, only to have it take hold again when Lavinia stumbled out of the car, her face a mask of earth and blood.

"Context matters," Mattie argued, and then she turned back to Lloyd. "She was driving a Nash Special Six we used to have, a beautiful three-window coupe our father bought just before the crash, and then a dust storm came up, a nasty one."

Stella closed her eyes, but in her mind, she still saw the towering wall of dust Lavinia must have seen that day, a mountain rushing toward her: thick, black, and unstoppable.

"She parked the car," Mattie continued, "and was covering her face and breathing through a handkerchief, but then some animal—probably a deer—frightened and blinded by the storm, slammed into the driver side window. The glass shattered and tore up the left side of her face. The wounds might not have scarred so terribly if the dust storm hadn't lasted another four hours. It was after dark before she was able to drive home, and we called a doctor."

"Damn," Lloyd breathed. "That must have been hell for her to go through. She's a brave woman."

Stella blinked at him. She hadn't heard someone react that way before, admiring Lavinia for her bravery rather than pitying her for her scars.

Mattie inclined her head. "How did you know?"

"How did I know what?" Lloyd asked.

"That the scars were caused by shattered glass. It's not something most people guess from looking. Strangers assume she was born that way."

He glanced at the tomato he was rolling between his fingers. "I've just seen similar scars before."

Stella couldn't help herself. "What did you think, Mattie? You'd met someone else with a 'second sight?'"

"Second sight?" Lloyd asked.

Mattie glared at Stella and then turned to Lloyd. "Our father's mother was Romani."

"Ro—what?"

"Most people know them as gypsies. But that's an insulting term, just so you know."

He nodded. "Thanks for setting me straight. The only *Romani* I've ever encountered is La Esmerelda in *The Hunchback of Notre Dame*."

"*You've* read it?" Stella asked doubtfully.

"My mamma loved the classics, sugar. Don't judge a book by its cover." He looked up at her, tilting his head. "I can see it. I always pictured her having black hair and green eyes, just like you."

"Except," Mattie said. "Esmerelda wasn't—"

"Wasn't really Romani," he finished for her. "She was stolen by them when she was a baby." He shot Stella a smug smile. "Quasimodo was the real Romani person."

"That's right!" Mattie exclaimed, and Stella rolled her eyes. "But," Mattie said, her face growing serious again, "that's another insulting lie people tell about the Romani. That they steal children."

"Understood," Lloyd said.

"Our grandmother left her *vitsa*, or clan, when she met our grandfather in Germany, and they came to America together," Mattie continued. "According to Romani tradition, the seventh daughter is blessed with a second sight and destined for greatness."

"And you're the seventh?" Lloyd asked. "There's more than the three of you?"

"Well, no."

Mattie paused and glanced at Stella, who explained.

"Our mother had four stillbirths between Lavinia and me. All girls."

"For a long time, our grandmother thought Lavinia would be their only child, especially because of her hair," Mattie said. "The Romani consider redheads to be lucky, so she assumed she might be the only one destined to live. Especially since no one else on either side of our parents' families had red hair."

"Lucky, huh?" Lloyd said, glancing back at the house, and Stella knew he was thinking about Lavinia's accident. While Stella didn't believe her grandmother's superstitions because they were silly, Lavinia didn't believe them for the reason Lloyd had guessed.

"In a way, she is," Mattie argued. "She survived. Not . . ." She trailed off and glanced at Stella, who saw the grief that flooded her own chest at the memory filling Mattie's eyes. Mattie cleared her throat. "Not everyone does."

Lloyd turned back from the house and looked at Mattie. "So, is the other thing true? You got the sight?"

Mattie shrugged, looking less sure than Stella had always assumed she was. "I'd certainly like to think I'm destined for greatness."

Lloyd smiled. "I wouldn't doubt it." He turned to Stella. "So, Mattie's the blessed sister and Lavinia's the lucky sister. Which one are you?"

Stella slammed the broom against the rug one final time, yanked it down from the line, and started inside.

"I'm the sister who is getting out of this heat."

In truth, people always called Stella the "pretty" sister, but "pretty" couldn't compare to "lucky" and "blessed." So far, "pretty" had not only been mostly useless, but detrimental. While it did help in situations like the one with the police officer that morning, it usually only made other girls hate her and made boys try to corner her when they got drunk at the few feeble town festivals Dodge still attempted to throw or paw at her during the movies if she agreed to accompany them for a free ticket to see her idols.

The stars Stella admired were beautiful, but also so much more. No one hated Barbara Stanwyck or tried to paw at Norma Shearer. They were worshiped by men and women, both onscreen and off. Because they weren't just beautiful. They were clever, sophisticated, daring, and bold.

And, of course, rich.

Stella wasn't rich, and in the deepest parts of herself, she feared she wasn't those other things either. That was why she had to get out.

She had to become *someone*.

CHAPTER 3

Considering how quickly Lloyd won over Lavinia and Mattie, Stella wasn't surprised when Aunt Elsa fell under his spell as well. He didn't seem to be *working* them, like Stella had done with the police officer, but no matter how genuine it might be, his affability profited him. When he offered to help Aunt Elsa sterilize jars and preserve the tomatoes, she invited him to stay for dinner, and when he regaled the boarders with tales of his travels from Oregon to Arizona, they insisted he stay the night on the sleeping porch.

Stella wasn't certain why it irritated her so much. Perhaps because Lloyd continued to call her "sugar" whenever Aunt Elsa was out of earshot or poked fun at her for "putting on airs," like a high-class city girl. Or perhaps it was because of the way he *enjoyed* damn near everything, not bothering to hide or subdue his delight like a decent person. He devoured Aunt Elsa's stew at dinner, emitting nearly obscene sounds of pleasure as he ate. And earlier, before lunch, when Aunt Elsa brought out a soapy bucket of water so they could wash up, he plunged his hands into the hot, thick suds and groaned in a way that made something strange squirm in Stella's stomach. Her breath had hitched as she'd watched him splash the water up over his neck, closing his eyes and sighing as the drops slid under his shirt.

It was uncomfortable. And distracting.

And Stella couldn't afford to be distracted. She had two problems to solve. One, she had an idea how to remedy, but not the means. The other, she *did* have the means to solve, but not the willpower.

It was unavoidable, however. So, after they finished the evening dishes, the boarders retired to their rooms, Mattie climbed to the second floor to draw a bath for Lloyd, and Lavinia went to the basement to wash his clothes.

Stella approached Aunt Elsa. She was in the hallway, retrieving a pillow and quilt for Lloyd from a closet.

"Aunt Elsa," Stella began. "I've been thinking about a way we could make more money."

Aunt Elsa closed the closet door and turned around. "Yes?"

"The sleeping porch is space that's going to waste. If we fixed it up and put walls where the screens are, we'd have another bedroom and could take on two more boarders."

"That would be wonderful," Aunt Elsa agreed. "But I don't see how we could manage it. We can't afford to buy the lumber or pay a carpenter."

Stella glanced at the floor. "I know. I'm still working on that part."

"It's a nice idea, honey," Aunt Elsa said, patting her shoulder. "But don't worry. We'll get by."

Stella bit her lip, closed her eyes, and forced herself to go on. "There's something else." She opened her eyes. "I know we have some bills due soon, and . . ." She slid her hand into the pocket of her overalls. "I didn't tell you before, but Jane's been cutting me in on her laundry business. I've been saving this up for the last three months."

She held out six dollar bills. In truth, she'd made them in only two weeks, but she couldn't tell Aunt Elsa that. Six dollars for three months of delivering laundry sounded believable, and it would be enough to cover the water bill, plus more. Aunt Elsa stared at her hand in disbelief.

"She can afford to pay you?"

"Her business is doing well. And her house is paid off, remember?"

"Yes, I remember," Aunt Elsa said with a touch of envy Stella felt as well. She reached out and took the bills. "Thank you, Stella."

"It's nothing."

But of course, it wasn't nothing. She'd saved twenty-five dollars since starting the moonshine business, and now she had only nineteen.

It's just a small step backward, she reminded herself. *You'll make more.*

"I'm going to put this away," Aunt Elsa said, pocketing the money. "Will you be a dear and take these out for Lloyd?"

Stella nodded and took the quilt and pillow from Aunt Elsa. Then she turned the corner and stepped out onto the sleeping porch. A cool breeze blew through the screens, carrying the scent of the honeysuckle bush from the side of the house. Stella had to admit, Lloyd was right; they smelled even better than roses. With a sigh, she walked to the wicker settee and set down the pillow and quilt.

"You lied to your aunt."

Stella jumped and turned to see Lloyd in the chair beside the settee, buttoning up what Stella realized was one of her father's shirts. She glanced down and saw he was wearing his pants, too. Lavinia must have loaned them to him while she washed his dirty clothes. Stella's chest twinged at the sight of her father's clothes on another person's body. It drove home the fact that he was no longer here to wear them himself. The material hung loosely on Lloyd, as he was taller and lankier than her father. Now that his hair was clean, she saw it was sort of a sandy brown. It was wet from the bath and curling softly over his forehead and ears, and she could smell the Ivory soap that clung to his skin from where she stood. He looked different, but also the same. The dirt was gone, but there was still something rough and wind-blown about him.

"You were listening?"

He nodded, closing the final button. "It was kind of you to give her that money."

"I didn't have a choice," she said, shoving her hands in her pockets. They felt cold and empty now.

"There's always a choice. And I know that was hard. Mattie told me what you're savin' up for."

Stella bristled. It felt too intimate. This boy wearing her father's clothes and knowing her fondest dreams.

"She talks too much."

Lloyd stood, walked to the settee, and gestured at the quilt and pillow. "Tell Miss Elsa I said 'thank you.'"

He spread the quilt out over the settee, tossed the pillow down at one end, and flopped down, stretching his arms. Stella had never really looked closely before, but at that moment, his eyes reminded her of Coca-Cola. Not just because they were brown but because there was something effervescent about them. They seemed to sparkle and dance with life, energy, and hope. Things that had been beaten out of most of the people she came across. He glanced up and saw her staring.

"I hope you don't mind me wearin' your daddy's clothes. After all, I did have a bath for the first time this century."

Stella's throat tightened with shame. "I shouldn't have said that. It was mean."

"Don't worry about it, sugar. I've been called worse."

Her eyes moved over his split lip, the scar through his eyebrow, and the yellowing bruise beneath the other eye. "What happened between you and that man at the station?"

"Like I told your aunt. Just a jungle disagreement."

"I don't believe that," Stella said, sitting down across from him on her grandmother's rocking chair. "You *spat* on him. You said 'you bastards' are all alike. What did that mean?"

He searched her face and then looked away. "He reminded me of someone."

"Who?"

He looked back, tilting his head. "Well, ain't you curious. I thought you were only interested in things that involved cash."

"You're changing the subject. Like you did in the garden. When Mattie asked why you left Texas and you started rambling on about your favorite smells."

He squinted at her. "Didn't realize you were paying such close attention." He looked her over and grinned. "You sweet on me, sugar?"

She glared at him, her face flaming, but kept her voice even. "You're changing the subject again."

"All right, all right," he said, propping himself up on his elbow. "I left some bad things behind in Texas. Things I'm not keen to talk about. But I promise, I'm no danger to you or your family. Is that enough?"

She looked in his eyes. No, she didn't think he planned to steal from her family or hurt them in any way. If that had been his plan, he'd have done it by now and run off, not spent the entire day working as hard as the rest of them.

And she supposed his past wasn't her business.

"Yes. It's enough."

She started to rise, but then Lloyd sat up and said, "Do you mind if I ask why y'all live with your aunt? Mattie said your father was looking for work in Wichita, but where is your mother?"

Stella sank back into the chair, grief weighing her body down before her brain even processed it. Recognition lit up Lloyd's eyes.

"I'm sorry. She passed?"

Stella remembered both of Lloyd's parents had died, and she nodded. "Four years ago."

"Too early on for it to have been dust pneumonia," he observed. "Was it some other sickness?"

A strangled laugh punched its way out of Stella's throat. "No, but it was the dust all the same."

"How is that?"

Stella licked her lips, now rough and dry, her lipstick long faded. "Mamma went into town, or that's what we assumed. Our father had just lost his car dealership, and when Mattie, Lavinia, and I saw her leave the house wearing all her jewelry, we supposed she was going to sell it. But then, while she was gone, one of the first truly bad dust storms came up. I remember my sisters, Daddy, Aunt Elsa, and I hid under the kitchen table with a wet blanket draped over us, coughing and wheezing for hours. The whole house shook, and everything went black. I thought the world was ending."

Stella closed her eyes, her heart throbbing, because in a way, she'd been right—*her* world had ended that day.

"When the storm finally passed, we searched for Mamma all over town but couldn't find her. The dust had knocked out the electricity and buried cars so deep, only the tops of them could be seen. Days passed, and no one saw her, and she never came home. Then, a few weeks later, my father and I visited the dry goods store and saw . . ." She swallowed. "Her hat there, for sale."

"Her hat?" Lloyd repeated. "You're sure it was hers?"

"It was a black, wool slouch hat she'd worn every day for the last two years," Stella explained, omitting that it looked just like the one Greta Garbo wore in *A Woman of Affairs* and that her mother looked just as elegant in it. "The clerk told us a drifter passing through had sold it to him, that he claimed he'd found it. The clerk hadn't noticed the spots of blood on the scarlet ribbon or the faux ruby-encrusted pin."

"Jesus," Lloyd breathed. "The tramp killed her then? To rob her?"

"We don't know. None of the jewelry she was wearing ever turned up, and it was worth much more. The tramp could have sold it in another town, or maybe he really did find the hat. It could have blown off in the storm after something hit her to her make her bleed, like flying debris . . ."

Stella paused and closed her eyes again, forcing the images from her mind.

"But you never found her?" Lloyd asked gently.

"No," Stella said, opening her eyes.

"I hate to say it but it's not all that uncommon," Lloyd said. "People get blinded by those storms, cars drive off roads, animals run wild—like with Lavinia. And things can get buried and lost forever—"

"I know," Stella snapped but regretted it when he shrank back and raised his palms.

"I know you know. I'm sorry." He lowered his palms. "You and your kin have lost more to the dust than most, that's for certain."

Stella blew out a breath. The storms had taken their mother and scarred Lavinia, but Lloyd was wrong—there were people who'd lost more. Not just their loved ones but their land, their way of life, their pride. Everything.

"It's all right," she said, relaxing her shoulders. "I'm sorry for jumping down your throat."

He smiled. "Don't sweat it, sugar. At least you didn't take a swing at me with a broom, like I thought you wanted to do while you were beating that rug out this morning."

A smile crept across Stella's lips as well. "Well, I still might, so watch your step." She started to rise again, but Lloyd raised a hand.

"Wait. If you don't mind, I got one more question for you."

"What's that?"

"You keep any of that product we discussed here? At your house?"

She did. The hairdresser bought some from time to time. Usually between boyfriends. "Why?"

"Because I finally got something you want bad enough to trade."

"And what is that?"

"Information."

"Information?"

"Information that will solve the problem you posed to your aunt just now."

She looked at him for a moment, then furrowed her brow.

"You're saying you've got information that will help us fix up this porch and bring in more boarders?"

"I do, indeed."

"What is it?"

He shook his head. "The moonshine first."

"How do I know you really have any information?"

"Cross my heart and hope to die," he said, swiping a finger across his chest. "You don't like what I got to say, and I will give you your product back and go back to the jungle."

Stella bit her lip. She only had half-pint jars anyway. It wouldn't be too much of a loss if his information was useless.

"Okay," she said, rising. "I'll be right back."

As quietly as she could, she hurried up both flights of stairs and climbed into the attic. She retrieved a single jar from beneath a pile of grubby sheets, dusted it off, and wrapped one of the sheets around the glass. If she ran into Aunt Elsa, she could claim Lloyd had asked for another blanket.

Then, she slipped back down to the sleeping porch.

"Here," she said, removing the jar from the sheet.

Lloyd sat up, took it from her, and gestured toward the rocking chair. "Have a seat."

"This information had better be worth twenty-five cents," she said, plopping down on the chair and placing the sheet on the floor beside her.

"Oh, it is." He unscrewed the lid from the jar and took a sniff. "Damn. I ain't had this in a long time. My mamma's side of the family brewed for decades. It was tradition."

"So, that's how you knew what the sugar was for?"

"Well, that and common sense." He looked up at Stella, grinned, and held out the jar. "Ladies first."

"I don't drink that stuff."

"You've never tasted it?"

"Hell no."

He sighed theatrically and glanced down at the jar. "I don't know if I trust a product the seller won't even touch."

She crossed her arms. "If you're trying to get me drunk—"

"I wouldn't do that."

His voice was suddenly cold, and so were his eyes. Stella stared at him, then quietly murmured, "I was only kidding."

Lloyd glanced at the jar again. "Sorry. Now I'm the one jumping down your throat."

Stella followed his gaze to the jar and then thought, *Oh hell. Jean Harlow would do it.*

She swiped the jar from his hand, imagining herself a brassy dame in a gangster flick. With an upturned chin, she looked into his eyes and took a confident gulp. The liquor seared her throat, and she sputtered and coughed, her eyes stinging. Now, she understood why they called it "white lightning."

"Yuck," she said, rubbing her watering eyes and handing it back. "Not that I'm complaining, but why do people want this stuff?"

"You know of any other product that can disinfect, numb pain, start fires, and help you sleep?" Lloyd asked, his smile returning. "This is a precious commodity, sugar."

He closed his eyes, took a sip, and released a sigh. The rough, relishing kind that made it hard for Stella to focus. He wiped his lips, and she shifted in her chair.

"So, what's the information?"

"I know where you can get enough lumber to fix up this porch. For free."

Her jaw dropped. "That's too good to be true."

"But it is. I guarantee. I'll take you there and help you load it up and bring it back to your place tomorrow."

He smiled and took another sip, and Stella's chest swelled with hope but then deflated.

"That only solves part of the problem. We can't pay a carpenter."

"That may be true. But you do know someone with experience building things who'd be willing to work for nothin' more than food and a place to stay."

She blinked at him. "You'd do that?"

"You got a nice setup here. I wouldn't mind sticking around for a while. I like your family. Like your food. Like the peace."

Stella couldn't imagine wanting to stay around Dodge. But then, she remembered guiltily, she wasn't homeless.

"You've got a deal. If what you say is true about the lumber."

He grinned and stuck out his free hand. She took it. His skin was rough, but warm. They shook, and he released her hand and took one more gulp of the moonshine. Then, he whistled, shook his head, and screwed the lid back on the jar.

"Sweet dreams, sugar. I know I'll sleep well tonight."

He slid the jar beneath the settee and scooped his shoes off the floor. Then he began to tie the laces together around his wrist.

"What are you doing?"

He glanced up at her, looked down at his wrist, and then laughed. Apparently, whatever he'd been doing was such an ingrained habit, he hadn't even realized he'd done it.

"Jungle protocol. This way no one can steal your shoes."

"No one's going to steal from you here."

Her voice had grown quiet. Pitying too. He didn't miss it.

"Don't sweat it, sugar."

He finished tying the laces around his wrists, and Stella couldn't help but be impressed by the one-handed accomplishment. Then, he stretched back out on the settee and closed his eyes. Stella rose from her chair, picked up the sheet, and walked into the hall.

Up in the attic, her sisters were already stripped down to their slips. Even with the window open, the summer air made the room stuffy. As Stella peeled her overalls off and stepped into her own slip, she told them about the money she'd given Aunt Elsa for the water bill, as well as the deal she'd made with Lloyd to fix up the sleeping porch.

"I'm glad," Mattie said, plopping down on the mattress and unraveling her braid. "I like Lloyd."

"Just because he's read the same old, boring book you have?" Stella asked.

"And because he irritates you," she replied. "But you like him, too."

"I do not," Stella scoffed, but Lavinia and Mattie glanced at each other, and Stella glared at them. "Are you two nuts? He's a dirty vagrant."

"He's not so dirty now," Lavinia said with a tiny smile.

"I like smooth, polished gentlemen," Stella argued. "Like Gary Cooper and Cary Grant."

"What about Clark Gable?" Mattie asked.

Lavinia nodded. "Lloyd does kind of remind me of Clark in *It Happened One Night.* Only younger and blond and without a mustache."

"His hair isn't really *blond,*" Stella said. "More like sandy brown."

Her sisters shared another glance, and her cheeks grew pink.

"Shut up!" she cried, grateful Lloyd wouldn't hear them three stories down, open window or not.

"Remember that part in the movie where he carried Claudette Colbert across the river, made her hold his suitcase, and then smacked her on the rear end?" Lavinia said to Mattie.

"Stella could definitely benefit from a spanking," Mattie agreed.

Stella seized a pillow and hurled it at them. It struck Lavinia hard in the gut.

"I hate you both."

The two of them burst into laughter, and Stella couldn't help but smile as well. She picked up another pillow from beside her Folger's can and looked out the open window. Perhaps, there were some things she liked about Lloyd. His practicality, for instance. She admired that, as well as the fact that he'd survived whatever he'd survived with that spark of hope and passion for life still intact. Stella had never wanted a boy for the boy himself, but for the world he was from.

That was why she had only ever desired movie stars. The men in the movies were sleek businessmen or powerful, filthy-rich gangsters. Stella had never known such men, but in Hollywood, she would.

If she was going to be *someone*, she needed to be a part of their world.

Not Lloyd's.

"Thank you for giving Aunt Elsa that money," Lavinia said as she sat down on the mattress. "When she gets tense and frightened, I get tense and frightened. I can breathe now."

"Thank goodness she doesn't know how I really earned it," Stella said, still gazing out the window.

"She'd never suspect that," Lavinia assured her.

"She'd never suspect it of Jane," Mattie said. "But Stella's another story."

Stella spun around and flung the second pillow at Mattie. It hit her square in the face, and they all laughed.

"What?" Stella demanded. "You didn't see that coming, Miss Second Sight?"

She joined them down on the mattress, and they all stretched out together. Stella slept in the middle, just as she'd been born, she supposed. It wasn't roomy or cool, but it was comforting somehow. For a moment, they were all quiet, staring up at the wooden boards, but then Lavinia spoke, her voice hushed.

"You don't think Daddy's ever had to . . . stay in a jungle? Like Lloyd?"

"Of course not," Stella said, her stomach tensing at the thought. "He told us months ago he has a room in a boarding house."

They both looked to Mattie. Though neither of them put much stock in their grandmother's traditions, that didn't stop them from wanting to have something certain to believe in.

"He's safe," she replied, still looking up at the ceiling. "There may have been times when he hasn't had a place to stay, but he's safe now. That's what matters."

Stella closed her eyes, trying to block out the image of her father tying his shoes around his wrist. "Things will get better," she said, forcing her eyes back open. "Once we get the sleeping porch fixed and we take on two more boarders. And maybe a job will open up in Dodge, and Daddy can come home."

Neither sister responded to the last statement, which they all knew to be a long shot, but Lavinia said with a sigh, "More boarders means a lot more work."

"But also more money," Mattie reminded her. "Which means less fear and tension."

"You're right," Lavinia said. She sighed again. "Sometimes, I hate money."

Stella snorted. "The only time I hate it is when we don't have it."

They were silent again for a moment. Then, Mattie chuckled.

"What is it?" Stella asked.

"Lloyd's thinking about you," she said. "He's angry with himself for it, but he is."

"Once again, you're a nut," Stella replied, hoping Mattie couldn't sense the heat rising in her cheeks. "You're just making that up or taking some wild guess. You're *not* clairvoyant."

Lavinia turned her face away, and a whisper escaped her lips.

"I wish . . ."

Stella knew she hadn't meant to say it out loud, so she didn't respond. If Mattie had heard her, she didn't either. Stella knew what she wished. That her face wasn't scarred, that a man somewhere would lie awake thinking about her. Stella wished she could tell Lavinia she was still beautiful, inside and out. She also wanted to tell her that men would never think of her if she never went anywhere near them. And also, that beauty could be as much of a curse as it was a gift. When

Lavinia did find love, she'd know the person thought of her as more than a pretty face, that she was worthy of being respected and valued for who she was. Stella had no such guarantee.

And wasn't entirely certain she *was* worthy of all those things.

"Well," Stella began, "if he drinks enough moonshine, he won't think much at all. Let's go to sleep."

Automatically, the three of them joined hands and murmured, "*Jekhipe.*" It was a Romani word their grandmother taught them that meant unity or oneness. None of them were sure how it started, but they'd said it to each other before bed for as long as they could remember. Even back when they slept in separate rooms.

As she settled into a comfortable position, Stella breathed in the scent of Lavinia's hair and brushed Mattie's arm with her fingertips. She'd miss them the most when she left, she knew. No matter how much they annoyed her at times, they were a part of her.

And no one would ever know her quite the way her sisters did.

CHAPTER 4

"Where the hell are we going?"

Sweat dripped down Stella's neck. Her palms were slick on the steering wheel.

"He said it wasn't much farther," Lavinia hollered. She was sitting beside Stella in the passenger seat, but the grumble of the gravel road beneath them was deafening.

Stella jumped as Lloyd's hand smacked the side of the door.

"Turn left at the crossroads!" he yelled through the open window. Then, he crouched back down in the bed of the truck, next to Mattie.

"We are in the middle of nowhere," Stella groaned, turning right. "If he makes us late, I'm going to kill him."

Aunt Elsa had agreed to let all three of them go with Lloyd to collect the lumber once they told her about their plans but only after the boarders left for work and only if they made it back in time to prepare dinner.

"I think I see something," Lavinia shouted, shielding her eyes.

In the distance, an iron fence and archway materialized. As she neared it, Stella saw that the fence was warped, and the archway was bent. A chipped wooden sign hung precariously from the archway. A word was carved into it, likely some family name, but the markings were so weather-beaten, she couldn't read it. Weeds climbed up and wrapped themselves around the rusty iron. Everything about the place had the air of abandonment.

"Keep going!" Lloyd ordered. "Through the archway."

Stella followed instructions and then drove up a gritty, overgrown drive. She continued over a hill, and then two buildings came into view. Or at least what *used* to be two buildings. They looked like they'd been razed to the ground by an earthquake. The mess to the left was nothing more than a massive pile of wood; the one on the right still had enough structure left for Stella to tell it had once been a redbrick house, big enough to be a mansion.

The dusty land between the two wrecks was dotted with the strangest trees Stella had ever seen. They were really nothing more than stumps, but they hadn't been cut down. Instead of a smooth, sliced surface, their tops rose up to a brittle point and curled over, like gnarled hands, and instead of brown, they were mottled gray, as if they'd been formed from ash.

"You can stop here!" Lloyd called, and Stella slowed to a stop and cut the engine. She and Lavinia slid out of the cab. Lloyd hopped out of the bed and helped Mattie down after him.

"Was this place hit by a tornado?" Lavinia asked.

Mattie waved the settling dust from the truck away from her face. "No. If a tornado had hit it, the rubble would be everywhere. This is all in the same place. It looks like these buildings just collapsed."

"Word in the jungle is God struck this place down with his own hand," Lloyd said. He was back in his own clothes now. They were clean, though worn and stained. He shoved his hands in his pockets. "They say the Devil lives here now."

"That's where you heard about this place?" Stella asked. "In the jungle?"

"I'm surprised none of you had heard about it before. It's a popular topic of conversation down there."

"Wait," Lavinia murmured, peering out at the strange, dusty trees. "I know what this place is. Or what it *was*."

"What?" Mattie asked.

"The Bright Cider Mill. Remember? Mr. Bright used to throw those big parties Mamma would never let us go to. She said they were wild and unfit for children, though I often argued with her, since I was nearly eighteen when . . . well, when I assume the parties ended. With the crash."

A memory stirred in Stella's mind. Men at the annual Boot Hill Fiesta and Dodge City Roundup holding green bottles labeled "Bright's Cider" and someone pointing out Mr. Bright as one of the judges at the Miss Dodge City Pageant. She remembered thinking he looked more like a field hand than a boss, wearing everyday work clothes instead of a suit and letting his dark, shoulder-length hair tumble freely instead of cutting it short and slicking it back with pomade like most men.

"Oh, I remember him," Mattie said. "He donated all that money to the school to replace the gym floor. He must have lived there." She pointed at the red bricks, then gestured toward the pile of wood. "And that would have been the mill. The trench behind it was probably once a creek. And these stumps were apple trees."

"They look diseased," Stella said. "I'll bet that's why the mill went under. Or the creek dried up. Or both."

"What's the story you heard?" Mattie asked Lloyd. "Why do they think the Devil lives here and that God himself struck it down?"

Stella glanced at Mattie. She looked pale and a little shaken. Of course she would be worried such stories were true.

"They say the owner made a deal with the Devil," Lloyd said. He laughed, and Stella was glad at least *he* had some proper sense. "It's probably because it's near the crossroads back there," he continued. "Everywhere I've been, I've heard stories and songs about deals with the Devil happening at a crossroads. Anyway, apparently the man broke the deal somehow. Then either God or the Devil, depending on which version you hear, destroyed this land and cursed it so nothing would grow."

"If that's true, God must have cursed the whole country," Stella muttered.

"There's folks who think that too, sugar."

Stella already knew that. It was why she'd hated going to church and was grateful when Aunt Elsa said they were busy enough as it was and stopped forcing them to attend. The preacher had ranted every week that the Depression would end and that the land would prosper again if Americans would repent and change their ways.

"Utter rot," Stella said. "Scantily-clad movie stars and bathtub gin didn't cause the Depression. If God were going to punish America for being sinful, you'd think he'd have done it for something like, I don't know, slavery or the Civil War or wiping out the Indians. Not for drinking and dancing and wearing short skirts."

Lloyd looked at her, his lips curling into a smile. "Amen to that."

"So, you've never been here before?" Mattie asked him. "You only heard about it?"

He nodded. "The way they described it, I figured there must be some wood up for grabs."

"You mean, you weren't sure?" Stella asked, her eyes narrowing. "You just heard about this place, knew how to get here, and *hoped* we'd find some lumber?"

"Hey, I was right, wasn't I?"

"But what if you'd been wrong?"

"No risk, no reward, sugar. You're a bootlegger. You understand."

He started toward the pile of wood, and Stella scowled at his back.

"Are you sure it's all right for us to take it?" Lavinia asked, following Lloyd.

"This place has been abandoned for years. If someone had wanted this wood, they'd have taken it by now."

Mattie followed the two of them, still looking a little wary. Finally, Stella pried up her feet and approached the pile as well.

They worked in silence as the wind picked up around them, hissing like an angry spectator and blurring the landscape with filth. Thankfully, it didn't take them long to fill the bed of the truck. Mattie and Lloyd would have to sit on the boards for the journey home, but they'd known that would be the case. As they were gathering the last load, Mattie stopped and looked around.

"Do you hear that?"

Stella paused to listen but only heard the bone-dry whine of the wind.

"Hear what?" Lavinia asked.

"The sound of someone . . . whispering."

Stella placed the boards she was carrying onto the bed of the truck. Unease skittered up her spite as she realized the wind was growing stronger, but she heard no whispered voices. She looked at Lloyd, who shrugged and wiped his brow, his shirt rippling in the breeze. Over his shoulder, the sickly yellow sky had darkened to muddy brown.

"It's coming from over there," Mattie said, walking around the pile of wood and toward the ghostly stumps.

"Mattie, what are you doing?" Stella called.

"You really can't hear that?" Mattie asked. "It's a voice. A pleading voice. It's asking for help."

Stella's pulse leapt, but then a clatter turned her attention back to the truck. A few of the boards had flown to the ground. The wind howled louder, and static electricity crackled through Stella's hair. The sky turned crimson, and a flock of birds shot by overhead, screeching as they tried to escape what Stella now knew was coming. She looked at Lavinia, whose face had gone so white, her scars looked like silvery spiderwebs.

"Dust storm!" Stella cried. She turned to Lloyd who took one look at Lavinia's ashen face and rushed to her.

"We have to get inside the truck," he hollered as another board banged to the ground, but Lavinia stared at the truck and shook her head. Stella knew she was thinking of the last time she hid in a car during a dust storm; of a sudden, violent impact, shattering glass, and tearing flesh.

"I'll keep my body over yours," Lloyd told her. "It will be okay."

"We won't all fit inside the cab," Lavinia protested.

"We have to try," Stella yelled.

The wind screamed as it slammed into them, shoving them sideways. Lavinia coughed on the dust and nodded, allowing Lloyd to guide her toward the truck. Stella turned back to Mattie, but she ran the opposite way, darting between the stumps.

"Mattie, stop," Stella yelled, but Mattie didn't stop. Stella ran after her, and Lloyd and Lavinia followed. The dead, twisted tree stumps were even creepier up close, and Stella recoiled as she passed them, the wind hurling dirt against her back. She continued through the cemetery of an orchard until Mattie came into view. She was standing before the dried creek bed, completely still. Stella stumbled to a stop beside her as Lavinia and Lloyd caught up.

"Mattie, the storm's coming!" Stella hollered. "We have to get in the truck!"

Mattie turned to her, eyes wild. "You really don't hear it?"

Stella's blood froze. Mattie had always been strange, but until that moment, Stella had never feared she might truly be crazy.

"Mattie, there is no whispering! How could you even hear whispering in this wind?"

Mattie turned back around and stared at the empty trench below her. Stella followed her gaze and noticed a discolored patch of dirt. The rusty, hardened soil was in the vague shape of an apple. Then, Mattie let out a shriek and jumped back.

"Tell me you see that!" she cried, pointing ahead.

"See what?" Lavinia yelled.

"That woman. She looks like a . . . ghost."

Stella looked from Mattie to the bare trench, her heart hammering. Lavinia gripped Mattie's arm.

"You're not well, Mattie. Come on, we have to get in the truck."

The wind screeched and knocked all four of them onto their hands and knees. Stella coughed and pushed herself up, wiping her eyes with the back of her hand. But then a cloud of dust rose up before them in the creek bed, swirling like a tornado, as if independent from the storm. Stella gaped at it, her lungs shrinking in on themselves.

Because within the whirling dust, she saw the outline of a woman.

I'm crazy too, she thought. *I've completely lost my mind.*

Or maybe she'd died in the dust storm, just like her mother, and this was hell.

"Do y'all see that?" Lloyd yelled.

Stella looked at Lloyd and then Lavinia, who had clamped her hand over her mouth. They saw it too. Stella and Mattie weren't crazy or dead.

Or they all were.

Stella turned back to the ghostly woman, who raised her swirling, dusty hand and beckoned them forward.

Hell, no.

But Mattie started to creep down into the trench.

"No!" Lavinia screamed.

The wind roared and static electricity crackled through the air. Stella glanced back to see a towering mountain of black dirt moving toward them, a few hundred feet behind the truck. She turned to scream at Mattie, but then the swirling cloud before them broke apart and the woman dissolved. Mattie continued across the empty bed, approached the apple-shaped mark, and stepped directly on top of it.

She vanished.

It was as though she'd stepped into a pool of water and slipped beneath the surface. She sunk down into nothing, leaving nothing—

no ripple, no dust. Stella gripped her head. This wasn't happening. It couldn't be real.

"Mattie!" Lavinia shrieked, then she turned to Stella and Lloyd. "Where did she go?"

Stella ran forward but stopped short of the mark. Lavinia and Lloyd joined her.

"Holy Moses." Lloyd's eyes were wide, his chest heaving.

"What happened to her?" Lavinia shrieked.

"I don't know," Stella yelled.

Lavinia gaped at the mark but then clenched her fists and said, "I'm going after her."

She moved toward the mark, but Stella yanked her back.

"No! We need to think about t–!"

Lavinia screamed again, and Stella stumbled backward. Mattie rose up from the place she'd disappeared in one fluid motion, breaking through the ground like it was the surface of a lake. She stepped back, looked up at them, and beamed.

"You have to come and see this," she gasped, stretching out her hand.

Stella and Lloyd backed away. Lavinia blinked, tears spilling down her dirt-caked cheeks.

"What happened? Are you all right?"

"I'm fine," Mattie cried, taking her hand. "Trust me. It's safe. Come see."

Lavinia touched Mattie's face with her free hand, searching her eyes.

"This is crazy!" Stella cried. "Where did you go? What's going on?"

"You have to see it yourself," Mattie said. "Come on. I'll show you."

She moved toward the patch, and Lavinia, still holding her hand, moved with her.

"No," Stella cried, but they stepped on the discolored spot and sunk down together.

Lloyd edged nearer, then looked back over his shoulder. Stella followed his gaze to see the approaching wall of dust swallow the truck.

"We have to go with them," Lloyd shouted, turning back to her.

"How? Where? We can't—"

"We don't have a choice!"

Lloyd placed his foot on the apple-shaped mark, slid down, and disappeared. Stella coughed against her arm, unable to hear anything but the wailing wind or see anything but the apple-shaped mark before her. She turned back around. The dust storm was vaulting toward her like a tidal wave, blocking out the sun. Lavinia's scarred face and her mother's bloody hat flashed across her mind.

There was no choice.

Though she'd never done it before, Stella made the sign of the cross like her grandmother used to do. Then she stepped where Lloyd had stepped and sank into the earth.

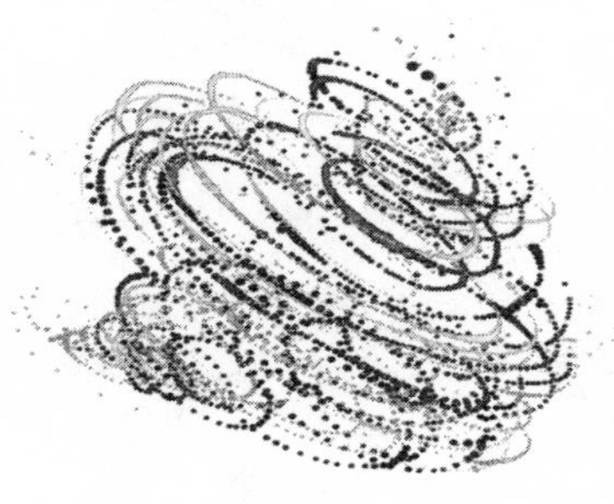

CHAPTER 5

It wasn't exactly *falling.*

Stella's feet both moved and didn't move. It was as though the ground withdrew beneath her and then reformed. But when she felt the sensation of being on solid ground again and looked around, she wasn't where she had been before.

Except, she was.

She was standing in the same creek bed, on the same spot, but cool, clear water was rushing past her, just over her knees. The cold that soaked through her overalls was jarring but also soothing, and when she sucked in a breath, she realized the air was clean. She inhaled again, her body shocked by the free and easy intake of air, a sensation she hadn't felt in so long, she'd forgotten what it was like.

She looked around, still bracing for the impact of the dust storm, but it was gone. Her muscles relaxed but then tensed up again as she took in her strange surroundings. An elegant, redbrick mansion stood where the crumbling wreck had been, and the pile of loose lumber had been replaced by a sleek, wooden mill. The area in between was no longer covered with eerie stumps, but lush, thriving apple trees that glistened in the sun—a sun that hung unobstructed in a blindingly bright, blue sky, no dust in sight.

"Oh my goodness, Lavinia," Mattie cried. "Your face."

Stella turned to see Mattie, Lloyd, and Lavinia a few feet to her right. She charged through the water toward them, her eyes seeking Lavinia's face.

It was clear. Her scars were gone.

Lavinia touched her cheek first, then peered down at her reflection. Her eyes widened. She bent closer to the surface, stared at herself, and then splashed water onto her face, washing away the dust from the storm. When she saw her scars were truly gone, a sharp cry escaped her throat.

"What is this?" she whispered. "Some kind of healing water?"

"I don't know. It seems like the same creek, only . . . different," Stella said.

"Let's go back," Mattie suggested, taking Lavinia's hand. "Just for a moment. We'll see if the scars are still there on the other side."

"No, wait—the storm," Stella said, but Mattie and Lavinia rushed past her to the discolored mark, still visible beneath the crystal clear water. They stepped on it and slunk down beneath the surface, vanishing just as they had when the bed was dry. No splash, no ripple.

Stella looked at Lloyd and stifled a gasp. The scar through his eyebrow, the bruise beneath his eye, and his split lip were all healed. He touched the side of his face, pressing his tongue to the back of his teeth.

"Jesus," he murmured.

Stella waded closer, shivering as the cold water continued to soak through her overalls. "What is it?"

Lloyd met her gaze, then laughed and shook his head. "I had this tooth, way in the back. Got knocked out a few years ago. And now it's . . . there. I can feel it." He slid his hand from his face to his neck and then down the back of his shirt. Stella wasn't certain what he was checking for, but whatever he found there caused him to laugh and murmur "Jesus" again.

He'd said the tooth was "knocked" out. How hard would a person have to be hit to lose a *back* tooth, she wondered?

The water stirred behind her, and she turned around. Mattie and Lavinia had returned. They were coughing up the dust from the storm, and Lavinia's unblemished face was heavy and drawn.

"The scars are still there, on the other side?" Stella asked.

They nodded. Stella glanced back at Lloyd. If he was disappointed, he didn't show it.

"I guess 'other side' is what you would call it," Mattie said, splashing toward the edge of the creek and climbing up onto the shore. "Or 'the real world,' perhaps."

"Then what is *this* world?" Stella asked, following her. "It seems real too. We can breathe the air, feel the water, touch the grass."

She climbed out as she said it, and her fingers brushed the grass. It was thick and soft as silk. It even *smelled* good, and Stella had never enjoyed the smell of grass.

"Maybe we've time traveled," said Mattie. "Like in H.G. Wells's book. Back to when the mansion and the mill were whole, the trees weren't dead, and the creek wasn't dry."

Lavinia and Lloyd clambered out of the water as well. The four of them stood there, watching the apple trees sway.

"It doesn't just seem like the past though," Lloyd said. "It's like another world. It's got a kind of . . . *glow* about it, you know? Like a fairy tale."

Stella agreed. The place radiated something that wasn't quite real. It was too beautiful and perfect. More like a movie than real life, but in lush, vivid color. She brushed the dust from her hair, which no longer crackled with static electricity. Her whole body felt lighter, as if the heaviness of her daily worries and drudgery had disappeared with the storm.

"Is that . . . someone moving up there?" Lavinia asked.

They squinted in the direction she was pointing. A figure was moving toward them from around the side of the mansion. Goosebumps rose on Stella's skin.

"What if it's the . . ." Stella couldn't force herself to say "ghost." "The figure in the dust. The woman we saw."

No one responded, but it soon became clear the figure was a man. When he came into view, Stella's mouth fell open.

"It's the owner," Lavinia gasped. "Archibald Bright."

He looked just like Stella remembered him: a tall, lanky man in his early thirties with dark, shoulder-length curls. They were currently tied back into a knot, drawing more attention to his strong jaw and warm, hazel eyes. He was wearing rough, denim-work clothes like the ones she'd seen him wearing at the Miss Dodge City Pageant, and as he drew closer, she saw he was breathing hard, his eyes wide and wet with tears.

"My God," he cried. "Where did you come from? How did you get here? Are you all right?"

The four of them stood stock-still as he reached them, their wariness coating the air. But the concern in his eyes compelled Stella to answer.

"Yes, we're okay."

"And we're not exactly sure how we got here . . . or where *here* is," Mattie answered. "You're Archibald Bright, aren't you?"

"Yes," he said, expelling a breath. "Call me Archie."

"Archie, why are you . . . I mean, where did we . . ." Lavinia stumbled, apparently as unsure where to begin as Stella. Archie looked at her, his lips parting slightly.

"If you don't mind, may I ask you a question first?"

"Of course," Lavinia said.

"What year is it?"

The rest of them glanced at each other.

"It's 1934," Mattie said. "July sixth."

Archie's face blanched. "Four years."

"Four years *what*?" Stella asked.

"I've been trapped here for four years." He shook his head, meeting each of their gazes. The clean, perfect breeze shifted through the leaves as they gaped at him, speechless.

"How did you find me?" he asked.

"We . . . well, we . . ." Mattie stammered, still blinking at him, stunned. "We were on your land when a dust storm came up. There was a figure of a . . . well, a woman in the dust, like a ghost, and she asked for help."

Archie stared at her. "A woman? A *ghost*?"

"Only Mattie heard her," Stella suddenly felt the need to clarify. "But yes, we all saw her."

"What did she look like?"

"She was just a shape in the dust. Faceless and . . . grainy," Stella said.

"She beckoned us toward an apple-shaped spot in the empty creek bed," Mattie said. Archie gaped at her.

"*Empty* creek bed? It's gone dry?"

"Oh . . . yes," Mattie said, looking guilty. "And the house and the mill are mostly rubble now. And the trees are . . . stumps."

Archie glanced around at his land, as if trying to picture what Mattie had just described in his thriving Eden. Mattie cleared her throat and continued.

"I followed the ghost, stepped on the spot and sort of . . . fell through. Then I was here, and the others followed. We were able to go back by stepping on the same mark again and then return the same way. Like a passage."

Archie looked at her, out at the creek, and then back again. "So, you've found a passage in and out, but it's in the creek?"

Mattie nodded, and his face fell.

"What's wrong?" Stella asked.

Archie sighed. "I'll show you."

He walked toward the creek, and the rest of them moved to the side. They watched as he stopped at the edge and stuck his hand out over the water. The moment it passed the land they were standing on, it disappeared. His arm simply stopped; there was nothing below his elbow. He pulled his arm back, and his hand and forearm materialized once more.

"Holy Moses," Lloyd spoke, giving voice to Stella's own thoughts.

"If I try to cross the boundaries of the land, one of which is the creek, I cease to be," Archie said, turning back around.

"Why?" Lavinia asked. "How did you get trapped like this?"

He flexed his jaw, pain hardening his features. "I . . . well, the fact of the matter is . . . I can show you."

"*Show* us?" Lloyd repeated.

"But it might . . . it might shock you."

"We can handle it," Mattie assured him, curiosity burning in her gaze. However, she inched closer to Stella and Lavinia, tucking herself between them.

"All right," Archie said, expelling a breath. He closed his eyes and raised his hands, palms up. Stella jumped as the world around them grew dark, the sun slipping behind the bright apple trees. The sky turned purple, then navy and filled with twinkling stars. Light bloomed inside the mansion and mill, streaming out through the windows, and strings of paper lanterns sprang up, glowing between the trees. The sound of a fiddle, followed by a cello and drums, soared through the air, and a band appeared on a raised platform, playing a dizzying song. Other people materialized, men and women all over the grounds, talking, laughing, and dancing on a smooth, wooden dance floor. The smells of corn bread, fried chicken, and corn on the cob filled Stella's lungs, and she saw tables piled with more food than she had seen in one place in years—ripe, firm fruits; gleaming vegetables; thick meats; and freshly churned cream. There was also a heady, yeasty smell in the air she easily recognized. Some people were drinking moonshine, some soft and hard cider, some even beer. It was like a scene from her memories of before the world changed forever, filled with the abundance, joy, and freedom she'd taken for granted. She turned to see Lloyd and her sisters barely breathing, just as transfixed.

"What is this?" she asked Archie.

"A memory of one of the parties I used to throw here," he explained. "Soon after I became trapped, I discovered I could bring my memories to life."

Stella gaped at the dizzying scene. She'd been too young to care about parties when the mill was in its prime, but she could see why Lavinia had begged their mother to let her attend one like this. Just then, a man and a woman dashed by, heading toward the creek. As they passed, the man called out "Hey, Archie!" and the woman shrieked "Great party!" Archie waved at them, and they grinned. When they reached the edge of the creek, they paused and started to strip off their clothes.

"Oh my," Lavinia squeaked, clasping both hands over her mouth. Once the man and woman were down to nothing but their undergarments, they leapt into the water, laughing and squealing.

"Come join us," the woman cried, and Stella realized she was talking to Lloyd. A grin split his smooth, untarnished face.

"That's all right, ma'am," he called back. "Just had a bath the other night."

"Suit yourself," she replied with a smile. She splashed the other man, who laughed and splashed back.

"They can see and hear us," Mattie marveled, turning back to Archie. "They can hear and see you as well."

"Yes. Memories like this have helped me to pass the days. And to keep my sanity," he added with a chuckle, though sadness glimmered in his eyes.

Though Stella's mother had told them the Bright Orchard parties weren't suitable for children, which the stripping couple seemed to confirm, Stella noticed a few kids scattered about. They were eating, dancing, and darting between the adults, playing tag. One boy ran up to Archie and grinned at him.

"Mr. Bright, the lads and I were wondering if we could explore the cave."

The kid had an Irish accent, which Stella had heard on the lips of men passing through Dodge. Archie beamed back at him.

"Now, Frankie, that cave is boarded up because it's dangerous. But you and the lads are free to climb the trees if you're tired of dancing. And remember, call me Archie."

The boy rolled his eyes but then smiled and stuck out his hand. "If you say so."

Archie's jaw popped, and he turned away. When he spoke, his voice was rough with pain. "Go on, Frankie. Have fun."

Frankie ran off, and once he was gone, Archie turned back around.

"Why didn't you shake his hand?" Mattie asked. Lavinia elbowed her, but Stella was glad she'd asked.

Archie turned to her. "I'll show you that too."

He held out his hand and Mattie reached out to take it, but once their skin met, his hand dissolved, passing through hers like a ghost's. She bristled and took a step back. The three gaped at her, and Stella could tell Lloyd was stifling another "Holy Moses."

"So, you can't . . . *touch* anything?" Lavinia asked.

"No," Archie said. "I can't eat or drink anything either. Apparently don't need to, which I'm grateful for." He glanced at the crowd and then stiffened. "Here she comes."

"Here who comes?" Stella asked, following his gaze.

"The woman who trapped me here. The one I conjured this party to show you."

Stella knew which woman he meant as soon as the words left his lips. Not because there was anything particularly nefarious about her, but because of the way she was gazing at Archie as she moved.

Hungrily.

Stella had seen that look on the faces of her idols on the silver screen. They wore it while clad in whisper-thin gowns, slinking toward the men they'd decided they wanted.

This woman wasn't wearing a sheer evening gown, but the undone buttons on her blouse and the sway of her hips sent the same message. She was lovely, with soft blue eyes and wheat blond hair curled into long ringlets.

"I'd never seen her before," Archie told the rest of them. "She simply showed up one night. Since then, I've tried to ask her name or where she came from, but her memory can't tell me more than she'd told me that night, and no one else knew either."

"I've heard you're the owner here," the woman said as she approached him.

"I am," Archie said, going rigid.

"Then it appears I owe you a favor."

"A favor? What for?"

She laughed, moved closer, and purred, "You know, you're cute when you play dumb."

Tension swept through Stella's muscles and discomfort twisted her stomach. "Can she not see us like the others?"

"No," he said, still watching the woman. "I'm choosing to replay the memory just as it was, rather than letting her interact of her free will like the others."

Her eyes still on Archie, the woman nodded at the mansion. "Let's go inside."

"Why?" Archie asked, his voice flat, as if reciting a line from a play.

She pinned him with her gaze and lifted a brow. "So I can pay you the favor I owe you."

"That's not necessary," Archie replied.

"I insist."

"I'm sorry. I must decline."

Stella watched as pain and then rage flared in the woman's eyes. "Why?" she demanded. "What's wrong with—"

The woman's image began to flicker, sputtering like the projection of a film when a reel ran out. Stella glanced at the rest of the partygoers, but they didn't seem to notice.

She looked back at the woman, whose voice cut out as well, swallowed by static as she disappeared completely.

"What . . . what just happened?" Stella asked.

"I'm not sure why, but something about the curse won't allow me to view the exact moment it happened," Archie replied.

"Curse?" Lavinia repeated.

Archie looked at her and shrugged helplessly. "That's what I assume it was. She chanted something I didn't understand, and then a mountain of dust formed in the distance. It tore through the orchard, wiping out everything—I couldn't see or breathe. When it passed, everyone was gone, and the world looked different. It had this . . . sparkle to it. Like you see now. I tried to leave but found out I was trapped. As time went by and no one else came, I thought I must be hidden, or the rest of the world was gone. I haven't seen another human being since then." He looked at each of them, tears starting in his eyes. "Not until now."

"My God," Mattie murmured. "It's just like a fairy tale. A curse like this always happens when a witch or fairy takes revenge on a human man for rebuffing her advances."

Archie's face colored, and Lavinia jabbed her elbow at Mattie again.

"You're acting awestruck," she hissed. "This is his *life*, not a fairy tale."

Mattie may have been amazed and Lavinia may have been sympathetic, but Stella felt the most practical emotion—fear. She turned to the others.

"What if the ghost we saw was that woman, and she brought us here to trap us just like Archie?"

"But we're not trapped," Mattie argued. "We can come and go as we please. Besides, she was crying out for help."

Stella pinched the bridge of her nose. "That's what people do when they're trying to trap you, Mattie. They pretend to need your help."

"I know what I heard in her voice, Stella. She was truly scared."

"Scared of what?" Stella exploded, dropping her hand. "She's a ghost or a witch or something. She was powerful enough to trap Archie here, so what makes you think she needs any help from us?"

Mattie lifted her chin and glared at Stella. "I never said I knew what she was scared of, only that she was scared. And whatever her motives, it couldn't have been a trap, because we're *not trapped*!"

"Hold on," Lavinia said, raising her palms. "I know this situation is crazy, but we're . . . well, we're being rude." She turned to Archie. "I'm Lavinia Fischer, and these are my two sisters, Stella and Mattie. And this is Lloyd. He's . . . well, he's—"

"A friend of the family," Lloyd offered. He stuck out his hand but then remembered himself and pulled back, ducking his head.

"Don't feel bad," Archie assured him. "It's hard to get used to. All of this must be hard to get used to."

Lloyd gave him a grateful smile and then glanced at the tables of food. "I don't know. I could get used to a bounty like this."

"Oh, it's nothing," Archie began, but Stella shook her head.

"It's not nothing to us. You don't know since you've been here since 1930, but the last four years have been nearly apocalyptic, and I'm not exaggerating. That dust storm you experienced? They happen all the time now. Drought and the Depression have destroyed the country. Nothing grows, and no one has money."

"My God," he whispered, horror twisting his features.

"But here," Mattie continued, looking around, longing flooding her eyes. "I know you're a prisoner here, but to us it's like . . . it's like—"

"Paradise," Lavinia finished, the same desire reflected in her gaze. Stella felt the same pull toward everything around them, and when she saw Lloyd inhale and expel one of his sighs, she knew he felt it too. They all wanted to do more than watch this party. They wanted to be a part of it, to live this reality with the others.

"I know you can't touch anyone or anything," Stella told Archie, "and I don't mean to be insensitive but . . ." She wet her lips. "Do you think *we* could?"

Archie gave her a kind smile. "It's not insensitive at all and only natural to wonder. But the honest truth is, I don't know."

Stella looked at the dancers, remembering the airy glee of dancing without a care, of using her body for joy instead of housework, of flying across the floor with a partner like two synchronized moons orbiting the earth.

"I'll find out," she announced, the ache for her old life overtaking her fear. She marched to the nearest partygoer, a man watching the dancers and smoking a cigarette. She reached out to tap him on the shoulder, half certain her hand would pass through him like Archie's, but her finger met the soft cotton of his shirt and the muscle beneath. She flinched as he turned around.

"Yes?" he asked, raising an eyebrow, and Stella looked down at herself, remembering she was wearing a pair of man's overalls.

"Oh, nothing," she said with a smile. "I must have thought you were someone else."

He took a drag on his cigarette and looked her over again. His lips curled as he exhaled. "I can be him too, sweet cheeks."

Of course. Even magical, memory men were creeps. Even when she was dressed like a grubby field hand.

"That's okay," she said. Then, she trudged back to the others and said, "Well, we can touch them. And be insulted by them as well."

Her gaze caught Lloyd's. He'd been watching her, but he quickly looked away.

"That probably means we can eat too?" he asked. "That corn bread smells like heaven."

He chuckled, as if he were joking, but Stella heard the yearning in his voice.

"I don't know," Mattie said. "In folklore and mythology, whenever humans enter a magical world, eating or drinking something from that world often lands them into trouble." She quirked a brow up at Stella. "*That's* when they get trapped."

"This isn't a myth or a fairy tale," Stella countered. "This is real life."

"And maybe it wouldn't be so bad being trapped here," Lavinia murmured, touching her cheek. She laughed a little then, as if she'd been joking, but Stella hadn't missed the sadness and longing in her voice. Lloyd hadn't either.

"I like havin' my face fixed up here too," he said to Lavinia. "But it ain't our world. We have to go back."

Lavinia looked at him, a rare flash of anger in her eyes. Stella understood it. Lloyd's scars weren't anywhere near as severe as Lavinia's, and besides, he was a man. His scars and injuries gave him a tough, experienced-looking air. The world applauded seasoned, street-wise men but demanded girls remain pure, unweathered, and blemish-free forever. The same scars that made a man look strong only made a woman look damaged.

Still, he was right about one thing.

"We do need to go soon," Stella said. "The dust storm has probably passed by now, and we promised Aunt Elsa we'd be back in time to make dinner."

"Of course. You have lives to get back to and loved ones who will miss you," Archie said. Stella turned toward him, guilt pricking her chest when she realized they'd been ignoring him. "But I don't mean to . . ." he continued, running his tongue between his teeth. "I mean, I know it's a lot to ask, but do you think . . . do you think you might come back?"

"Yes, of course," Stella said, the guilt in her chest ballooning.

"Now that we know you're trapped here all alone, how could we abandon you?" Lavinia agreed. Stella could tell she was earnest and felt as guilty as Stella did, but the longing in her eyes told her another truth as well. A world with clean air, green earth, and a beautiful, unscathed face called to Lavinia as hypnotically as the music, colored lights, and spinning dancers called to Stella. When she glanced at Lloyd, his gaze still lingering on the food, and Mattie, her face alight with fascination, she knew they felt the same. None of them could resist the pull of this magical paradise.

"And more than that," Mattie told Archie. "We'll find a way to free you. We'll solve the riddle or undo the curse or whatever needs to be done. There's a reason we were brought here, and I think it's because we're the ones who are meant to help you."

Archie glanced at each of them, shaking his head in wonder. "Thank you. All of you. Words can't . . . I just can't tell you how grateful I am." With a wave of his hand, Archie dismissed his memory, and the party blew out like a candle.

They made plans to come back the following night after Aunt Elsa and the boarders had gone to sleep. The group waded into the water, leaving Archie in the buttery, unreal sunlight. Stella glanced back before she stepped on the discolored patch of dirt to see him hold up a hand in farewell. He flexed his fingers, paused, and then glanced at his hand, as if remembering for the first time what it was to be able to touch, the intrusion of their solid, tangible presence wrenching his heart. Then Stella slipped through the earth, and he disappeared from her view.

CHAPTER 6

The dust storm might have passed, but so much filth still hung in the air. The four of them couldn't stop coughing as they trudged toward the truck. Stella's lungs felt like claws tearing at her chest, begging her to return where the air was clean. The boards they'd collected had been scattered, and the truck was covered in dust, but neither were buried. It only took a few minutes to load the boards back into the truck and drive off through the brown-yellow haze.

They were silent during the drive. The cab seemed more sweltering than before, the air more stifling. Stella could still see Archie's glowing world in her mind, hear the dizzying music, smell the food, and feel the lightness in her bones. Beside her, Lavinia ran her fingertips over her scars. Their bodies had left the cider mill, but their minds had not.

Thankfully, they arrived home in time to wash and prepare dinner, and Aunt Elsa was elated to see they had made it home safely, especially with the free lumber. Stella helped set the table and cook the meal in a mindless daze, but eventually, the routine brought her back to reality. By the time she and her sisters took their places in the after-dinner assembly line of Lavinia washing the dishes, Stella drying them, and Mattie putting them away, it seemed Archie and his ethereal world had only been a dream.

Still, it was a dream none of them could stop thinking about.

"I'm going to go to the library tomorrow," Mattie told them, her voice low. "I want to look for books about spells and curses. Maybe they can help us figure out how to free Archie."

"I can go with you," Lavinia offered. "Since you mentioned folklore and fairy tales, it might be helpful to look through those books as well."

Stella didn't believe in fairy tales, but she could no longer deny there was more to the world than she'd previously imagined. The idea that something so vast and confusing existed made her anxious. She hated unpredictability and anything she couldn't understand or control. She wanted answers as much as she wanted to dance in Archie's world.

"I was thinking I might talk to the boarders," she told them. "Especially the older ones. If they went to Archie's parties or know people who did, they might know who the woman who cursed him was."

Mattie looked at her, surprised. "That's a great idea, Stella."

Stella arched a brow. "Well, I do have them now and then."

"Actually," Mattie continued as if she hadn't spoken. "I already have a few volumes of fairy tales in the attic. Do you two mind finishing up so I can look through them?"

"Go on, Mattie. I can take over."

Stella looked up to see Lloyd in the kitchen doorway. His eye and lip had healed a little since the previous evening, but it was still odd to see the wounds again after they'd vanished in Archie's world. Her eyes flitted to his jaw, where she now knew a tooth was missing.

"You don't know where everything goes," Stella found herself saying, though she wasn't sure why. It was impractical to refuse his help, and after what they'd experienced together, it felt as though the four of them were in the same secret society. But maybe that *was* why. Stella could handle sharing a frightening mystery with her sisters. The three of them had existed in their own, private world since birth; their shared experiences and closeness, something no one could replicate. Lloyd was now a part of something intimate and cloistered Stella wished was theirs alone. It brought him too close to her sacred, personal space. Too close to her.

"I'll dry, then," he said, extending his hand for the towel. "You can put them away."

There was nothing she could say to argue, so Stella gave him the towel.

"I'll let you know what I find," Mattie said. Then, she hurried from the room.

"What's she lookin' for?" asked Lloyd.

"A story like Archie's," Lavinia replied. "Or something that might explain it."

"It's a mighty strange story," Lloyd said, taking the plate she'd handed him and wiping it with the towel. "That is, if it's true."

"You don't believe him?" Stella asked.

"I'm not sayin' I don't believe him. I'm just sayin' I don't take his word as gospel. I only just met the guy. I don't know what he's about."

"He's about being trapped alone for the last four years," Stella replied.

"And not being able to touch anyone or anything," Lavinia added.

"I'm just sayin' refusing a girl seems a peculiar reason for that girl to up and curse you."

Stella snorted and swiped the dry plate from his hands. "Now I get it."

"Now you get what?"

"You can't imagine a man refusing a girl at all."

Instead of becoming indignant, he laughed.

"What is it about me that makes you think I ain't all that picky, sugar?"

An unwelcome flush filled her cheeks. "Picky?"

"Choosy. Selective. Particular. All of which, I happen to be."

"What are you, a dictionary? Besides, women aren't *food*."

"But that's how you think men see them, ain't it? That we're all like that lawman down by the station or that man in Archie's orchard?"

You are *all like that*, she thought, but then she realized it wasn't true. Her father wasn't like that. He had always treated her mother, Aunt Elsa, and every other woman with respect. The male boarders treated Stella cordially as well, and other beautiful girls, like Jane, didn't seem to constantly attract unwanted advances.

So maybe all men didn't treat every girl they met like a cheap meal. But plenty *did* treat Stella that way.

What did that say about her?

"I believe Archie," Lavinia said. "We saw that woman with our own eyes, and his explanation is no crazier than the existence of his world in the first place."

Stella set the plate on the shelf and took the next one from Lloyd. "Speaking of which, why do you think your injuries healed there?" she asked them both. "And why was everything so beautiful and perfect? That doesn't seem like much of a curse."

"It is if you have to look at that perfection and can't enjoy it," Lloyd said.

"And maybe our healing is part of that perfection," Lavinia offered, glancing at her reflection in the window. "In that world, everything is the way it's *supposed* to be."

THEY FINISHED THE REST of the dishes in silence. When they were done, Stella grabbed the broom and swept out the front hall. As she emptied the dust bin outside, she caught sight of Lloyd on the sleeping porch. He sat down on the wicker settee and retrieved the jar of moonshine hidden beneath it. Stella went back inside and crept through the hall toward the room. He was raising the jar to his lips when she entered.

"How did your tooth get knocked out?"

He took a sip, then lowered the jar. "Feeling curious again?"

Stella didn't answer. In truth, she *was* curious. Until that day, her life had been dully and painfully familiar, but even after meeting an intangible man in a magical realm, she found Lloyd mysterious. Maybe because he was like that magical realm in his own way—he defied the rules of behavior for most of the men she came across.

While most of them were predictable and dim, Lloyd was smart and able to surprise her and catch her off guard, and though he certainly loved to tease her, he'd never made real advances. He had that spark of life in his eyes, even though he'd clearly been through some terrible, painful things. She wanted to understand him the way she wanted to understand the mill. Until she did, he would always have the upper hand.

"You got a kind of . . . glint in your eye," he said when she didn't respond. "Like you're on edge. You want to sit down? I already know you don't want a drink."

She propped the broom against the wall and sat down across from him on the rocking chair.

"You don't think we're all nuts?" she found herself asking. "The four of us. That we simply had some kind of shared hallucination this morning?"

He chuckled. "It does seem less real now, don't it? Now, that we're back."

"Exactly. I feel like, when I wake up tomorrow, it will all have been a dream."

"It would be a good dream, if it was. Better than most of the dreams I have."

"You have bad dreams?"

"Most of the time."

"What are they about?"

He studied her face, his Coca-Cola eyes bright in the lamplight. “What kinda dreams do *you* have?”

“There you go, changing the subject.”

“It’s a talent.”

“It’s annoying.”

He leaned forward, resting his elbows against his knees. “You know who you remind me of? Ruth Chatterton in *Female*. When she plays the CEO of that big company.”

“I love that movie,” Stella gasped. “And I *love* Ruth Chatterton. You . . . you have the time and, well, the money to—”

“I manage to scrape enough together to go to the pictures now and again. That or the good old barter system, of course.”

Stella scooted forward. “How do I remind you of her?”

“She’s a business girl. No-nonsense. She knows what she wants and how to get it.”

He nibbled the edge of his bottom lip, the part that wasn’t injured. His gaze was sharp, almost penetrating, and Stella felt the urge to grab the moonshine and take a swig.

“I hate how that movie ends, though,” she said. “When she gives the company to her fiancé and says she’ll have nine of his children.”

He laughed. “You don’t want kids?”

“Hell no. And I sure as hell wouldn’t give up a million-dollar company to have them.” She paused and laughed. “Did you know, there are a surprising amount of Romani stories about women becoming pregnant by eating apples?”

“No kidding?”

She nodded, laughing harder. “When I was a little girl, I refused to eat them. I must have been eleven or twelve before my parents convinced me it was safe.”

“Even as a kid, you were cautious.”

“More than I should have been.”

She met his gaze. It was . . . *nice* laughing with him.

"So, is that what you dream about?" he asked. "Being Ruth Chatterton?"

"Or Jean Harlow or Greta Garbo or Norma Shearer or Barbara Stanwyck. Any of them would do. Who are your favorite stars?"

Lloyd leaned back against the settee. "I don't really go in for pictures much. When I was a kid, though, I . . ." He chuckled and took a small sip. "I liked to read the *Hopalong Cassidy* books and other dime novel Westerns."

"You wanted to be a cowboy?"

"I did indeed. You know, lots of those stories took place in Dodge City. I was sort of excited to stop here."

"I'll bet you were disappointed," Stella muttered. "It's no longer the wild frontier town of Wyatt Earp. Just a dusty prairie village like all the others."

"It's been pretty different so far," Lloyd countered, and Stella couldn't argue with that. "My mamma disapproved of those books, though," he continued. "Like I said, she loved the classics."

"How old were you when she died?"

Stella immediately regretted the question. His smile dissolved, along with the mirth in the air.

"Fourteen. She and my daddy took sick at the same time. They died of influenza—her first, then him just two days later."

"I'm so sorry."

They shared a look of understanding, just as they had the previous night when they discussed Stella's mother's death. Stella was lucky enough to still have her father, but she'd also been fourteen when her mother died.

When the entire world turned upside down forever.

"At least it was quick for both of them," Lloyd said. "And I . . . well, your story about your mamma made me grateful I at least had their bodies to bury. I dug their graves with my own two hands."

Stella's brow puckered in pity, but he raised a palm.

"No, it felt good to do that, to be *able* to do that for them. Putting them to rest beside each other on the land they'd loved so much."

A smile found its way onto Stella's face, despite her twisting heart. Lloyd had a true talent for finding the silver lining. But then, she remembered something.

"How old are you, Lloyd?"

"Eighteen."

Stella was surprised. She'd thought he was at least two or three years older than she was, though perhaps the scars and air of hard living he carried made him seem older. Even so, the math didn't add up.

"You said you'd been riding the rails for two years. If your parents died and you lost the farm when you were fourteen, where did you live for the two years before you left Texas?"

He looked at her, his body now eerily still, his eyes wary. The quiet lasted so long, Stella thought he might not respond. But then he looked at the floorboards, and took a long, deep drink of the moonshine.

"I went to live with my uncle." He looked back up and met her gaze, though his own was still guarded. "He's the one who knocked out the tooth. Gave me this, too." He gestured at the scar through his eyebrow. "You and Mattie asked how I knew where Lavinia got her scars. It's because I've got the same ones, on my back. He . . ." He rolled his shoulders, his eyes flitting down. "He threw me into a mirror. A tall, freestanding one. The mirror and I both fell, and it shattered on top of me."

Stella stared at him, horrified. "Why?"

"He always made up excuses. I cooked the dinner wrong, mucked the barn out wrong—hell, *looked* at him wrong. But the truth is, he did it for kicks, plain and simple. He liked feeling bigger and stronger than me, loved throwing his weight around. He . . ." Lloyd paused, wet his lips, and looked back up. "He liked to hurt people, you know?"

Stella didn't know and had a feeling she didn't want to. Still, she asked, "So, that's why you ran away? Why you're riding the rails?"

He took another drink and didn't look at her when he answered. "Yeah."

She didn't believe him. Not entirely. There was a terrible storm within him now. She could see it in the lines of his face, in the desperate, almost violent way he had raised the jar to his lips. They'd waded into something deeper and darker than Stella understood, and she didn't know how to climb out.

"Is that who the man at the station reminded you of?" she asked, but then she closed her eyes and cursed herself. *Keep digging, Stella.*

"Stella?"

She looked up. Lavinia was peeking around the corner.

"What is it?"

"Mr. Donaldson is here. He's talking to Aunt Elsa on the front porch."

Stella gaped at her. Had she been so absorbed she didn't hear his car? "What?"

"Who is Mr. Donaldson?" Lloyd asked.

"He's our account manager at the bank," Stella explained. "He holds the mortgage on the house, but there's no reason for him to be here. We've never missed a payment."

She stood, and she and Lavinia walked inside and around the corner. Through the window beside the front door, they could see Aunt Elsa talking with Mr. Donaldson, but heard nothing. Then, a moment later, Aunt Elsa opened the door, and they both jumped.

"Goodnight," she said, not pausing for a reply before closing the door behind Mr. Donaldson. Stella had never heard her voice sound so cold, even when scolding. When she turned around, her cheeks were flushed, and her eyes were burning with anger.

"Aunt Elsa, what is it?" Lavinia asked, rushing to her. Stella followed, anxiety creeping through her chest. Aunt Elsa blinked, took a breath, and smoothed her skirt.

"Nothing, girls," she said with a stiff smile. "Mr. Donaldson was just stopping by."

"Why would he stop by? And this late at night?" demanded Stella.

"Don't worry. He won't be doing it again," Aunt Elsa said, rage flaring again in her eyes as she glanced at the door. "We've never missed a payment, and he knows it."

"Aunt Elsa, what's going on?" Lavinia asked.

"Nothing," she said, turning back to them. "I told you. He won't be coming by again. Now, let's go to bed."

She strode toward the stairs but then paused and turned back around. "Lloyd said he would be able to start on the sleeping porch tomorrow?"

They nodded.

"Good. Like I said, everything's fine," she added quickly. "But the sooner we can bring in more boarders, the better."

She turned back around and jogged up the stairs. Stella and Lavinia shared a pointed glance, an agreement that they would discuss what they'd witnessed later. Lavinia followed Aunt Elsa, and Stella began to follow as well, but she heard Lloyd's voice behind her.

"Everything all right?"

She turned around. He was standing in the doorway between the hall and the sleeping porch. Stella walked back to him.

"No. Aunt Elsa said everything's fine, but she's terribly upset. She's also even more eager for you to fix the sleeping porch."

"I'll get to work on it first thing in the morning."

"Speaking of being terribly upset," Stella said, wincing a little and knowing she should probably leave it alone. "I'm sorry I upset you just now. I shouldn't have pried, and I didn't mean—"

"Water under the bridge, sugar. That's the thing about the past—it's past. Doesn't bother me now."

He grinned, turned around, and ambled back to the sleeping porch. Stella watched him go before she headed toward the stairs, certain she'd been lied to for a second time that night.

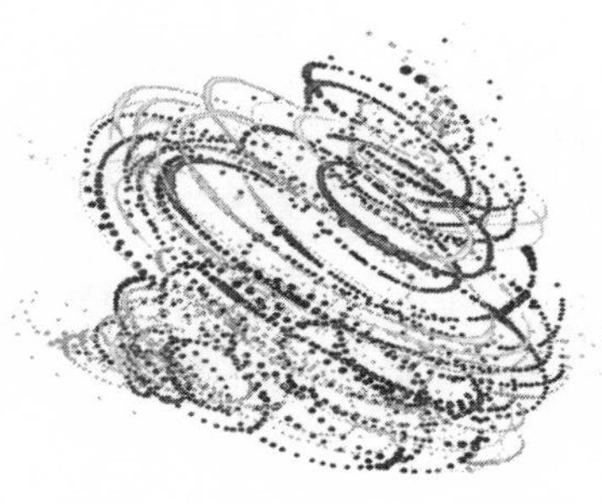

CHAPTER 7

Mattie scoured her fairy tale books that night but didn't find anything helpful. Eventually, she gave up and crawled into bed with Stella and Lavinia, who still hadn't figured out what Mr. Donaldson had said or done to anger Aunt Elsa so much. The next morning, they threw themselves into work, hoping to make enough time for their research that afternoon. Lloyd spent the day taking measurements and sawing the lumber, and Stella, Mattie, and Lavinia did their chores in a mindless frenzy. Their eagerness seemed to permeate the air, but Stella knew it wasn't only to solve Archie's mystery and free him. All of them were desperate to enter his magical world again, starving for the bounty, excitement, and freedom that had been leeched from their world long ago.

After lunch had been served and cleaned away, Lavinia and Mattie took the truck to the library. Most of the boarders returned to their jobs, so Stella decided to speak with the only one left at the house—old Mrs. Kelly. Stella approached her room—which had once been hers—to find the door open, the antiseptic, menthol scent of Vicks VapoRub wafting into the hall. Stella peeked in. Mrs. Kelly was seated at Stella's old desk, reading a book, her gas mask within arm's reach. Stella rapped her knuckles against the door.

"Mrs. Kelly?"

Mrs. Kelly looked up from her book, lowered her spectacles, and squinted at Stella.

"Hello there, Stella. Do you need something?"

"Yes, actually," Stella said, edging into the room. She realized she hadn't yet thought of how to bring the subject up. "I . . . I was wondering if I could ask you something. It's for school—I mean, not school *now*, since it's summer—but *over* the summer, for school, we are supposed to do some research about . . . about local businesses. From the past."

If Mrs. Kelly thought her rambling was strange or unbelievable, she didn't show it. Nor did she seem to remember Stella had graduated last month and wasn't returning to school in the fall.

"Of course," she said, gesturing at Stella's old bed. "What would you like to know?"

Stella took a seat on the bed, but as she sank onto her old quilt, the familiarity of her previous life swamped her. The bed was old, but it had been *hers* and so much more comfortable than the mattress she shared with her sisters.

Don't think about that now, she told herself.

"Do you remember anything about the Bright Apple Orchard?" she asked. "Mr. Bright sold apples and cider, and I heard he sometimes threw parties?"

"Oh, of course," Mrs. Kelly said, her creased face brightening with a smile. Then she paused to cough, her dust pneumonia acting up. "My son frequented those parties often," she said when she recovered. "Before he left to work for the railroad, of course. Mr. Bright was such a generous man. Anyone was welcome, and he refused to take a dime for the food or drinks. I might have gone myself once or twice if Mr. Kelly hadn't needed me so much in those final years."

Her smile turned sad, and Stella shifted, glancing at her lap. It didn't feel right to ask Mrs. Kelly if her son ever mentioned an evil witch or fairy attending the party when she was thinking about her dead husband.

"You know, even though I never went there, I always thought there was something, sort of . . . strange about the orchard," Mrs. Kelly continued.

Stella's head shot up. "How so?"

"Well, it seemed to me an orchard should takes years to thrive," she explained. "Years for the trees to grow, mature, and bear good fruit. But it seemed like Mr. Bright's orchard appeared overnight. It was just before the Great War. He moved into town, and then there was an orchard."

Stella knit her brow. Mrs. Kelly must have been mistaken about the year. Archie would have been barely a teenager in 1912. Unless he was genetically blessed to appear thirty when he was forty. Though, for all Stella knew, he was.

"Maybe he'd planted it earlier and you only heard about it later, when he was making money and throwing the parties," Stella offered.

"Oh, of course that must have been the case," Mrs. Kelly agreed, stifling another cough. "Although, I still thought it strange to plant an apple orchard in Kansas. It isn't unheard of, mind you, but I always heard the best apples came from back east or further north. No matter. I always liked the man, and so did Mr. Kelly. Though he was one of the richest men in town, you would never know it. He dressed like the rest of us and never acted as if he were better."

Stella couldn't help but smile. "Yes, he has—*had*—warm eyes, and wore his hair long, like a cowboy's."

"Yes," Mrs. Kelly said, smiling as well. "And of course, you know what he did for all those orphan children brought in from the east coast by the Children's Aid Society, don't you?"

Stella inclined her head. "No."

"He took in the ones who couldn't find homes, the wilder ones with criminal records. He employed the older ones at his orchard and paid for the younger ones to attend boarding schools in Kansas City, since he didn't have a wife to help him raise them."

Stella thought of the Irish boy at the party, the fondness in Archie's eyes when he spoke to him, and the pain in his voice when he couldn't shake his hand. Her admiration and empathy for Archie grew, but more importantly, Mrs. Kelly's comment gave her an opening.

"I suppose there were many women who wanted to marry him though," she said. "A nice-looking, rich man like that would attract attention."

Mrs. Kelly chuckled. "Oh yes. And he was gentleman, too. In fact, I heard . . ."

She trailed off, and then glanced away.

"You heard what?" Stella pressed.

"Well, do you . . . do you know what a cat house is, Stella?"

Stella blinked in surprise, but then nodded. She'd heard of houses of ill repute, and though most of the courtesans in her beloved films were filthy rich, she'd seen some films, like *The Story of Temple Drake* and *Safe in Hell*, that dealt with women who worked in rough places like that.

"Well, there used to be one on the edge of town," Mrs. Kelly continued. "It was run by a woman called Old Clara. It was a terrible place a woman would turn to only if she were desperate, where the girls were beaten by the men and Old Clara herself. But a nurse friend told me Mr. Bright would pay the nurses to let him know when a girl was admitted so he could hire her to work at his orchard for twice what she made at Old Clara's."

Stella thought of the forwardness of the woman who'd approached Archie, her easy sexuality and insistence she owed him a "favor."

"Did you know of any of those girls?" she ventured. "Their names perhaps?"

Mrs. Kelly's eyes bulged. "Goodness, of course not." A coughing fit overtook her, and she hunch over, digging a handkerchief out of her pocket. As she hacked into the fabric, Stella raised her palms.

"I'm sorry. Of course, you wouldn't. That was a silly thing to ask."

"It . . . it's all right," Mrs. Kelly wheezed. "These attacks . . . they happen. I think I need to . . . to lie down if you don't mind."

"Not at all. Thank you so much for your help."

WHEN NIGHT FINALLY FELL and Aunt Elsa and the boarders went to sleep, the four of them crept through the creaking house as quietly as they could. Once outside, they pushed the truck to the end of the block before starting the engine. The trip to the mill took about thirty minutes, so the plan was to get there, stay for an hour, and arrive back home at midnight, which would give them plenty of time to rest before the following morning.

The abandoned archway and crumbling buildings looked even more ghostly at night, even without a pending dust storm. After Stella turned off the headlights, Mattie led them toward the creek with a flashlight. Its beam illuminated the dust in the air, but there was no trace of the ghost, and Mattie didn't report any whispers. When they found the discolored mark, Lavinia placed her foot on it first. She disappeared, followed by Mattie, and then Lloyd. Before Stella stepped forward, she removed her shoes, placed them in one hand, and gathered her skirt above her knees. As an experiment, she'd worn what used to be her best dress and shoes—a bright red sweaterdress that was now rusty and black T-strap heels that were worn through at the soles and moth-eaten—and she didn't want to get them wet when the creek materialized.

Her plan worked. Once she was in the other world, the water rose above her knees but below her gathered hem. She glanced up and caught sight of Lloyd. His eyes flitted over her knees and exposed thighs. Then he met her gaze, unashamed, and raised a questioning eyebrow. She ignored him, climbed out of the creek, and looked down at her dress. It was bright red again, intact, patch-free, and as new as the day she bought it, and her restored heels were so polished, they glinted in the moonlight.

"Oh my goodness," Mattie said, looking her over. "Your damaged clothes are mended just like Lloyd's and Lavinia's scars."

Stella beamed. "I thought that might happen. That's why I wore them tonight."

Lavinia, who'd been grinning and cupping her smooth cheek in her hand, turned to the mansion and called, "Hello? Archie?"

A few seconds later, he appeared, jogging around the mansion and through the trees.

"You're back," he called with a grin. "It's so good to see you." He trotted to a stop. "You brought a camera?"

He nodded at their father's Kodak in Mattie's left hand as she clicked off the flashlight in her right.

"Yes. I thought I would try and capture the things we see here, if that's all right," she said.

"Of course."

"We've done some research on how to free you," she continued, laying the flashlight in the grass. "Though, I'm afraid we don't have much yet."

"Oh, I wouldn't expect that you would. After all the time I've been here, I'd hardly bank on anyone finding an immediate solution."

"We do have a lead, though," Mattie said. Then she grinned at Stella. "Tell him."

Heat flooded Stella's cheeks, and she glanced at Lloyd. She'd told her sisters what she'd learned from Mrs. Kelly, but not him.

"I . . ." she said, turning back to Archie. "Well, I heard you used to help women who . . . well, women who worked at a place called Old Clara's. She said you hired them here so they wouldn't have to . . . work there. And I wondered if the woman you showed us, the woman who cursed you . . . from the way she carried herself and how she said she wanted to thank you . . . I just wondered if she might have been one of those women."

Archie's lips parted. "I'd never thought about that. She might have been."

"You aren't sure?"

"I paid the nurses at the hospital to pass along my offer, but my foremen dealt with the direct hiring, so I never knew who came from where."

"But they or your other workers might know who she was, right?" Mattie asked. "The woman would never tell *us* who she was, but they might be able to find out, wouldn't they?"

Archie knit his brow. "I suppose, but I don't know which ones would know. I could conjure a party most of them would have attended from around that time if you'd like, and we could ask them."

Mattie clapped her hands together. "Yes! That's a brilliant idea."

Stella detected an extra note of elation in Mattie's voice, which she understood. The reason for summoning the party was for Archie, but she knew Mattie was as eager for the excitement and splendor as she was. When she saw the light in Lloyd's and Lavinia's eyes, she knew they felt the same way.

Archie closed his eyes and raised his hands. The band appeared first, followed by the people, the lanterns, and finally, the food. Music, chatter, and laughter rose through the air, bright as the stars. Stella exhaled, her blood singing as she turned toward the dance floor, where everyone was bouncing to a wild, ravishing polka.

"Pardon me, miss," a voice said, and Stella turned to see a young man approaching Lavinia. "Would you care to dance?"

Lavinia blinked at him and then glanced at Archie.

"Go on," he said, his smile luminous, as if nothing would give him more joy than to see her enjoy herself.

"Yes," Mattie agreed. "We've got plenty of time."

Lavinia turned back to the man. A grin broke across her face, more confident and brilliant than Stella had seen since before the accident. She gave a curtsy and took the man's hand. He led her onto the dance floor, and they joined the swirling crowd.

"How 'bout it, sugar?"

Stella turned to see Lloyd extending his hand.

"You know how to polka?" she asked.

"Polka, waltz. Even foxtrot. Dancing was the way my daddy won my mamma's heart."

Stella glanced at Mattie, glaring in response to the knowing smirk on her face.

"Go on," Mattie said. "Archie and I will ask around on our own first."

"You're sure you don't mind?" Stella asked Archie.

"Not at all," he insisted. "Have fun."

Stella smiled at him, turned back to Lloyd, and took his hand. It felt smooth and soft, rather than rough and calloused like in the real world. Strangely, rather than pleasant, Stella found the sensation unnerving. When he led her onto the floor, however, his grip was strong and reassuring, and she couldn't fight the shiver that ran up her spine when he touched her waist.

"Ready?" he asked, and she looked up at his healed, unblemished face. He did look younger that way, more like the boy he might have been if not for his uncle and riding the rails. She wasn't sure how she felt about this face that was his and not his. But the next thing she knew, they were dancing, and every other thought disappeared.

She'd forgotten what it was to simply dance without a care. It was thrilling to use her body for something other than dusting, washing, sweeping, or hauling jars of moonshine; to be breathless from exhilaration rather than wheezing from exhaustion. She loved the click of her heels against the wood, the whip of her skirt against her knees, and

Lloyd was a strong partner, sweeping her up in dizzying circles. The sweet night air and flickering lanterns added to the magic, and soon, she'd nearly forgotten every worry she'd ever had. She wasn't Stella Fischer, a poor, nothing girl from a prairie town. She was Norma Shearer in *Strangers May Kiss*, gliding over the floor of a millionaire's ballroom in southern France. She was Ginger Rogers, twirling on the balcony of a fancy, Brazilian hotel in *Flying Down to Rio*.

When the song came to an end, it took her a moment to catch her breath. She looked up at Lloyd. He was breathing hard too and smiling down at her. The band struck up a waltz.

"Do you want to—" Stella began, but then a girl with lovely blond curls crept up behind Lloyd and tapped his shoulder.

"May I have this dance?"

Lloyd glanced at Stella. She smiled to hide the surprising disappointment that flooded her chest. "Go ahead. I'll see how Archie and Mattie are doing."

She backed away, her gaze lingering on the girl's waist as Lloyd placed his hand there. A flash of apple red hair caught her eye, and she saw Lavinia waltzing across the floor with a different partner. Stella turned, walked onto the grass, and spotted Mattie and Archie near the trees.

"Any luck so far?" she asked as she approached them.

"No," Mattie said with a sigh. "And apparently, we've already talked to everyone."

"It does seem strange that none of them know anything," Archie agreed.

"It's like she dropped out of the sky," Stella said, resting her hands on her hips.

"I told Archie about Lavinia and I visiting the library to research curses and folktales," Mattie told her. "Though, like I told *you*, none of them seem to apply so far. He hasn't lost a precious object or made a deal with a supernatural creature, like in most of the stories we read.

But if the woman's identity is a dead end, more folk and fairy tales are the only place left to look." She raised a brow at Stella. "Did you have fun dancing with Lloyd?"

"It felt good to dance again," Stella replied, ignoring her pointed look.

Mattie raised her camera and turned to Archie. "Is it all right with you if I go and take more pictures?"

"Of course. Snap away."

She trotted off into the crowd, and Stella glanced at Archie. It was easy to forget he was intangible, especially so close. He appeared as solid and substantial as anyone else, his denim work shirt lifting with the breeze and his musky grown man scent wafting toward her. Memories of her father pinched her throat, and she swallowed.

"I know you conjured this party to find the identity of the woman," she said. "But being here, enjoying this, it's more than magical for us. It's a paradise compared to the world we know, and we're all grateful."

He breathed a laugh and shook his head. "No. It's *me* who is grateful to you. Four, kind kids who are willing to keep me company and help me regain my life. The least I can do is show you a good time while you're here." He nodded at the dance floor. "Lavinia seems to be having an especially good time."

Stella followed his gaze. Lavinia was spinning about, her back straight and face alight.

"This is wonderful for her," Stella said. "It's like she's her old self again."

"What do you mean?"

Stella froze. She hadn't meant to open the door to Lavinia's pain like that. And yet, Archie might have some answers.

"Well," she began, "we're not sure why, but things seem to . . . *heal* for us here. In our world, this dress and these shoes are worn through, and . . . Lavinia has scars covering the left side of her face. They're from an accident during a dust storm three years ago. But here, they're gone."

Archie shifted his gaze to Lavinia. His brows sloped downward, as if he were trying to picture the scars on her smooth, clear face. "That poor girl. All because of another dust storm."

Perhaps it was the sympathy in his eyes, or maybe the knowledge of what he'd lost as well, but Stella added, "The dust has taken a lot from our family. We lost our mother because of a storm, too."

Archie turned to her, his brow furrowing deeper. "Lost?"

"She died in a dust storm."

Archie pressed his lips together and then ran his tongue between them, as if searching for the right thing to say. "I am sorry for your loss," he finally said. "I've lost loved ones as well. It never gets easier."

"No, it doesn't," Stella agreed. The years since her mother's death seemed both like the blink of an eye and a lifetime, and every day was as difficult as the last. "So, do you have any idea why Lavinia's scars heal here? Why our worn things mend?"

"I wish I did, but it's as much of a mystery to me as everything else." He looked back out at the crowd, a smile lifting his lips, though the sadness remained in his eyes. "I am glad Lavinia can be happy here, though. Feel beautiful again."

Stella shifted her weight. While she was happy to see Lavinia bright-eyed and carefree, she also wished she could find a way to be those things in the real world, to realize she had the same beautiful face, even with her scars. That no matter what the world may think, she was no less perfect because of them. Mattie had moved past the dancers and was now snapping photos of the creek and the back of the mill. The waltz ended, and Lavinia hurried toward Stella and Archie.

"Goodness," she said, fanning herself with her hand. "I haven't danced this much in years."

"You look as though you were born for the dance floor. A natural," Archie replied.

He smiled at her, and Stella's chest twinged because she'd seen that look before.

On the face of their father.

It was the kind of admiration she only saw in the eyes of adults—a wonderment and delight at what the next generation had wrought. Lavinia must have recognized it too, because she swallowed and glanced at her shoes.

"Thank you, Archie." Then, she cleared her throat and turned to Stella. "You should dance again too. I think I saw Lloyd—"

She clamped her mouth shut when she glanced back out at the party, and Stella followed her gaze. Lloyd was no longer on the dance floor, but standing beside a table piled with barbecued ribs, mashed potatoes, creamed corn, and glistening cakes and pies. He was at the dessert end, laughing with the girl with the curly, blond hair. She swatted his arm playfully, and in response, he dipped his finger into the icing of a cake and smeared it onto the end of her nose. She bent over in a fit of giggles, then straightened up, grabbed a handful of cake, and shoved it into his mouth. He stumbled backward, laughed, and licked his lips.

"Oh no," Lavinia murmured. "Remember what Mattie said about eating the food?"

"Well, if it *is* some kind of magical trap, that's his own fault," Stella snapped, her cheeks unreasonably hot, and her voice unnecessarily cool. "I don't need to dance with him anyway. I won't have trouble finding a partner."

And she didn't. She danced one waltz and two more polkas, each with different partners, one of whom was at least as good as Lloyd. She saw him dance with another girl once, and when her second polka ended, she spied him resting against the steps of the mill with a group of men. Apparently, the cake he'd eaten had given him the confidence to consume other things as well, as he was drinking from one of the green Bright's Cider bottles in long, deep gulps. Worry for him twisted her stomach, but then reminded herself he'd made his choice, and it wasn't her concern. She looked away, spotting Mattie heading toward the mansion, camera in hand.

"Are you going inside?" Stella called as she caught up to her.

"Yes. Have you been in there yet?"

"No."

"Come on. Let's explore."

The two of them climbed the front porch of the towering, redbrick building. Old-fashioned gas lamps and flickering candelabras glowed through the windows. Mattie pulled open the massive, oak front door, and they stepped inside. Everything in the spacious parlor gleamed. The chandelier that hung from the ceiling, the banister, and the fireplace mantel were polished to perfection.

It was still so strange to be in a world where a fine film of dust didn't coat everything in sight. Mattie raised her camera with a *flash*, and Stella moved farther into the room.

"This furniture is beautiful," she said, running her fingers along the back of a cashmere sofa. "And so *clean*."

"I've never seen anything so elegant," Mattie agreed.

Stella hadn't either. Except in the movies, of course. In fact, the room reminded her of Greta Garbo's sumptuous palace in *Queen Christina*. She approached the broad front staircase, which was made of glossy oak and adorned by a red velvet carpet. She climbed a few steps, imagining herself a queen ascending to her throne, but stopped when she passed a window. Through its spotless panes, she could see the dancers twirling about on the lawn.

Suddenly, she screamed and stumbled back.

A blurry, disembodied face was staring at her from the window.

"Stella, what is—oh my God!" Mattie cried.

"You see it too?" Stella gasped.

"Yes!"

Stella remained frozen as Mattie dashed up the stairs beside her. The ghostly face was just distinct enough to discern it belonged to a woman. She stared at Stella and Mattie, her eyes the only clear feature in her swirling, grainy face.

"It has to be the ghost from before, right?" Stella gasped.

"Yes. She—" Mattie doubled over, nearly dropping the camera.

"What's wrong?" Stella asked.

"You don't hear that?"

"Hear what?"

"She's—she's screaming!"

Stella turned back to the woman. Her shadowy lips didn't seem to be moving. The camera *thumped* to the carpet as Mattie cried out and clutched her ears.

"Let's go," Stella said, seizing her arm and scooping up the camera. She dragged her down the stairs, through the parlor, and toward the door.

As they passed the front window, the woman's face emerged in the glass, even larger now. Stella jumped back, and Mattie screamed and covered her ears again, though Stella still didn't hear anything.

"Come on," Stella yelled, gripping her tighter and hauling her through the door. Once they were out on the porch, she slammed the thick, oak door behind them. Mattie dropped her hands and released a breath.

"Has the screaming stopped?" Stella asked.

"Yes."

They looked back at the window. The woman was gone. There was nothing but glass.

"Oh no!" Mattie yelped, staring down at the camera.

"What?" Stella asked.

Mattie swiped the device from her hands. "Why didn't I take a picture?"

Stella stared at her. "A ghost was screaming inside your head, and you're upset you didn't stop to *take her picture?*"

"You honestly couldn't hear her?"

"No. Just like none of us heard her whispering. Apparently, you're the only one who can hear her."

They climbed down the porch steps without speaking, but the silence seemed to say what Stella knew they were both thinking. The idea of Mattie's "second sight" seemed a lot less crazy now.

"What was she screaming?" Stella asked as they rounded the side of the mansion.

"Something that makes me even more sure she's the ghost of the girl who cursed Archie."

"What?"

Mattie sucked in a breath, released it, and looked up at Stella.

"'Vengeance.'"

CHAPTER 8

They discovered a few new things about Archie's world when they left that evening. First, eating and drinking in his realm didn't trap them there, as Lloyd had no problem emerging through the creek bed. Second, they couldn't bring objects from Archie's world into their own, as the handkerchief Lavinia had borrowed from someone and stowed inside her pocket disappeared on the other side. However, objects they brought in returned, such as Mattie's flashlight and camera. They would have to wait until she developed the film to see exactly how the realm appeared in the photos.

Another thing they'd discovered was that time seemed to pass more quickly in Archie's world, if only for the fact that time often did when fun was involved. When they arrived home, they found it was nearly two in the morning. None of them had thought to wear a watch, something they would have to remember for next time.

Because, of course, there was going to be a next time.

They'd promised Archie they would return as soon as they could, and Stella sensed the rest of them, like her, were hoping the opportunity would come the very next night. Even the frightening encounter with the ghost hadn't dimmed the allure of the mill. Mattie wanted to explore and learn, Lavinia wanted to feel her smooth face and dance, and Lloyd wanted to "kick back and relax in paradise." Stella wanted to dance as well and to wear her mended clothes. And now that she knew she could eat, she wanted to devour every scrap of food on that table.

In the morning, however, when sunlight crept through the attic window and Mattie nudged her awake, Stella couldn't imagine wanting anything other than sleep.

Unfortunately, that wasn't an option. There were chores to be done, and as they were making breakfast, Lloyd informed them he needed some more supplies to work on the porch—more nails and something to use for insulation. He suggested old newspapers as a cheap way to go about it, but Stella's family had stopped taking the paper when the dealership went under. Stella knew Jane took the paper and likely saved her old ones, as she tended to save everything, so Aunt Elsa agreed to let Stella and Lloyd drive to town to purchase the nails and ask Jane about the papers.

Stella had downed two cups of Aunt Elsa's strong black coffee but still felt worn and sleepy as she drove to the general store. She nearly nodded off while Lloyd went inside to purchase the nails. Aunt Elsa had given them enough money, but Stella regretted not bringing a bit of her own from the Folger's can. When she looked at the fuel gage, she realized they would need more gas before returning to Archie's, and if Aunt Elsa noticed, she'd wonder how they'd run out of gas so quickly.

Once Lloyd returned, Stella drove to Jane's, hoping she'd be home. In the past, Stella would have called first, but her family had disconnected their phone when they stopped receiving the paper. Thankfully, when she and Lloyd climbed out of the truck, Jane's old Chevrolet was parked out front. Stella started up the drive but frowned when she noticed her sleeves were frayed, the threads hanging loose over her arms. She was still wearing her sweaterdress from the night before, the formerly red one that had been perfect in Archie's world, but now it seemed even more damaged than before.

"That's a whole lot of wind chimes," Lloyd observed, jerking his head toward Mrs. Woodrow's porch. Stella winced as the chimes clanged and echoed inside her head, which was starting to ache.

"Apparently, Mrs. Woodrow thinks they ward off evil spirits."

She glanced at the widow's house, and then noticed a polished, red Cadillac parked in the drive. She knew that car. There was only one man in town who could afford it. Lloyd noticed it too.

"That ain't Mrs. Woodrow's car, is it?"

"No. It's Mr. Donaldson's. The banker who came to our house last night."

"He's got some flashy taste."

Stella had the urge to insult the car too, but seeing it made her uneasy. "Why is he going around making all these house calls lately?"

"Hey, Stella. What are you doing here?"

Jane was leaning against her porch railing, smiling down at them.

"Hey, Jane," Stella replied. "I came by to ask for a favor." She walked up the drive, and Lloyd followed. "This is Lloyd. He's staying with us and helping to convert our sleeping porch."

"Nice to meet you," Jane said, sticking out her hand. He took it and grinned.

"Pleasure's all mine. So, you're Stella's business partner?"

She froze for a moment, then glanced at Stella.

"He's fine," Stella assured her. "I sold him some the other day."

Lloyd met her gaze, his grin curling at the word "sold." Then he turned back to Jane and released her hand. "You make an excellent product. I've been thoroughly enjoying it."

"Thank you," she said, her dimples popping as she smiled and brushed a silver-blond lock of hair from her lovely face.

"Where's Jasper?" Stella asked, her voice a bit louder than necessary.

"He's with the girls. Come on in."

"What girls?" Stella asked as she and Lloyd followed her inside. Her question was answered immediately. Mrs. Woodrow's twin, ten-year-old girls were seated on Jane's carpet. They were playing Scrabble, and Jasper was kicking and cooing beside them.

One of the girls tickled Jasper's belly, and the other let out a huff and glared at her.

"Amelia, it's your turn."

"I'm playing with Jasper."

"You're playing with *me*."

"Oh, all right." The other girl turned back to the board and peered down at her letters.

"I'm watching them for Mrs. Woodrow," Jane explained. "She wanted to meet with Mr. Donaldson alone."

"Why?" Stella asked as she and Lloyd followed her into the kitchen.

"She didn't say."

"He came to our house last night, too," Stella said.

"Mr. Donaldson?"

"Yes."

Jane waved them deeper into the kitchen, lowering her voice.

"I don't know what he's meeting Mrs. Woodrow about," she said, "but I have wondered how she's been making her mortgage payments. Her husband didn't leave her much when he passed. And Amy and Amelia told me she cries in her room a lot. It's been over a year since his death, so I don't think she's crying for Alex."

"That's terrible," Stella said. She couldn't imagine being alone with two girls and no way to support herself. Mrs. Woodrow cleaned a few homes and took in sewing now and again, but if her husband's insurance money was gone, Jane was right. It couldn't be enough.

Jane sighed. "But enough sad talk. What brings you two here?"

"We need insulation to convert the sleeping porch. I was wondering if you had any old newspapers we could use."

"Of course," Jane said, brightening. "I have piles up in the attic. My parents saved them even before I was born. There are still some up there from when they moved here from Wisconsin. Come on."

She rose, and so did Lloyd.

"I'll help you haul 'em down."

"Thanks so much. Stella, could you keep an eye on the kids?"

"Sure," said Stella, standing, but as she watched them walk away, she had a sudden, irrational urge to throw something at Jane. Irritated, she trudged to the living room, where Amelia was once again ignoring the game and playing with Jasper.

"Amelia, pay attention!" Amy yelled.

"But he's so cute!"

"Here," Stella said, sitting down beside them. "You play with Jasper, and I will play with Amy."

"Who are you?" Amy asked.

"My name's Stella. I'm friends with Jane. I have sisters too, and I know how annoying they can be."

The comment brought a smile to Amy's face. "Okay. It's your turn."

Stella continued to play with Amy while Lloyd and Jane made a few trips from the attic to Stella's truck. Amy had been winning when they began, and her lead had only increased by the time the truck was loaded. Feeling even more annoyed, Stella shoved herself onto her feet when Lloyd and Jane finally finished.

"Thanks so much," she said to Jane. "We appreciate it."

The kitchen door swung open, and Stella turned to see Mrs. Woodrow. Her face was ashen, and her shoulders were hunched, as if she were fighting the urge to faint or be sick.

"Honey, what's wrong?" Jane said, walking toward her.

"Oh, nothing. Thank you for watching the girls. Mr. Donaldson's just left."

Stella moved into the kitchen, knitting her brow. Mrs. Woodrow was lying. The Cadillac had pulled out of her drive ten minutes ago. Stella studied Mrs. Woodrow. She wore a high bun, but the hair at the base of her neck was freshly wet, and the scent of lavender soap rose from her skin and filled the room. She'd just bathed. Why would she bathe in the middle of the morning immediately after meeting with her bank manager?

Something cold twisted in Stella's stomach. She tried to tell herself Mrs. Woodrow had simply wanted to pamper herself and relax in the tub while her children were away, that her midmorning bath had nothing to do with Mr. Donaldson. But then she remembered Jane's worry that Mrs. Woodrow couldn't make her mortgage payments, and the sickened look on Mrs. Woodrow's face, the fact that she'd asked Jane to watch her children, and the overwhelming scent of that lavender soap took on a new meaning.

And so did Mr. Donaldson's late-night visit to Aunt Elsa.

Stella lunged forward and opened her mouth to find out if she was right.

"Pleasure to meet you, Jane," Lloyd jumped in. "Thanks again for the papers."

Stella looked down to see he'd caught her arm. She blinked through a red haze as he led her out the front door, only vaguely aware of Jane saying she'd see her that coming Monday. Stella didn't even realize she was sitting in the passenger's seat until Lloyd had already driven them down the block.

"That bastard!" she yelled once she found her voice. "That evil bastard! He's trading her mortgage payments for—for—"

"I know."

"Did you see how sick and disgusted she looked? She's helpless and he knows it. She'll do anything to keep a roof over her daughters' heads."

"I know."

"Why did you pull me out of there?"

"Because you were gonna confront her, and she was feelin' shame enough. She didn't need to know you knew her shame."

Stella sucked in a breath and dug her fingernails into her palms. Perhaps he was right, but still . . .

"Aunt Elsa," she gasped, her anger rising again. "He must have tried to make her the same offer last night at our house. Oh, if my father were here—"

"She didn't need him," Lloyd reminded her. "She threw him out on his ear, all on her own."

"Because she could. Because *we* aren't desperate. But Mrs. Woodrow . . ."

The truck jostled, but Stella's nausea had nothing to do with the bumpy drive.

"Why are men such beasts?" she spat.

"Because the world lets them be."

Stella looked at Lloyd, thinking she'd never heard a truer statement. Then she muttered, "No offense."

"None taken. I know what I am. And I'm *not* that."

There was a burn in his voice. Stella looked at his hands on the steering wheel. His knuckles were white.

"Well, at least we got the newspapers," she said ridiculously, overwhelmed by all the awful things in the world she couldn't control. Lloyd nodded and flexed his fingers.

"I like Jane. She's a sweet girl."

Stella's stomach tightened with a different kind of discomfort. "Well, she's not really a girl. I mean, she's old."

"I thought she was Lavinia's age."

"She is, but . . . well, she's a mother. It makes her seem older."

She crossed and then uncrossed her arms. Lloyd looked at her, the hint of a smile on his lips.

"What?"

"Nothing," he said, looking back at the road. "It sounds like her husband was—"

"Another man who's not worth my spit."

"Well-put," Lloyd said with a chuckle. "Poor girl. Abandoned twice in her life."

Stella blinked and then turned to face him. "She told you about her real parents?"

"Yeah. While we were up in the attic."

Stella turned back to the road. Jane had not only been adopted, but literally left in a basket on the front porch of the parents who'd raised her, like in a fairy tale.

They'd been an older couple with no children and considered Jane a miracle. Jane had loved them, but never stopped feeling abandoned by the biological parents she never knew.

"What's wrong?" Lloyd asked.

"Nothing," she said, forcing a shrug. "I'm just surprised she shared something so intimate with someone she'd just met."

"Well, you know me, sugar. I've got that disarming Southern charm."

Stella rolled her eyes but found herself smiling. "How was Archie's cider, by the way?"

A low moan escaped in his throat, and Stella shifted in her seat.

"Delicious," he said. "You have got to try it tonight."

"Do you really think we should go back tonight? We shouldn't . . . wait a while?"

"Why?"

"I don't know. To rest? Aren't you tired?"

"I'm used to runnin' on little to no sleep. And I want to taste every dish on that table, drink from every bottle they got, and dance to every song that band knows. We've got access to an honest-to-god, bona fide magical world. You can bet I'm going to sample every last bit I can."

Stella thought of the girl with the sleek bob and wondered what other things Lloyd might want to "sample" in Archie's world.

"You're right," she said, tipping her chin in the air. "There are plenty of men I still haven't danced with, and I have a moth-eaten dress that will look gorgeous with my new heels."

Lloyd didn't respond, which made her feel moderately satisfied. But as they drove on, her thoughts drifted back to Mrs. Woodrow.

Her wind chimes hadn't succeeded in warding off evil after all.

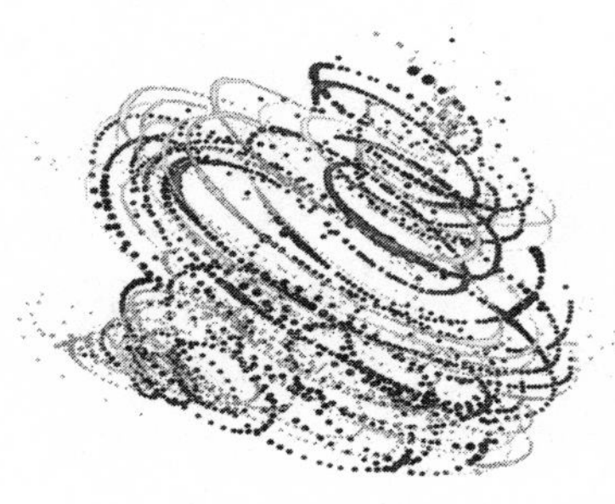

CHAPTER 9

"And now, ladies and gentlemen, Miss Lavinia Fischer will be singing you two songs!"

The crowd broke into wild applause as Archie waved Lavinia on to the stage. She beamed as she climbed the steps, and Archie returned the smile and slid behind the band. The idea had been Mattie's. Lavinia used to love to sing at church and in school plays. The pianist and fiddle player struck up the song's first chord, and Lavinia turned her radiant face to the crowd and began to sing.

"Birds do it, bees do it
Even educated fleas do it
Let's do it, let's fall in love"

Stella smiled and lifted her glass of fizzing champagne to her lips. She'd never had champagne before, but her idols seemed to drink it in every film, so when a man had brought out a bottle and offered her some, she'd gladly accepted. It was crisp and sweet, and the bubbles seemed to have climbed up into her brain. She was halfway through her second glass, and Archie's shimmering world seemed even more brilliant than usual. A *flash* split the air. Mattie had snapped a picture near the stage. Though Stella thought she'd taken enough pictures already, Mattie insisted on finishing the roll of film before she developed it. She took one more of Lavinia, then turned and strolled through the crowd. The people had seated themselves on the dance floor after Archie's announcement, and now they were resting their heads on each other's shoulders, watching Lavinia. Mattie snapped a few pictures of them before plopping herself down as well.

"Romantic sponges, they say, do it
Oysters down in Oyster Bay do it
Let's do it, let's fall in love"

Her voice was like rich velvet, rolling and lilting in all the right places. Stella could feel it pulling at her from across the twinkling lawn. She loved Lavinia's singing voice but hadn't heard it in years. Her desire to hide her face had caused her to hide the rest of herself as well, including her talent, and Stella wished more than ever she would share it in the real world.

But just thinking about the real world stoked flames of rage in Stella's stomach. She cursed herself and drained the rest of her glass to put them out. She'd managed to keep her mind off that terrible morning since they'd arrived, but now Mrs. Woodrow's shame, Aunt Elsa's fury, and the urge to kill Mr. Donaldson had resurfaced. The air where she was standing, like all the mill's air, was pure and fresh, but suddenly she needed to breathe more freely, away from the crowd. She placed her empty glass on a table and headed toward the orchard.

"In shallow shoals, English soles do it
Goldfish in the privacy of bowls do it
Let's do it, let's fall in love"

As she walked through the trees, Stella's perfect heels sank into the earth. She slipped them off and dangled them from her hand as she continued. Her bare feet felt so light on the silky grass, she could hardly feel them.

"Where you off to, sugar?"

She stopped and turned at the sound. Lloyd was strolling around from the side of the mill with another man. They were smoking cigarettes that looked factory-made, as opposed to the cheap, lumpy roll-your-owns Stella often saw railway bums smoking. Two amber bottles glistened in each of their hands.

"Just taking a walk through the orchard," she replied. "Where have you been?"

"Franklin here was showin' me a cave."

"Oh, the one that boy mentioned the first night we came here?"

"Yeah."

"It's a few yards beyond the mill. Beneath a hill," Franklin told her.

"It's boarded up with stones though," Lloyd said. "Not sure why he said it was dangerous." He took a drag from his cigarette and squinted out at the crowd. "Is that Lavinia singing?"

"Yes."

"Damn. She's good."

Stella chewed the inside of her cheek as Lloyd exhaled, unsure why she suddenly wished Lavinia would hit a sour note. Franklin tipped his hat.

"I'm heading back. Catch you later, Lloyd. Ma'am."

Lloyd raised his bottle. "See you, Franklin. Thanks for the beer and the cig."

Applause erupted as Franklin ambled off toward the crowd. Lloyd finished his cigarette and stamped it out in the grass. Then, the band began the opening strains of "Night and Day." It was a haunting, smoky tune, and Lavinia's voice rose over it, just as sultry and hypnotizing.

"Night and day, you are the one

Only you beneath the moon and under the sun"

Lloyd took a swig from his bottle and sighed. "Damn, does this taste good. I haven't had a beer in years." He turned to Stella and held it out with a grin. "You want a taste?"

Stella's warm cheeks grew warmer, though she wasn't certain why. Her fingers closed around the cool, damp glass, and she took a sip. The thick, yeasty bubbles were bittersweet, but not unpleasant.

"I like it," she said, her already cozy veins growing more relaxed. She returned the bottle, and Lloyd cocked his head to the side.

"Been drinkin' yourself, sugar?"

She lifted her chin. "I had some champagne."

"Fancy." He tipped the bottle back. The breeze picked up, rustling the leaves of the apple trees. Lavinia's voice drifted in on the air.

"Night and day, why's it so

That this longing for you follows wherever I go"

Lloyd caught Stella staring at him as he lowered the bottle and wiped his lips with his sleeve. "What're you thinkin'?"

Stella cleared her throat and fingered a leaf on a nearby branch. "How much I wish we could bring the objects from this world back to ours. Can you imagine how much people in Kansas would pay for champagne? Or bottled beer brewed in a legitimate brewery?"

Lloyd chuckled. "Always the business girl. Thinkin' like Ruth Chatterton."

"What's wrong with that?"

"Nothin'." He tipped the bottle back, holding her gaze. "Nothin' at all."

"Night and day, under the hide of me

There's an ooh, such a hungry yearning, burning inside of me"

Stella released the leaf and ran her fingertips over a ripe, gleaming apple.

"Be careful with those," Lloyd said. "I've heard funny stories about them."

Stella laughed. Lloyd finished his beer and placed it on the ground. Then he sat and leaned against the base of a thick, wide tree. He patted the grass beside him.

"Come sit with me."

Stella hesitated. "I don't want to get my dress dirty."

"That dress has a big, black scorch mark on its rear end."

"Not in this world," she snapped, color rising in her cheeks.

"Well, then maybe in this world, it won't get grass stains on it either."

Stella emitted a huff but sat down beside him. The ground felt smooth and soft, more like satin sheets than grass, though admittedly, Stella had never encountered satin sheets. Lloyd leaned his head back, closed his eyes, and sighed.

"This is the life."

He raised one leg, resting the crook of his arm against his knee, and Stella became acutely aware of his body's nearness to hers. She could smell him, and the aroma was different from anything she was used to—beer and tobacco mingling with a foreign, sort of masculine scent that reminded her of the woods.

It was delicious.

Stella squeezed her eyes shut. What in the world was the matter with her? Too much champagne? The song? The magical world? She could admit Lloyd was attractive, and even that she liked him, but she'd never felt the *pull* she was feeling toward him with anyone before. She opened her eyes and looked at him, remembering the conversation they'd had about their favorite smells. Lloyd liked the smells of tomatoes and earth, but Stella wanted the smells of big city life, of Hollywood. Men who slicked their hair back, wore tailored suits, and drank fine wine.

So, why did she feel the urge to touch Lloyd's face? To breathe in his skin?

"And this torment won't be through
Till you let me spend my life making love to you
Day and night, night and day"

He turned and caught her staring again. "What're you thinkin'?"

She turned away, a frantic drumbeat pounding against her ribs. "Why do you keep asking me that?"

"I'm curious. Like you are with me."

"I'm not all that curious," she argued, turning to face him. "Besides, you already know everything about me."

"Not everything."

His voice was soft, thoughtful even, but there was something knowing and *older* in his eyes. It stole the breath from her lungs, and she found herself asking, "Such as what?"

"Such as why are you're itchin' to get out of Dodge."

She choked out a laugh. "You're kidding, right?"

"You got a good family here. A nice house. A thriving business."

He winked at the last remark, but Stella didn't return the smile.

"What I've got is a family that isn't whole, a house that isn't mine, and a business that only exists to get me somewhere I can be *someone*."

He inclined his head, his smile fading. "You don't think you're *someone* now?"

She glanced away, twining a blade of grass around her finger.

"Stella."

She blinked at the ground. He'd never called her by her name. She looked back up. His brows were drawn together. The concern on his face, and knowing he knew her fear, made her want to sink down into the earth.

"Maybe we should head back," Lloyd said. Stella started to rise, but at the same time, Lloyd leaned across her, his hand outstretched. Their chests met, and she yelped and scooted backward.

"What are you doing?"

He looked at her. When Stella saw his confusion, she glanced down. His hand was on the bottle, which had been on her other side. He'd reached across her to pick it up. The crease between his brows deepened.

"Did you think I was trying to—"

"No. I mean, I don't know what I was thinking."

He released the bottle and sat back. "I wouldn't do that."

"What?"

"Come at you like that."

Her face flamed, and she scrambled to her feet. "I didn't think—"

"That's happened to you a lot, though, hasn't it?"

She froze as he rose to his feet as well. Her silence answered his question.

"I know . . ." He glanced at his shoes and ran a hand through his hair. "What I mean is, that won't happen with me. Not ever."

His voice was firm. So firm, she actually felt a bit . . . offended.

"Well, I guess that's good to know," she said, straightening her spine. "Of course, Jane might always be interested or maybe that girl you danced with the other night—"

"Whoa—hold on." He pinched the bridge of his nose and burst into laughter. The sound scraped Stella's insides like flint igniting sparks of rage.

"Are you laughing at me?"

"No."

"Then what the hell are you laughing at?"

He stopped and cleared his throat. "The fool idea that I don't want you."

The air stilled. Or it seemed to. Every sound in the night dissolved.

"What?"

"You think a man only wants a woman if he pounces on her like a dog?"

Stella couldn't form a reply. In truth, the answer was *yes*.

"I've wanted you since I saw you haulin' that sugar out to your truck," he said. His eyes were dark in the moonlight, his gaze unflinching and mesmerizing. "I want you whether you're sweeping the porch or twirling out on the dance floor. I want you at home in your overalls and here in your fancy heels." He inched closer, his movements slow, but purposeful. "I can hardly even look at that mouth of yours without wanting to kiss it."

Stella's lips parted. There wasn't a breath in her body. "You want to kiss me?"

"I want to lay you down in the grass and take you right here if I'm honest, sugar."

Heat filled Stella's body from her toes to the tips of her ears. "Then, why—"

"Because I ain't some rutting dog chasin' after a piece of meat. I won't lay a hand on you until you tell me you want me to. Until you say, 'Lloyd, I'm liable to die if you don't kiss me.'"

Stella's heart tumbled, as did the next words from her mouth. "I've never said 'liable' in my life."

He laughed, and the tension eased a bit. "Well, something along those lines."

Stella crossed her arms and fought the smile that tugged at her lips. "What makes you so certain that day will come?"

"I'm optimistic."

He grinned, and she couldn't help but return it, feeling as warm and luminous as the moonlight on his skin.

"Are you two enjoying yourselves?"

Stella jolted and turned to see Archie walking toward them.

"Sure are," said Lloyd. He winked at Stella, who flushed, picked up her shoes, and slid them back on.

"Did you hear Lavinia?" Archie asked.

Stella glanced back at the crowd. She hadn't realized the song had ended. The band had begun a waltz, and Lavinia and Mattie were headed toward her, just behind Archie.

"Yes," Stella said to Archie, and when Lavinia reached them, she told her, "You were amazing."

"Thank you," Lavinia said, beaming. "Everyone was so kind."

Mattie held up her camera. "I finally used up my film. I can't wait to get it developed."

"What time is it?" Stella asked.

Mattie looked at her watch and winced. "Twelve thirty. We should go."

"I understand," Archie said. "However, if you do want to stay the night sometime, you'd be more than welcome to. I have some comfortable tents, and you could camp out on the lawn."

"Why not in the mansion?" Lavinia asked, but then she covered her mouth and looked at Stella and Mattie, remembering. They'd told her and Lloyd about the ghost the previous night but hadn't yet mentioned it to Archie.

"What about the mansion?" Archie asked, stiffening. "Is something . . . wrong?"

"We didn't tell you this the other night, Archie," Mattie explained. "But Stella and I came across a ghost in your mansion. The same one who led us here. She appeared in the parlor windows, looking like swirling dust, like before."

Archie paled. "Oh no! Are you all right?"

"Yes, we're fine," Mattie assured him. "She didn't try to harm us, just to communicate, like before. But instead of asking for help, she screamed the word 'vengeance.'"

"Vengeance?" Archie repeated, scratching his cheek. The fact that he could touch *himself* was one of the things that often made Stella forget he was insubstantial, so much so that she jumped when a glowing firefly flew through him.

"What if . . . what if it *isn't* a ghost?" Lavinia pondered.

"What do you mean?" Stella asked.

"Well, Archie," Lavinia said, turning to him. "You said after she cursed you, she disappeared. She didn't *die*, did she?"

"Not as far as I know. She was just gone, like everything else." He glanced at the mansion. "Either way, it might be better if you stayed away from the house."

Stella didn't need to be told twice. "I agree. Now, we ought to be going home."

"But we'll keep working on how to free you," Mattie told Archie.

"And we'll be back tomorrow," Lavinia added.

Stella bit her cheek, irritated Lavinia would make such a promise without so much as a glance at the rest of them for confirmation.

"Thank you so much, as always," Archie replied. "I truly can't thank you enough."

"Before we go, I wanted to ask you somethin'," Lloyd said to Archie. "I saw the cave that boy mentioned tonight, but it was boarded up with stones."

"I wondered about that, too," Mattie said. "I found it while I was exploring and took a few pictures. I didn't see why it was dangerous if it was boarded up.

"That's why I did it," Archie explained. "I didn't want the kids getting hurt. I guess I probably didn't need to keep them away from it once the stones were in place, but I thought 'better safe than sorry.'"

He closed his eyes, raised and lowered his hands, and the party vanished.

"Thank you again for coming."

They said their goodbyes and walked out of the orchard toward the creek. Archie remained between the trees, his hand raised in farewell. As she hurried over the lawn, Stella glanced back, but then she froze. She was far away, and the light was dim, but she could have sworn she saw a falling leaf land on Archie's shoulder. She squinted more closely, but then the leaf continued down to the ground, falling through his body as if it were air. Perhaps, she shouldn't have had more than one glass of champagne. She turned back around and followed the rest of the group toward the creek.

CHAPTER 10

"Goodness, Stella. Leave some coffee for the boarders."

Stella glanced up from the mug she was pouring her third helping into. She placed the pot back on the stove and swallowed what little remained in her mug.

"Sorry, Aunt Elsa."

"All three of you look like death this morning," Aunt Elsa continued. "Did you get any sleep at all?"

Mattie looked up from the toast she was cutting into triangles. It was a trick Aunt Elsa had devised to make the boarders' plates look fuller than they really were. Lavinia was supposed to be watching the eggs she was frying, but she'd been staring at her reflection in the kitchen window instead. She blinked, glanced at Aunt Elsa, and flipped the eggs. When neither of them answered, Stella said, "We slept fine. We're just tired, like every morning."

She wished that was the case. They'd gotten more sleep than the night before last, but it was starting to add up. They couldn't keep this up forever, not every night. It wasn't only taking its toll on Stella's energy, but her shoes. Her already worn heels were chipped and the insides were fraying now. It was as though they received twice the damage while restored in Archie's world. Maybe their bodies did too, because if Stella appeared anything like she felt, she *did* look like death.

"I'm tired, too," Aunt Elsa said. "But there's work to do. Stella, come and help me set the table."

Stella did as she was told, and Lavinia and Mattie got back to work. They served the boarders' breakfast and then ate their own in silence. When Lloyd appeared, he looked tired too, but not as run-down as the rest of them. He really must have been more used to running on less sleep. Once the dishes were finished, Aunt Elsa drove the truck downtown to purchase more groceries, and Stella was thankful she'd filled the tank with her Folger's money. The fact that she had, however, only reminded her of the impracticality of their current arrangement. The trips to Archie's were fun, but they weren't bringing Stella any closer to her goal. If anything, they were impeding her progress, as every cent from that can was a step away California.

Aunt Elsa had left Stella with instructions to dust the house, and Lavinia and Mattie to help Lloyd with the insulation. Once she'd made it down to the first floor, however, Stella stopped dusting and approached the sleeping porch. She needed to talk to her sisters while Aunt Elsa was away. As she passed the hall mirror, she jolted when she saw how pale and drawn her face was. She almost *did* look like death.

On the sleeping porch, Lloyd was smearing mud on the boards he'd put up where the screens had been, Mattie was in the rocking chair scribbling in a notebook, and Lavinia was seated before the piles of Jane's parents' papers, scrunching them up.

"We shouldn't go back tonight," Stella said.

They all stopped what they were doing and looked at her, but Lavinia's head shot up first, and her face was drawn with surprise and even horror.

"Not go back? But we have to. We promised—"

"No, *you* promised," Stella reminded her. "Without even asking the rest of us how we felt about it."

"But why wouldn't you want to go back?" Lavinia asked.

"Because we need a break. Don't you feel terrible this morning?"

"Not *terrible*," Lavinia said, though the purple smudges beneath her eyes told another story. "Not as terrible as Archie feels, anyway. He's out there all alone, all the time."

"Keeping Archie entertained isn't our job."

Lavinia's eyes narrowed, and she rose from her pile of papers. "How can you be so selfish?"

"*Selfish?*"

"Yes, and heartless too. Archie's been alone for four years because of a curse he didn't deserve, and he's been giving us beautiful parties he can't even enjoy himself. He's one of the most generous and kind men on earth, and you want to desert him, just because you're *tired*."

"I don't want to 'desert' him, just to take a break for a while," Stella replied, her voice rising. "And who's paying for the gas to get us there, Lavinia? *I'm* the one making sacrifices. It doesn't cost you a thing to go out there and enjoy those parties."

"Let's calm down," Mattie interjected. "There's no need to fight."

"It's only a little money, and you have *plenty*," Lavinia spat, ignoring Mattie.

Stella glared at her, her blood burning. "I've already spent everything I made from last week. A whole week's batch, *wasted*–"

"Wasted?" Lavinia repeated. "As if you're not benefiting as well? Don't pretend it's some kind of 'sacrifice' to look beautiful in your fancy, mended dresses."

"Well, as long as we're not pretending, why don't you drop the act as well?" Stella cried. "You're not desperate to go to the mill because of your sympathy for Archie. You only want to go there because–"

"Stella!"

Stella turned to Mattie. She had a warning look in her eyes.

"No," Lavinia said, glaring at Stella. "Let her finish."

But Stella knew she wouldn't. It wasn't only Lavinia's pain she couldn't face, but her own guilt. She had what Lavinia wanted more than anything in the world, something Lavinia lost through random chance and no fault of her own. Stella couldn't blame her for wanting to go to a place where she felt beautiful again. And she couldn't point it out while looking into her scarred face. She glanced at Lloyd, who was watching them silently, muddy paintbrush in hand. Then she swallowed and turned back to Lavinia.

"Mattie's right. There's no reason to fight about this. I'll go back tonight, because we said we would, but Lavinia, you have to agree we can't go *every* night."

Lavinia's jaw flexed as if she wanted to argue more, but after a beat, she glanced down and mumbled, "No. Not *every* night."

"I was having similar thoughts to Stella's this morning," Mattie said. "No matter how often we end up going, this isn't something we can continue indefinitely."

Lavinia sat back down and began crumpling newspapers again.

"And our ultimate goal is freeing Archie, agreed?" Mattie asked.

Lloyd and Stella nodded. After a moment, Lavinia did too, but then, without looking up, she said, "If we freed him, would we still be able to go with him to that world?"

"Maybe. Maybe not," Mattie said. "There's no way to know."

Lavinia crumpled the next paper without a response, and Mattie continued.

"I've been writing down some of the Romani stories Puri Daj used to tell us. They've given me a few ideas."

"Puri Daj?" Lloyd asked.

"It means grandmother," Stella explained. Then, she turned back to Mattie. "Like what?"

Mattie stood from the rocking chair and glanced down at her notebook. "Last night, when Lavinia mentioned the fact that we don't know for certain if the woman who cursed Archie died, it made me think, instead of a ghost, she could be a *tchovekhano*."

"Sorry to keep askin', but—"

"It's sort of like a vampire," Lavinia said to Lloyd, picking up the next newspaper on the pile and glancing absently at the text. "Except, it doesn't drink blood or anything. It's just a person who's . . . undead."

"'Revenant' and 'specter' are also decent translations," Mattie added. "They have bodies, but they aren't alive. And they're usually evil, of course."

"But the ghost doesn't have a body," Stella argued. "She's more insubstantial than Archie. She only exists in windows and dust."

"True, but what if she's the *ghost* of a *tchovekhano*? Or a *mullo* or some similar creature? And when she cursed Archie, her spirit got trapped as well?"

Stella considered this. She supposed it made sense for a person who had the ability to curse people to be some kind of creature, rather than a regular person.

"It also fits with the story of the *tchovekhano* Puri Daj told us," Mattie continued.

Before Lloyd could ask, Stella turned to him and explained.

"A girl goes to a party for three nights, and each night she meets the same handsome man and, well . . . goes to bed with him."

Lloyd raised his eyebrows. "Interesting children's story."

"These stories are older than our society's puritanical conventions," Mattie said, her intellectual snobbery almost tangible in the air. "They don't shy away from the necessary and factual components of everyday life."

"Hey, I ain't complaining," Lloyd protested. "You just started, and it's already more interesting than 'Jack and the Beanstalk.'"

"Anyway," Stella continued, rolling her eyes. "He always disappears by the morning, so on the final night, in order to find out who he is, the girl sticks a needle and thread in his clothes so she can follow the trail when she wakes. She does, and when she finds him, he is sitting on a grave, and she realizes he's undead."

"In one version, she finds him eating a corpse inside a church," Mattie interjected.

"Mattie," Stella groaned when she saw the horror on Lloyd's face. Then, she continued. "The undead man finds her the next day and asks what she saw at the cemetery—"

"Or the church," Mattie added.

"Or the church," Stella said with a sigh. "But she won't tell him, so he kills her entire family and eventually kills her."

Lloyd's eyes widened. "Damn."

Stella shrugged, conceding, and Lavinia closed the newspaper she'd begun to open and took up the story.

"But when he kills the girl, she turns into a beautiful flower, and a nobleman finds her and picks her. He keeps her in a vase beside his bed, and every night she becomes a girl again, and well . . ."

"Has relations with him as he sleeps," Mattie said for her.

"Heavy sleeper," Lloyd observed with a grin. His gaze found Stella's, and she glanced at the floor and continued the story.

"One night he *does* wake up, and when he sees how beautiful she is, he decides to marry her. After that, she stops turning into a flower. She's just a regular girl."

"But, of course, the *tchovekhano* finds her again," Mattie continued. "And he threatens to kill her new husband if she doesn't reveal what she saw that night with the thread. But this time, she stands up to him and says, 'May God shatter you.' And God does. The *tchovekhano* literally shatters with rage because she stood up to him. His body rips itself apart."

"It's actually sort of a happy ending," Lavinia said to Lloyd, whose lips had curled in disgust. "The girl takes his heart and uses the blood to bring her family back to life."

"Yeah. Enchanting," Lloyd said. "So, how do you figure this relates to Archie? Does he need to find the ghost and tell it to burst?"

Mattie shook her head. "No. Stella was right. The woman doesn't seem to have a physical body *to* shatter. I only thought the story was similar because it involves an evil creature seeking relations with a human to whom it brings suffering."

Though once again about to open her newspaper, Lavinia set it down and looked at Mattie. "But the girl *did* agree to have relations with the creature. Archie didn't, and that's what caused the curse."

Stella glanced at Lloyd. He was picking dried mud from the end of his brush. Apparently, he still didn't buy the story as wholeheartedly as they did.

"I know," Mattie said, plopping back down in the chair and nibbling her pencil. "That's why I'm still thinking of stories."

"Maybe Archie can tell us more when we go back tonight," Stella offered. "Some detail he hasn't mentioned that will help."

"Archie . . ."

Stella, Lloyd, and Mattie all turned to look at Lavinia. She'd murmured the word in shock, as if he'd just appeared before her, but she wasn't even looking up—she was looking down at the paper in her hands, which she'd finally opened. Stella inched closer to Lavinia and followed her gaze. Lloyd did the same when Stella gasped and jumped back, her heart in her throat. Mattie rose to her feet, and when she looked over Stella's shoulder, she shrieked and clasped her notebook to her chest. On the old, yellowing copy of *The Milwaukee Sentinel*, beneath the headline "Cider Mill Prospers" was a picture of Archie. He looked exactly the same.

But the date read September 24th, 1894.

"Maybe you weren't wrong about the creature, Mattie," Lloyd murmured. "Maybe you were just wrong about which person the creature was."

CHAPTER

Archie's world was cool, silent, and beautiful as always when Stella, Lavinia, Mattie, and Lloyd climbed out of the creek that night. Stella kicked the water from her bare feet and slid on her heels, though she wasn't entirely certain she would be doing any dancing. Not unless Archie could give them an astoundingly reassuring explanation for what they'd discovered. She'd almost been too frightened to come at all, but Mattie had reasoned if Archie intended to hurt them, he would have already. Stella knew, in truth, Mattie was burning for an answer, and Stella was too—they all were.

Still, when Archie jogged toward them, Stella's blood grew cool, and she moved a bit closer to Mattie.

"You're back," he cried as he neared them. "Have you found out anything new? Would you like another party?"

"We . . . we did find out something," Mattie said, glancing at the rest of them and then at the paper in her hands.

"What's wrong?" Archie asked. "Is it something bad?"

"No. Well, sort of. You see, this newspaper is from 1894 in Wisconsin, and—"

"And you're in it," Stella finished. "Looking like you look now. And it says you're a thirty-year-old man with a prosperous cider mill."

Archie's smile dissolved. Mattie unfolded the paper and held it up so he could look. He scanned the words and the picture and then turned away.

"So, it's true?" Lavinia asked, her voice hushed. "This is you? It's not a . . . mistake?"

Archie squeezed the back of his neck. "I'm sorry. I didn't want you to know."

"Know what?" Mattie asked, her chest heaving.

Archie turned back around. Misery and regret shone in his eyes. "My . . . my family grew apple trees in Connecticut since before The Revolutionary War. I was born shortly after. In 1794."

Though she'd already known he was alive in 1894, the idea that he'd been born nearly one hundred and fifty years ago made Stella step back, her skin prickling.

"Shortly after, my wife, Eliza, gave birth to our son, William—"

The words snapped off in Archie's throat, and he squeezed his eyes shut as if something had pierced through him.

"Here. I'll show you."

He closed his eyes and raised his hands. A woman in a long, old-fashioned dress and a boy with Archie's curly hair appeared on the edge of the orchard. They smiled and laughed as they played together, darting between the trees.

"When I first became trapped, I played memories like this over and over," Archie said, opening his eyes. "But it was more torture than relief."

Stella watched the way Archie's eyes followed his son, the pain that seemed to radiate from his core.

"We decided to travel west to make our own way," he continued. "We planted an orchard and built a farm in Ohio, but the harsh, muddy land gave little. We worked relentlessly to tame it, to make the apple trees thrive, to produce enough food to survive each winter. We were weak, hungry, and exhausted. Then, the August William turned eleven, I developed swamp fever, a malady contracted by many who lived near the Great Black Swamp when mosquitoes swarmed in summer. The disease wasn't always fatal—Eliza and William had survived it—but I knew I was dying. I also knew they wouldn't last without me. Harvest was coming, and without me, the crops would rot, and they would starve. Panicked and mad with fever, I stumbled into the orchard and fell to my knees, praying for deliverance, but it wasn't God who heard my prayer. It was . . . another being."

He closed his eyes and waved the memory away. Mattie moved closer, realization lighting her face.

"You made a deal, didn't you? To survive and save your family."

He nodded, and Stella wet her parched lips.

"A deal with who?" she asked.

Archie opened his eyes, his mouth tight, as if he were fighting being sick. Then he closed them again and raised his hands. A figure rose up from the ground a few feet away. It was a man, but not a man. He was wearing a long, black coat that seemed to be made of soot and dust. It billowed behind him, though there was no breeze, crumbling in the air but never completely falling away. What should have been the whites of his eyes were black, and his irises burned like flames. He moved toward Archie, and when his boots hit the ground, the grass around it slithered away like snakes.

"Archibald Bright," he said, his dry voice scraping like stone on stone. "I can help you."

Stella knew it was just a memory, but ice pooled in her stomach. She grasped Mattie's hand beside hers. It was as clammy as her own.

"But you must grant me something in return," the man grated, moving closer to Archie.

Stella's pulse leapt, and she squeezed Mattie's hand.

"Archie, please, make him go," Lavinia cried.

Archie closed his eyes and swept the man away. With a shuddering breath, he opened his eyes and turned back to them.

"Who, or *what*, was that?" Lloyd asked.

Stella looked at Lloyd. She'd never seen him so pale.

"He called himself Ruin," Archie replied. "But it's obvious who he was. The dark woodsman, the black miner. The one my grandmother called Old Scratch."

"So, those stories of a deal with the Devil were true," Lloyd murmured.

"The Devil. A devil. He wasn't of this earth. But I was desperate. I would have done anything to save my wife and son, and that's what I did. I shook his burning, soot-covered hand and sealed my fate. The moment I let it go, my fever disappeared. I felt stronger than ever before, no trace of hunger, thirst, or pain. He said I would stay that way forever—never fall ill, age, or die. And as long as I lived, whatever land I worked on would flourish, no matter the location, condition, or weather."

"Is that why my . . . why things heal here, on your land?" Lavinia asked.

"I've considered that," Archie admitted. "But it never happened before."

"You mean before you became trapped?" Mattie asked. Archie nodded, and she bit her thumbnail, thinking. "In a sense, a body that never ages is a body that's constantly healing, continuously regenerating cells and renewing life. The same can be said for the land. Before, it only affected you, but perhaps, since it's become a sealed, veiled world in which only you reside, that healing extends to anyone who comes inside the restorative bubble."

Stella supposed that made as much sense as anything else, but it was hardly the most pressing question.

"So, what was the deal?" she asked. "What did Ruin want in return?"

Archie glanced down.

"At first, nothing. For seven years, my land prospered, and I never heard from him again. I began to think I was merely lucky, that he'd been nothing but a hallucination brought on by the fever. But then, on William's eighteenth birthday, he, Eliza, and I were celebrating with a picnic in the orchard. Ruin appeared before us and he . . . he said . . ."

Archie turned away, his fingers curling into fists, and though he was trying to blink them back, a single tear slipped down his cheek. He wiped it away and turned back, agony blistering in his eyes.

"He said William was the payment. That in exchange for living forever, I owed Ruin any child I fathered the day that child came of age. Eliza and I begged him not to take our son, but he wouldn't hear it. William tried to run, but Ruin moved like billowing smoke. He opened his filthy, smoldering coat and enveloped William. Then, when he opened the coat . . ."

A sob broke in Archie's throat, and Stella covered her mouth, dread coiling in her stomach.

"When he opened the coat, only William's bones were left. They collapsed to the earth with his shapeless clothes, splattered in his blood. Ruin repeated the terms—that any child I fathered would meet the same fate when they came of age. Then he vanished."

A breeze rippled through the leaves as Stella, Mattie, Lavinia, and Lloyd stared at Archie in speechless horror.

"Soon after, Eliza took her own life, unable to bear the loss of our son and what I'd done to cause it," Archie continued. "I tried to do the same but couldn't, no matter how hard I tried. The deal I'd made with Ruin had made it impossible for me to die, even by my own hand. Realizing I had no choice but to live, I moved around the country, planting orchards wherever I went. I could usually stay in one place for about fifteen years before the wrinkles and gray hair that never made an appearance drew any questions."

Stella's lips parted as she remembered Mrs. Kelly telling her the Bright Orchard seemed to have popped up overnight. Perhaps it had, but—like Mrs. Kelly—anyone who noticed or harbored suspicions would have told themselves they were mistaken, just as she had.

"I filled my empty life with parties like the ones I've shown you," Archie said. "Easing my pain with people to whom I could never become truly close to, knowing I could never share my secret or—God forbid—have more children."

Silence fell over the orchard again. Stella thought of Archie helping all those women from Old Clara's, taking in the unwanted orphan children, and the fond, wistful way he'd looked at the Irish boy. He'd been trying to make up for what he'd done, to replace what he'd lost.

"So, becoming trapped in here had nothing to do with a woman?" Mattie asked.

Archie shook his head. "No, it did."

He conjured the same woman he'd shown them before, only this time he also conjured a second person—himself. Stella blinked at the memory Archie. He was wearing similar clothes, but his hair was down. He and the woman began the same scene he'd shown them the first night they met him. As before, the woman lashed out when he refused to go inside with her.

"Why not?" she demanded. "What's wrong with—"

"Please, don't shout," Archie whispered, raising his palms, but the woman seized his wrists.

"You think you're better than me? Is that it?"

"What?" Archie twisted his wrists free, and the woman stepped back, tears filling her eyes.

"You can keep your lousy job."

She turned to dash away, but Archie caught her hand.

"Wait, do you mean . . ." He glanced around, lowering his voice. "You're one of Old Clara's girls?"

"As if you didn't—"

"I didn't know. And I don't think I'm better than you." He released her hand, and she cradled it in her chest, watching him wearily. "You don't have to do that here," he continued. "Not to keep this job, not for any reason. You don't owe me anything."

She wiped her eyes, keeping her face hard, but her voice was small when she asked, "Do you really mean that?"

"Yes. So, please stay. There's no reason to go."

"I thought . . ." She looked at her shoes, her cheeks coloring. "I thought you were disgusted by me, knowing what I—"

"Never," he said, stepping closer. "Listen, I . . . I'm in no position to throw stones."

She tilted her head, her hardness melting. "Maybe not, but you're a good man."

"Trust me. I'm not—"

"Trust *me*. I know men. Whatever you may or may not have done, you're a good one." She nodded behind her. "Would you . . . like to dance?"

He let out a breath, smiled, and took her hand. Then the real Archie wiped the scene away.

"So, she didn't curse you?" Stella asked.

"No," Archie replied. "But she is still the reason I became trapped. After we danced that night, I invited her back to the mansion for some hot chocolate. She'd never had it. We talked, and she was so grateful and kind . . . and I had been *so* lonely . . . and she was beautiful, and she wanted . . . we both wanted . . ."

His cheeks flamed, and he turned away. Comprehension washed over Stella. When she glanced at the others, she saw they understood too.

"I sort of told you the truth when I said she'd disappeared," Archie continued. "After that night, I searched for her in town but never found her. I even went to Old Clara's but no one knew where she'd gone or what her real name had been. As the years passed, fear grew and clawed at me, but I tried to ignore it."

"As the years passed?" Stella repeated.

"Yes. The night I just showed you was twenty-two years ago. In 1912."

At first, Stella thought that must be impossible, that she would have noticed the partygoers wearing clothes from two decades ago. But then she remembered fashion wasn't the same in Kansas as it was in big cities.

Without the time or means to follow the trends of magazines and movies, most farm women wore the same cotton dresses and homespun blouses and skirts their mothers and grandmothers had worn.

"But you *did* become trapped in 1930," Lavinia said.

"Yes, which was—"

"Eighteen years after you and the woman were together," Mattie finished, her eyes expanding. "The year any child you might have fathered with her would have come of age."

Archie let out a breath. "Yes. When the dust storm arose that day, I thought Ruin had created it, because he'd appeared amid the swirling cloud and announced I'd broken the deal."

"Because you fathered a child without knowing who it was or where to find them," Mattie gasped. "He thought you were trying to hide the child from him, but the truth was you didn't know the child existed."

"Exactly," Archie confirmed. "He told me I would be trapped here as punishment for attempting to outwit him."

"Then the ghost—" Stella began.

"Must be my child," Archie said gravely. "When you told me the ghost was a woman, I knew I must have had a daughter, and that Ruin ended up finding her and taking her, just like William."

Stella knit her brow. "But William didn't become a ghost, did he? So, why would she—"

"William understood what I'd done and why Ruin took him," Archie explained. "Because of that, I can only hope he is at rest. That, unjust as his murder was, he had closure. But my daughter wouldn't have known what was happening, who Ruin was, or why he'd taken her, which is why—"

"Which is why her spirit is caught here, seeking vengeance," Mattie breathed.

"Yes." Archie looked at each of them. "I am sorry I lied to you. I couldn't explain why I was trapped here without telling you what I'd done, and I was too ashamed. I didn't want to relive what happened with Ruin, and if I'm honest, I thought he might terrify you and make you not want to help me. Not to mention what you would think of me, knowing I made a deal with that creature and cursed myself to be trapped here with one night of weakness—"

"Don't be ashamed," Lavinia insisted, stepping forward. "You made that deal because you were trying to save your family. Anyone else would have done the same."

"And who wouldn't be lonely after living like that for so long?" Stella found herself agreeing.

"*And* I still think there's a way to free you," Mattie added. "Now that we know what really happened, we have a better chance of discovering what that is. I just need to reexamine those 'deals with the Devil' stories I dismissed before."

Lavinia glanced at the mansion. "Now that we know the ghost is Archie's daughter, maybe it wouldn't be too dangerous to go back and—"

"No," Archie interrupted. "I don't want to risk putting you in danger. However . . ." He glanced at each of them, his mouth softening with a small, hesitant smile. "Now that you do know the truth, would you . . . would you like me to conjure parties from further back in the past?" His gaze settled on Mattie. "When you told me about your love of H.G. Wells and his time travel book, I thought you'd delight in examining real people and objects from the last century, though obviously I couldn't offer to conjure them for you then."

Mattie's face lit up. "You could do that?"

Her excitement infected Stella, and likely Lavinia and Lloyd too.

The idea of traveling further away from her dusty, barren home? To enter not only a world of leisure and bounty but another time and place? Past times and foreign places only existed in the movies—to venture inside them would be the same as stepping inside one herself.

Still, her practicality told her to be cautious. "Wait just a second," she told Archie. Stella looked at Lloyd and her sisters and then gestured for them to follow her a few paces away. They did, and Stella lowered her voice. "Do you think it's still safe to trust him?"

"Yes," Lavinia asserted. "You saw his wife and his son and . . . Ruin. He showed us the whole truth this time."

"Yes, *this time*," Stella emphasized. "But he lied to us before."

"It's easy to see why he would," Mattie reasoned. "He didn't want to scare us off, and Ruin probably would have, just like he feared. And it only makes sense he'd hide something so personal and painful from us back then when we were all strangers."

Stella pursed her lips and turned to Lloyd. His face reflected how she felt—hesitant, but yearning for what other wonders might lie in store.

"I think what we decided before we came tonight still holds true," Mattie continued. "If Archie wanted to hurt us, he's had plenty of chances to do so."

Stella looked at Mattie. As much as she hated to admit it, she trusted her intuition. And she was right. Archie was a good man who'd done nothing but give to others for over a hundred years of his life. Even now, he was offering to give them a gift he couldn't enjoy himself. She understood why he'd lied and believed he wouldn't hurt them. After all, how could he, when he couldn't even *touch* them?

"All right," she said, then she looked at Lloyd, who nodded.

"All right with me too."

The circle dissolved as the four of them turned around and walked back to Archie.

"We'd love to see the last century," Mattie told him.

Archie smiled, his eyes glistening with gratitude. "It would be my pleasure. I don't deserve you all."

He closed his eyes and raised his hands. The sounds of guitars, fiddles, snare drums, and mandolins rose through the air. A band materialized on a raised platform, similar to the one they'd seen before, only these men were wearing long coats, ascots, and bowler hats. Instead of jewel-toned paper lanterns glowing on strings of electric bulbs, old-fashioned lanterns lit by candles hung across the yard, their delicate, golden flames dancing like moths behind the glass. Horses whinnied in the distance, and men and women appeared, twirling over the dance floor. The men wore the same fashions as the men in the band, and the women wore dresses with corseted bodices, thick, gathered bustles, and cake-like tiers of fabric, just like in the movies.

"Oh my goodness," Lavinia whispered.

"Where and . . . *when* is this?" Mattie asked.

"It's what you read about in the newspaper," Archie said. "My place outside Milwaukee. September of 1894."

Stella glanced at the mill, mansion, trees, and creek, which remained the same. "But you can't change—"

"No, I can't change the landscape," Archie said, reading her thoughts. "I can only bring in whatever once crossed my land, not the land itself. Otherwise, I could make the creek disappear or change the borders and escape. I'm sorry, as I would have loved to show you the ocean view from my orchard in Virginia Beach."

"Don't be sorry," Lavinia said with trill of disbelieving laughter. "This is astonishing."

A couple walked off the dance floor but stopped when they saw Archie, their confused eyes darting between Stella and her sisters. Immediately, Stella realized what they were staring at. She and Lavinia were wearing dresses that stopped just below their knees, and no other woman from this world had their hair cut as short as theirs. Mattie's long braid wasn't out of place, but she was wearing a man's button-up shirt and overalls. The change in men's fashion was subtle enough for Lloyd not to cause a stir, but the girls were probably nothing less than shocking to these people.

"Oh," Archie murmured, apparently coming to the same realization. "Wait—I have an idea."

He closed his eyes and flourished his hands again, and a large covered wagon appeared near the creek.

"A traveling salesman came through once that summer. You can look inside and see if he had anything that would fit."

"Clothes from the 1800s," Mattie murmured. "Come on. Let's look!"

LAVINIA, STELLA, AND MATTIE emerged from the wagon a few minutes later. They'd managed to locate enough clothing that fit their needs, after bumbling through the strange layers of underwear and figuring out the corsets. Lavinia had been lucky enough to find a crimson gown that fit perfectly, and Mattie had tucked a puffy-sleeved blouse into the waist of a skirt she'd rolled up a few times to make short enough. Stella's dress fit the least comfortably. The length was good, and the corset helped to cinch it around the waist, but the sleeves pinched her upper arms, and her breasts swelled up above the neckline. But it was sumptuous silk and a gorgeous emerald green that she couldn't resist.

Her eyes found Lloyd's immediately when she climbed down from the wagon. She waited for his gaze to drop and linger over her cleavage, but it didn't.

"You found one that matches your eyes," he said.

She smiled, and Mattie walked up to Archie.

"Could you introduce me to some people? Imagine—learning about history from the people who actually lived it!"

"Of course," Archie said. "This way."

He walked toward the crowd by the buffet table, and Mattie followed. Lavinia moved near the dance floor and was quickly approached by a man. He must have complimented what would have been a daring haircut to him, because she grinned and patted the curls above her shoulders. Then, they were dancing, and Lloyd turned to Stella.

"May I have this dance?"

"You may."

They walked to the dance floor and joined the waltz. Stella's dress was tight, and the corset was far from comfortable, but it did help her keep her back straight as she danced. She wasn't used to holding her skirt in her hand either, but as Lloyd spun her backward in graceful circles, the heavy *swoosh* of her gown made her feel like Miriam Hopkins in *Barbary Coast*—a Gold Rush courtesan twirling in California's finest dance halls.

She looked up at Lloyd. His gaze had finally slipped down to her neckline. She cleared her throat, and he looked back up, meeting her gaze with a broad, shameless smile.

"Sorry, sugar. I can't help admiring beautiful things."

Her heart nearly rose through her chest, which now felt quite bare. "You're insufferable."

"You find honesty insufferable?"

She chewed her cheek. No man had ever been so blatant about being attracted to her before. Other men wrapped their suggestive comments in protective ambiguity, and the aim of those comments was always to get something from her in return. But Lloyd had made it clear he didn't plan to make such advances. She didn't understand him.

Or why she liked what he'd said so much.

"What do you think about Archie's story?" she asked.

"Now you're the one changing the subject."

"I learned from the best."

He chuckled and spun them away from the edge of the floor. "Well, I don't like sayin' 'I told you so,' but . . ."

"All right, all right. Fair enough. But do you think . . ."

She glanced around as they turned, looking for Archie. He was introducing Mattie to people near the buffet table.

"Do you really think we can trust him?"

"I don't know. I can understand why he lied. And I'm in no position to judge him."

She raised an eyebrow. "You've made a deal with the Devil too?"

"No. But I ain't no angel."

She looked at him, expecting to see a flirtatious smirk on his face, but instead, his smile had vanished, and his eyes were dark and distant. He was still leading the dance, but his movements were stiff and mechanic. All his former grace and playfulness had disappeared. Stella had never seen him without either quality, and it disturbed her.

"Well, who is?" she asked. "When I was six years old, I chopped off one of Lavinia's braids."

Lloyd blinked and glanced back down at her. "What?"

"I cut off one of Lavinia's long, red braids with a pair of scissors."

"Why?"

"Because she called me a baby, and I was mad."

He stared at her for a moment and then burst into raucous laughter.

"It worked," Stella said with a shrug. "She never called me a baby again."

Lloyd continued to laugh as they revolved around the floor. After a breath, he said, "Remind me never to make you angry."

She snorted. "You make me angry ten times a day. Probably more."

"And yet, you've never taken a pair of scissors to me."

"You don't have enough hair. Besides, you've never called me a baby."

He grinned, his eyes dancing again. "No. If there is one thing you ain't, sugar, it's a helpless child."

She met his gaze and then found herself unable to look away, as if some kind of bolt had clicked inside her at the contact. Lloyd didn't look away either. They continued to dance, but the people around them dissolved, blurring and blending in with the flickering candles and twinkling stars. Stella felt lost and breathless in a way she'd only felt when staring up at the silver screen. It was like a movie.

No. It was *better* than a movie.

Whether or not it made sense no longer mattered. She wanted Lloyd. In that moment, she wanted his words, his smile, his touch. Everything. She bit her lip and saw his chest rise. He looked at her mouth and wet his lips, as if imaging the contact. She shivered, but then applause jerked her awake like shaking hands. Lloyd halted, and they both looked around. The song and dance were over.

"Stella," Mattie cried, weaving her way through the crowd. "You won't believe who's here. Victor Berger!"

"Who?"

"He's a famous politician–the first socialist elected to the House of Representatives. Or, I suppose, he *will* be. In 1910. Right now, he runs a newspaper dedicated to social reform in Milwaukee. You must come meet him. You should come too, Lloyd. Now, where is Lavinia?"

She grabbed Stella's hand and jerked her through the crowd. Stella glanced back at Lloyd. He was following them and smiling, but there was tension in his frame, and Stella was certain the same tension was mirrored in her own face. She turned back to Mattie, still yanking her obliviously through the crowd.

So much for her "second sight."

CHAPTER 12

The most relaxing time of the week for Stella used to be Sunday mornings, when the boarders were at church and there were, for once, no chores to be done. She used to spend those mornings lounging on the back porch reading *Photoplay*, *Screenland*, or another movie magazine, but now she was too tired to read a word if she wanted to.

She, Lavinia, Mattie, and Lloyd had gone back to Archie's every night since he told them the truth. A week and a half since discovering the mill—since agreeing they couldn't continue going *every night*—and every night, that was exactly what they had done.

It was easy to be logical and make promises in the daytime, but once the sun went down, those solid lines began to blur.

Stella wished she could blame Lavinia, but all four of them were to blame. During the day, their exhaustion made them slower at their chores, which not only irritated Aunt Elsa but gave them less time to figure out how to free Archie. Mattie and Lavinia visited the library when they could, and on her moonshine runs, Stella asked if anyone knew the names of women who'd worked at Old Clara's, but to no avail. As the hope of freeing Archie dwindled, they began to focus more on enjoying themselves in his world.

Stella would have felt guilty, but Archie didn't seem to mind. Every night, he welcomed them as if they were his own children, beaming at them and conjuring every delight they could desire.

Today, however, they were sprawled on the half-finished sleeping porch—Lavinia on the floor, leaning against the wall, Mattie lying with her head in Lavinia's lap, Lloyd stretched out on the wicker settee, and Stella almost nodding off in the rocking chair. She hadn't realized how long they'd been sitting in silence until Mattie broke it.

"It's going to rain tonight."

Stella squinted at one of the open walls Lloyd had yet to board up. The morning sun was bright and, for once, the air was still. There was no sign of rain, but she wasn't going to argue. Mattie had proven she could hear ghosts, after all. Even if she had terrible timing when it came to Stella and Lloyd.

Stella looked at Lloyd, who was gazing up at the ceiling. His split lip had healed and so had the yellow bruise beneath his eye. Now, the only difference between his appearance at home and at Archie's was the scar through his eyebrow, the missing tooth she couldn't see, and the scars on his back he'd told her about. Stella had thought before that Lloyd reminded her of Archie's; something foreign and mysterious she couldn't understand.

Now, the similarities seemed even more acute. Like visiting the mill, the idea of involvement with Lloyd seemed much less practical in the sunlight, but when she was dancing with him, those daytime worries evaporated. And just as thoughts of Archie's invaded her mind more and more at home, so did thoughts of Lloyd. Even when he wasn't around, Stella found herself thinking about his scent, the strength of his arms when they danced, and the way he'd looked at her mouth and wet his lips . . .

Stella rose from the chair to stretch and shake the thoughts from her mind, but the moment her foot hit the floor she heard a *snap*, and she stumbled off-balance.

"You all right?" Lloyd asked, sitting up.

"Yes," Stella groaned, reaching down and removing her shoe. The heel had broken off and was hanging from the sole-like flap. "Dammit."

"I guess that's what happens when you've been doin' as much dancin' as we have," Lloyd said.

"It shouldn't," Stella argued. "These were worn, but not *that* worn." She turned to Mattie and Lavinia. "Have either of you noticed your clothes or shoes fraying more than they should after wearing them to Archie's?"

"You might want to keep your voice down," Lloyd murmured.

"Aunt Elsa's up in her bedroom reading her Bible," Lavinia assured him. "She does that every Sunday now that we don't go to church anymore."

Lloyd reclined on the settee again with a chuckle. "Maybe we all ought to do that. Now that we've seen the Devil."

"Ruin wasn't necessarily the Satan of Christianity," Mattie interjected. "Every culture, even non-Christian ones, have stories of evil spirits making deals. Stories that existed before Christ was born."

"Can we please get back to what's important here?" Stella said.

Mattie rolled her head in Stella's direction. "You really think your shoe is more pressing than theological concepts of evil?"

"Yes," Stella cried. "I mean, no—not my shoe specifically, but the fact that our things get more worn out than they should in Archie's world. And don't you think we're all more tired and drained than we ought to be? You two are pale as ghosts, and I have deeper circles under my eyes than Mrs. Kelly. We look terrible. Well, except for Lloyd. He looks fine."

Lloyd inclined his head and flashed her a crooked grin. "Why, thank you, sugar."

"You know what I mean," Stella said with another groan. She turned back to her sisters. "Come on. Don't you think that's strange?"

"I don't know," Mattie pondered. "I suppose it makes sense that there would be some kind of recompense for the healing we gain while we're there. A swapping of energy. To maintain balance."

"That doesn't make sense to *me*," Stella said.

Lavinia released an exhausted sigh. "Stella, what part of any of this makes sense?"

"I just don't understand why it affects us more than Lloyd," Stella replied, but Lavinia closed her eyes and rested her head back against the wall.

"Maybe he's more resilient," Lavinia responded.

Stella turned back to Lloyd, who lifted a shoulder.

"It makes sense to me. I'm used to not sleepin' much. Spent the last two years doin' it with one eye open, ready to scram if I needed to."

Stella thought of the night she'd watched him tie his shoes to his wrist. She didn't like picturing Lloyd like that, ready to fight off a stranger who might attack him in his sleep. She slumped back down in the chair and examined her broken shoe.

"I'll have to hide this from Aunt Elsa. I'm not sure how I would explain it."

Lloyd shifted on the settee, resting his head against his fist. "You know, that reminds me of a fairy tale my mamma used to tell me."

"My shoe made you think of a fairy tale?"

"Yeah. There are these twelve princesses, and even though their daddy locks 'em up in their room every night, every morning, their brand-new shoes are worn to pieces. Turns out, they have this tunnel to a magical world in their room, and every night they slip out to go dancin' there."

"Our grandmother used to tell us a story like that," Mattie said, sitting up and glancing at Lavinia and then Stella. "Do you remember The Three Sisters?"

Stella did, but she didn't see the connection. "How is it the same?"

"It starts the same way—with the shoes," Mattie said. "Only there are three sisters instead of twelve. And their father hires someone to stay the night with them and find out what they're up to."

"That happens in the princess story, too," Lloyd said.

"But the three sisters don't go to a magical world," Stella said. "They go to hell. Literally. They dance with devils."

"They do more than dance with them," Lavinia reminded her. Stella glanced at Lloyd, who met her gaze with a glint in his eye.

"If that happened in my mamma's story, she decidedly left it out."

"Like I said before, our grandmother told us old, original stories. She didn't tame them or water them down with puritanical mores," Mattie replied. "But it is interesting how the same ideas and even the same story elements exist across different countries and cultures. I guess it goes to show how connected we are by universal truths."

Stella rolled her eyes, and Lavinia turned to Lloyd.

"How does your story end?"

"Oh, the man who follows the girls finds out the truth and tells the king. The king closes the tunnel and rewards the man by sayin' he can marry one of the daughters. Either the youngest or the oldest. I don't remember."

"No one ever picks the middle daughter," Stella muttered under her breath. She wasn't sure why she'd said it, or even why she thought it, but when she glanced up and saw Lloyd's smile, she looked away.

"How does yours end?" Lloyd asked Mattie.

"When the father finds out his daughters went to bed with the devils, he kills them, slits them open, takes the devils out from inside them, buries the girls in a church, and the next day they come back to life."

Lloyd stared at her for a beat, and then said, "I'm starting to see a trend with y'all's stories. Lots of supernatural relations, murder, and comin' back from the dead."

"Thankfully, the only thing *we* have in common with either story is my shoe," Stella said, glancing at the snapped heel. "Well, and dancing in a magical world, I guess."

"And a devil," Lloyd added.

Lavinia lifted Mattie's head from her lap and crawled to her feet. "I'm going to go lie down before the boarders get back and we have to start making lunch."

"You just got up," Mattie said.

Lavinia walked out the door with a shrug. "I'm still tired."

Mattie sighed. "Maybe we all should sleep while we've got the chance."

"Don't need to tell me twice," Lloyd replied, lying back and closing his eyes.

Stella rose from the chair, and Mattie pushed herself up off the floor. As they walked out and trudged up the stairs, Stella thought the only fairy tale she wanted any part of was Sleeping Beauty.

BECAUSE OF THEIR BONE-DEEP exhaustion and growing inability to accomplish or focus on anything in the real world but their chores, they'd forgotten about the pictures Mattie had taken until she'd remembered that afternoon. She'd planned to develop the film in their bathroom, like their father had always done, but realized she couldn't do it without Aunt Elsa seeing the pictures. So Lavinia walked across the street to the Johnsons', who sometimes let them use their phone, and called a girl she'd gone to school with who worked at the town newspaper. The girl agreed to let Lavinia and Mattie come in and use the paper's darkroom, so the two of them drove the truck downtown once they'd finished the evening dishes. They told Aunt Elsa they were visiting Lavinia's old school friend, and Stella seized the opportunity and gave them some of her Folger's cash to fill the near empty tank.

The pocket where she had stuffed the money felt empty as she walked back up the front porch, and just as the truck pulled away, she heard a distant roll of thunder. She looked up at the sky. Thick, gray clouds were converging overhead.

Chalk another one up for Mattie.

When she stepped back into the parlor, she saw Aunt Elsa and a few of the boarders who had yet to retire to their bedrooms listening to the radio. Bing Crosby was singing "Brother, Can You Spare a Dime?" Stella thought of sitting down with them but then hammering from the sleeping porch drew her attention. She walked down the hall and stepped into the room. Lloyd was driving a nail into a board over one of the open walls.

"Your aunt wanted me to board these up—just for tonight. Since it looks like rain," Lloyd explained. "I was going to work on the window first, but that can wait 'til tomorrow."

Stella nodded, now understanding why Aunt Elsa and the other boarders hadn't been surprised by the banging.

"You need any help?" she asked.

He paused and turned to her with a quizzical smile. "You bored or somethin'?"

She crossed her arms. "If you don't want my help—"

"No, no," he said, raising his hands. "I do. You just took me by surprise. Come hold this board while I nail it."

She joined him beside the frame and pressed her hands against the board. He looked down at her.

"You seem shorter, sugar."

"I'm wearing an old pair of flats. Since my heel is broken."

He glanced at her feet and then hammered the nail into place. As he poised the next nail, he said, "You think those heels will still be mended when we go back to you-know-where?"

"It's okay. I don't think they can hear us," she replied, craning her head toward the door. Bing's velvety voice was loud as it floated in from the parlor. She turned back to Lloyd. "I hope so. Those shoes in that wagon from the 1800s look like a nightmare to wear."

"I've been meanin' to ask you somethin' about that," Lloyd said after striking another nail. "Does it ever feel strange for you to be back there? As a woman?"

"What do you mean?"

"I mean, you're going back to a time when women couldn't even vote, when they were more property than people."

"I never really thought about it before," Stella admitted. "I don't know that it makes much of a difference. I'm too young to vote now anyway, and women being able to vote hasn't stopped men from being in charge of everything or men like Mr. Donaldson from doing whatever they want."

Lloyd's smile dissolved. "I ain't gonna argue with that." He gave the nail one final *slam* and bent down to pick up the next board. "And it doesn't bother you to wear all those layers and corsets and stuff?"

"Why? You made it clear you enjoy them just fine."

He smiled. "Not sayin' I don't. But I'm askin' how *you* feel."

She watched him place the board flush with the one he'd just secured. Somehow, the simple question created a pocket of warmth in her chest.

"It's a little like playing dress-up, I guess," she answered, joining him and gripping the sides of the board. "Fun, but not something I'd want to do every day."

"I feel that way about Archie's place in general," Lloyd said, placing another nail against the board. "It's fun, but I sure as hell wouldn't want to live there forever."

She frowned at him as he hammered, and then, when he'd finished, asked, "Even if you could touch and taste everything? Like you can now?"

"Yeah. Don't get me wrong—it's a hell of a lot of fun, but it ain't real. And sometimes, when we're there, I find myself forgetting about the real beauty in the world."

"Like what?" Stella asked, unable to think of a single thing in the barren, dust-covered, godforsaken world they lived in that compared to the beauty of Archie's.

Lloyd pounded the final nail into place. Now there was only one gap in the wall, about as tall as Stella and a bit wider than a window. A gust of wind blew through it, bringing with it the fresh, wet scent of imminent rainfall.

"Like that," Lloyd said, closing his eyes and taking a savory breath. "The smell of the coming rain after there ain't been none for months." He opened his eyes and looked outside. "There ain't nothin' like that smell."

Stella took a breath as well. She had to admit he was right. The clean, earthy scent was delicious, intoxicating, even. She closed her eyes, and when she opened them, she saw Lloyd looking at her.

"See what I mean? That out there—" He jerked his head toward the window. "That's real. Natural and good." Off in the distance, a peal of thunder rolled softly through the air. "And sounds like that," he continued, turning back to the darkening sky. "The purr of that thunder. Ain't nothin' like that in Archie's world."

Another swell of sweet, damp air blew into the room. Lloyd sighed again, and the sound was so raw and laced with so much pleasure, Stella's pulse leapt, and she found herself asking, "Why do you do that?"

"Do what?" he asked, turning around.

Stella sucked on her tongue, unsure how to describe what she meant. "Enjoy everything so much. Or rather, so *loudly*. It's like the whole world is the best dinner plate you've ever seen and you haven't eaten in weeks. And you don't even try to hide it. You're always sighing and moaning and . . ." She clenched her jaw, unable to go on. Lloyd smiled, inclining his head.

"Does that bother you?"

"It's just . . . not something I'm used to."

"So, you like it, then?" he asked, his smile widening.

She tossed her head back and barked out a laugh. "I did *not* say that."

"Then tell me what you do like."

He took a step toward her, his dancing eyes fixed on her own.

"What?"

"What do you like, sugar? What do you enjoy?"

She laughed again. "Why do you want to know?"

"So I can give it to you."

Her mouth went dry. In that moment, she wanted anything he would give her. She stared at him, distantly realizing Bing Crosby's song had ended. Now, Ruth Etting was singing "Glad Rag Doll." The words drifted into the room, along with another roll of thunder.

"I know you're admired

I know you're desired

But only by fellows who soon grow tired

Poor little Glad Rag Doll"

Stella took a step backward, her stomach sinking into her feet. Her skin felt suddenly cold, and she hugged herself. Then, out of nowhere, the sharp prickle of tears stung her eyes. She blinked and turned away, confused and ashamed.

"Stella, what's wrong?" he asked, but the sound of her name on his lips only sharpened the pain in her chest. She hunched her shoulders and shook her head.

"Nothing."

"You're just a pretty toy boys like to play with

Not the kind they choose to grow old and gray with"

There was silence from Lloyd behind her. Then, she heard his footsteps move to the door, the hall, and then back. It was only once he'd returned that she realized the song was no longer playing.

"They've all gone to bed now," he said. "They just left the radio on."

Stella didn't move, still not entirely sure why she'd frozen or why she couldn't look at him.

"I've never heard that song before," he continued. "Have you?"

Stella swallowed and forced out, "Yes. It's from a movie called *Glad Rag Doll* with Dolores Costello."

She could almost hear Lloyd's smile. "Of course. If it's from the pictures, you know it."

They were quiet a moment. The gentle pelting of rainfall began outside.

"Stella," Lloyd said. "Can you look at me? Please?"

The "please" was so soft and earnest, she couldn't help but turn around. Lloyd's gaze was fixed on her, his mouth drawn into a line. After a moment, he wet his lips and said, "Can I tell you something?"

Stella nodded.

"It's only a song."

She wanted to laugh but couldn't. Her throat felt thick, her stomach sour. "It's what people think."

"It's not true."

"About me?"

"About anyone." He glanced down, then raised his eyes again, the line of his shoulders sharp. "No one should be treated like a toy. Like a thing with no feelings."

Stella tightened her fingers around her arms. "People do get treated that way, though."

He laughed, and there was something dark inside it. "I know."

Stella's eyes drifted to the scar through his eyebrow, and she thought of the missing tooth and the glass cuts she couldn't see. His words about his uncle rang in her ears. *He liked to hurt people, you know?*

"You've felt that way," she dared. "With your uncle."

He held her gaze as if it were painful, but necessary. Like prying a shard of glass from his skin. "Yeah."

The rain picked up outside. The sound, the scent, and the breeze were still mild, but the room felt dark and frigid. Lloyd ran a hand through his hair and then took a step toward her.

"I'm not a toy, you're not a toy, and the people who *do* treat people that way don't deserve to walk this earth." He swallowed, and she shivered at the violence in his voice. "And if anyone *tries* to treat you that way, you punch them square in the jaw, you hear? And if you don't want to, and I'm around, you can bet I'll do it for you."

She shook her head, emboldened by the naked vulnerability in his eyes. "I don't understand you. You say you want me but that you won't touch me. You look at my body and tell me how much you like it, and then you say I should punch men like that in the jaw."

He smiled, and though it was sad, a bit of the darkness deserted the room. "I can see how you've gotten it mixed up in your mind, given the pricks you've come across, but wanting someone and disrespectin' them don't go hand in hand."

"What?"

"And while you are beautiful, sugar, that ain't the reason I want you."

"It's . . . not?"

He released a relishing sigh, holding her gaze. "Mm-hmm. That killer ambition that shines in your eyes makes me absolutely crazy. I can barely breathe when I think about how you'd gut anyone for your sisters. I get all tingly when you argue with them about being practical, and when you talk business and dollars and cents . . ." His breath hitched, and he bit his lower lip. "You look finer than a frog's hair split four ways to me then, sugar."

Her eyes flitted over his face. "*What?*"

"I feel bad sayin' this, 'cause I know what it means to your family, and I'm hopin' you won't slug me for it, but I could have had this sleepin' porch finished a day or two ago."

Thunder crashed, and the sprinkling rain outside swelled to a downpour. Stella opened her mouth, but Lloyd raised his hands.

"I ain't been draggin' it out for the shelter or the food, though I love your aunt's cookin', and not because I like your sisters, though I do. Not even because I got access to a magical world with good food and beer. Every night, when we come back from there, you're the reason I lie awake thinkin' of ways to make myself useful enough for your aunt to keep me around. Now, I know you'll think it's only to get you into bed and move on, but it's not."

She opened her mouth again but then closed it, the tips of her ears burning.

"I'm layin' it all on the line here, sugar," he said, his gaze sober and fierce. "I don't only lie awake thinkin' of reasons to stay here neither. I lie awake thinkin' of ways to make you want me like I want you. To make you feel the way I feel when you're in my arms on that dance floor." He took a step closer. "I got it bad for you, sugar. In every way."

Stella stared at his face, as if her gaze were physically locked there. Then she pursed her lips and said, "Why should I believe you?"

"I don't know what I can do to convince you," he said with a helpless shrug. "Name the task. I'll do it."

Another crash of thunder preceded another surge of rain. Stella glanced through the window to the dark, wet garden outside.

"Jump out that window," she told him. "Stand in the rain and get soaked to the bone."

Lloyd glanced behind him, turned back, and laughed. "You serious?"

"Completely. Go out and stand in the rain, and I'll believe you."

His lips slid into a grin. "Why didn't you pick somethin' hard?"

He turned around, and in one fluid motion, leapt down into the garden. Stella approached the open space and watched as he sauntered a few feet away, turned around, and spread out his arms.

"Here you go," he proclaimed, his hair matted to his head and his shirt and pants plastered to his skin.

The wind swept through Stella's hair, carrying the scent of the rain and honeysuckle. Before she could convince herself not to, she pried off her flats, climbed over the edge, and splashed down onto the grass. The wet earth squished between her toes as she hurried through the garden. By the time she reached Lloyd, her curls were straight, and her dress was completely drenched.

He lowered his arms and beamed.

"Have I proven it to you now?"

She shook her head, causing strands of dripping hair to stick to her cheeks. "No."

"No?"

He blinked at her through the rain, his face falling, but she smiled.

"Lloyd, you've already proved it to me a hundred times. You've been honest with me, kind to my sisters, and respectful to Aunt Elsa. You've had countless chances to act like a selfish ass, and you never have."

The shock began to melt from his face, and he planted his hands on his hips. "Then, why did you make me come out here?"

"I thought it would be funny. And kind of like a movie."

Lloyd threw his head back and laughed. Then he looked back down at her, ran a hand through his rain-soaked hair, and grinned, his teeth bright in the darkness. "You're a devious little vixen, you know that?"

She smiled and moved a bit closer. "Have I ever told you I love the way you talk?"

"Not that I can recall, but it sure is nice to hear it." He looked her over. "Have I ever told you you're drop-dead gorgeous when you're soppin' wet?"

Her heart fluttered. "Would you like me to explain the effect of supply and demand on the prices of bootleg liquor?"

"Jesus," he murmured. "I want you so bad right now, sugar."

"Do you?" she asked with a shiver that had nothing to do with the rain.

"Mm-hmm." He looked her over again as if savoring the sight, his tongue pressed to his teeth.

"Lloyd?"

"Mm-hmm?"

"I'm liable to die if you don't kiss me right now."

His head shot up, and he met her gaze, his pupils blown wide. Then she was in his arms, and his mouth was pressed to hers. She parted her lips, and he moaned into her mouth. Her toes curled, and she gasped. "I lied. I love the sounds you make."

He laughed, clasping her face. "Let's make them together, then."

He kissed her again, and her breath hitched as he pulled her to the side of the house and pressed her back to the wall. She drank him up as greedily as the parched soil at her feet soaked up the rain. Lloyd moaned again, dragging his hands from her face to her shoulders, and then past her collarbone. He started to slide them further, toward her chest, but then he stopped.

"Is this all right?" he whispered, his breathing ragged against her lips. She answered without hesitation.

"Yes."

Lloyd continued, and Stella gasped. Whenever boys had touched her like that before it was either in feigned, accidental brushes or outright unwelcome grabs, and in either case, her body had never reacted the way it did now. Fire tore through her, and she arched her back with a sigh that was almost a whimper. Lloyd froze, his muscles taut, and she wondered if her reaction had repulsed him, but then he buried his face in her neck and rasped, "Oh, sugar. I like the sounds you make, too."

She clutched his wet hair and pulled his face back up, kissing him wildly. In response, he gripped her hips and hoisted her up against the wall.

"Is this all right?" he murmured.

"Lloyd, I've liked everything you've done so far. Consider the light green until I say 'red.'"

She tightened her legs around him and kissed him again, as if to prove it. But then, a pair of headlights flashed through the darkness and the sheets of rain.

"Red, red," she squeaked, and Lloyd put her down and backed away.

"I'm sorry."

"No, it's not that," she said, laughing and wiping the rain from her eyes. "It's my sisters. They're pulling up."

He glanced over his shoulder and turned back to her with a smile. "Oh, right. I guess we should get back inside."

They crept back to the makeshift window. Lloyd helped Stella back through first and then hauled himself inside. The two of them blinked in the lamplight, looked at each other, and burst out laughing.

"Shh," Stella said, pressing her finger to her lips in an attempt to calm her own giggles. "I'll get you a towel. And some of my father's clothes."

She turned to go, but he caught her wrist and gently pulled her back. His warm cola eyes were bright and more effervescent than ever.

"What's your middle name?"

She quirked up a brow. "Marie. Why?"

"Stella Marie Fischer, I had a wonderful time tonight."

She beamed. "What's your middle name?"

"Eugene."

"Lloyd Eugene McCormick, the pleasure was all mine."

His grin widened. "Oh, I promise you, it wasn't." He pressed his lips to her hand, and she flushed from her head to her toes.

"I'll be right back."

"See you soon, sugar."

By the time Stella brought Lloyd the towel and clothes, the light was on in the attic. She smiled and found herself giggling again as she climbed the attic ladder. She would have to tell her sisters something about what had happened. She was no longer dripping, but her hair and dress were still wet, and Mattie would have an inkling the moment she took a look at her face. And Stella *wanted* to share some of it, but she wasn't sure how much. What parts did she want to confide in her sisters and what parts did she want to keep locked up in the intimate place within herself she and Lloyd had created?

Deciding simply to wing it, she crawled up into the attic. She expected her sisters to gape, grin, and ask questions the moment they saw her, but they didn't look up from the mattress. They were staring down at the stack of photographs they'd returned from developing. Lavinia's face was pale, and Mattie's brows were drawn.

"What's happened?" Stella asked, approaching them.

Lavinia didn't look up. Her eyes were glued to the photos. But after a moment, Mattie raised her head.

"The pictures of Archie's world. There's something strange. Something . . . wrong."

CHAPTER 13

For the first night since they'd discovered it, they didn't go to the mill. They told themselves it was because of the rain. Two of them would, as always, have to ride in the bed of the truck and get soaked to the bone. But even though neither Mattie nor Lavinia said it, Stella knew they felt the same way she did.

The pictures had made them uneasy.

The moment Mattie had shown them to her, Stella had understood what she'd meant about them being strange. There was *color* in them. No matter what night they'd been photographed or what angle they'd been shot from, a handful of objects always showed up in one glaring color—red—instead of black and white. The first ones Stella noticed were the apples, which stood out like crimson paint smears among the branches of the orchard and then Lavinia's hair, as vividly red as it was in real life. The pile of stones that walled up the cave were scarlet rather than gray, and the topmost window in the back of the mansion was red from top to bottom. But most disturbing of all were Archie's own bare hands, which were red in every picture, as if he were wearing bloody gloves. By the time they showed Stella the pictures, Mattie and Lavinia had already discussed whether or not there was simply some malfunction with the camera, the film, or the developing process. The camera and film were both old, and the newspaper's dark room had slightly different chemicals than they were used to, so it was possible. It was Mattie who finally voiced Stella's fear; that the strange coloration had something to do with Archie's deal with Ruin. But then Lavinia reminded them of the thing that upset Stella most.

In every picture of Lloyd, his hands were the same deep red as Archie's.

It was only the two of them—not Stella or her sisters or any of Archie's other guests. Only Archie and Lloyd looked as though they'd dipped their hands in red paint, whether the shot was up close, far away, posed and still, or blurred in motion.

Which was why, in the end, they decided the coloration must be a fluke, the result of trying to capture a magical world on non-magical film.

And also why they decided not to mention the pictures to Lloyd.

Still, taking a break from the mill for at least one night seemed best. Stella was grateful for the extra rest, since the next day was Monday, and she had to wake up early to do her moonshine run. Although, she had so much trouble falling asleep, the extra time didn't make much difference. As she lay between her sisters, knowing Lloyd slept a few floors below, it was all she could do to keep from creeping back down to the sleeping porch.

When she awoke the next morning, she felt excited and energized. She left before Lloyd woke up, and while making her deliveries, she realized if she cut him in on the business, he might be able to make enough money to stay in Dodge, maybe to even pay rent to Aunt Elsa. As a man, he could go places she couldn't, like men's clubs and barber shops and political meetings, which would mean more contacts and clients, and his charm and affability would make him an excellent salesman.

She told him about her idea once she arrived home. He agreed, and when she explained how if he also helped make deliveries, she and Jane could expand enough to pay him without decreasing their own income, he gave her a roguish look that made her shove him against the sleeping porch wall and kiss him until they were breathless.

That day, Stella's chores didn't feel like drudgery at all. As she dusted, beat out the rug, and helped hang the laundry, she felt like humming. It was as if her body were truly awake for the first time. Whenever she looked at Lloyd, heat flared beneath her skin.

She was so content that when night fell, she didn't feel like going to Archie's. The evening could be spent just as well on the sleeping porch with Lloyd, but Lavinia was twice as eager to return after missing a night, and though she'd dismissed the pictures along with the rest of them, Mattie was even keener to explore Archie's world and ask questions. Lloyd said he didn't care where he was as long as it was with Stella, who felt the same, so the four of them snuck out once again and drove to the ghostly mill.

Stella could tell their absence the night before had saddened Archie. When he saw them, he lit up, as if they had died and come back to life. They explained how the rainstorm had kept them away, but when Stella added that the visits were also making them exceedingly tired, Archie offered a calm, peaceful picnic instead of a dance. The moon disappeared, the sun rose, and people on blankets appeared on the lawn.

"What year is this?" Mattie asked.

"Around aught nine, I believe," Archie answered. "In Pennsylvania—the last place I put down roots before I moved here."

Stella glanced around. The year matched the picnickers' attire. It was almost enough for her and her sisters to have to change clothes, but not quite. No one gaped at Stella's knee-length dress, short hair, or modern-day heels—which had indeed mended once she passed into Archie's world. She loosed a grateful breath, having been in no mood for a corset.

After eating and drinking their fill on a soft, gingham blanket, she, Lloyd, and her sisters wandered off in different directions. Mattie hopped between groups on the lawn, listening and asking questions, Lavinia and Archie took a stroll through the sun-soaked trees, and Stella and Lloyd decided to explore the empty mill. A few nights ago, Stella had asked a worker for a tour, and he'd explained the milling process, shown her how to work both the hydraulic press and the hand press, and demonstrated the different steps for making regular cider, apple cider vinegar, and fermented hard cider. Lloyd listened as she explained everything she'd learned and followed her as she climbed the steps to the business office above.

"If this mill were operational in our world," she said, picking up an inventory sheet from the desk in the middle of the room, "it could produce not only the cider products but also whiskey. The still down there is twice the size of Jane's. Could you imagine how much we'd be able to produce with access to something like that? We'd make a fortune."

She put the paper down and turned back to face him. He was drinking her up, the corners of his lips curled into a grin. She flushed and returned the smile.

"Why do you wanna be in pictures?"

Her brows drew together, her smile faltering. "What do you mean?"

"I'm not sayin' you wouldn't look great on the screen or that you don't know how to turn on that movie star charm. I just wondered why you want it so much."

"What girl doesn't want to be in the movies?"

"No, I get that. I do. But if I didn't know better, I would think your dream was to be in charge of a company, or . . ." He gestured around them. "Runnin' a mill or somethin'. You got a good head for business. And . . ."

"And what?"

"You seem to love it."

"Love what?" she asked, laughing again. "Running things?"

"Well, yeah. Organizing, planning, overseeing. You get this fire in your eyes when you talk about it. I'm surprised *that's* not your dream."

Stella glanced down at her perfect shoes, including the heel that swung like a flap in the real world. "I don't know," she said, hopping up on the desk. "It never occurred to me. I've never known a woman who ran anything. The only powerful women I knew were in the movies. So, that's what I wanted."

Want, she corrected herself silently. *What I want.* Why had she used the past tense?

"So, what's *your* dream?" she asked. "Assuming you've moved past the idea of being a dime novel cowboy."

He grinned. "I don't know. For the last few years, I suppose it's been havin' a place I can call home. Somewhere peaceful and safe."

He met her gaze, and a sudden wave of panic spread through her chest.

What was she doing?

She slid down from the desk and moved to the window. That look in Lloyd's eyes . . . when he'd said he wanted a home, he'd meant Dodge.

He'd meant *her*.

And why wouldn't he? Just that morning, after only one night of kissing, she'd offered to cut him in on her business, to find him a reason to stay. What had she been thinking? Had her first moments of passion been so blinding and intoxicating, she'd lost all sense of her goals?

She was leaving. As soon as she'd saved enough money, she was leaving for Hollywood. She'd never heard of women becoming CEOs in real life, but she had heard of them becoming stars. Clara Bow, her childhood idol, had been plucked from obscurity and become America's "It Girl" after winning a magazine contest. That was Stella's chance—her only chance.

"Hey, what's wrong?"

She heard Lloyd's footsteps behind her. After a breath, she turned around. His face was drawn with concern. She knew he wanted her, believed he respected her, and could tell he cared about her. But girls like Lavinia and Jane were meant to be someone's home. They were selfless, kind, wholesome, and good.

They were safe, soft places to land. Lloyd had proven he wouldn't treat Stella like the glad rag doll of the song, but that was only because he was either blinded by desire or didn't know her well enough yet. Eventually, he would realize he was wrong; she was like that doll. Pretty on the outside, but a mess of insecurity, longing, and incompleteness inside.

If those things were true about any of the movie stars she worshipped, no one ever knew, because no one could touch them. No one could see anything but the image they projected. *That* was real safety.

That was real power.

"I'm sorry," she said, clearing her throat. "I thought—in the window just now. I thought I saw the ghost."

He paled a bit and looked at the window, and guilt swarmed Stella's stomach.

"It was just my mind playing tricks on me though," she assured him. "There's nothing there."

He relaxed his shoulders, met her gaze again, and smiled. "You know, I wasn't really all that keen to come out here tonight."

"You weren't?"

"Nope. I'd have been just fine on the good ol' sleeping porch. With you."

Heat crept up her neck, and she admitted, "I'd had the same thought."

His grin widened, and he stepped closer. "I like the way you think."

Her pulse leapt, even as her mind screamed, *Tell him no. Tell him you're leaving. This can't be what he wants it to be.*

"I like the way you taste, too," he murmured.

She melted.

I'm not leaving yet.

Her breath drained from her body as she whispered, "Right back at you."

He bent down and kissed her, his lips like the flutter of butterfly wings on her own. She tilted her head back, her eyes sliding shut, wanting more of him. He cupped her face with his magically-smooth, callous-free hand, and she flinched. In truth, she preferred the worn, rough feel of his skin in the real world. But then his other hand gripped her waist and pulled her flush with him, and every thought of otherworldly healing evaporated. She parted her lips and coaxed his mouth open, tasting him more deeply, and he released one of the aching sighs that set her blood on fire. She clutched his hair, tugging him closer.

"You really like that, huh?" he whispered, grinning against her lips.

"Yes. Do it again."

His grin broadened. "How 'bout you give me a reason to?"

Her heart flipped, and she slid her mouth to his neck.

"Jesus," Lloyd bit out. "You don't do nothin' halfway, do you?"

She trembled in satisfaction as goosebumps rose up under her tongue. She couldn't deny this was a kind of power all its own. It was beautiful, exciting, and perhaps, most strangely—safe. She trusted Lloyd, and being with him like this, teasing, exploring, and discovering what she liked, was not only electrifying, but tender as well.

Lloyd lifted her face back up and kissed her, breathing her in. Then he lowered his hands, his fingers brushing the buttons of her dress.

"Is this all right?" he whispered.

"Green light."

He fumbled a bit as he started undoing the buttons, and she kissed him to reassure him. When he reached her waist, he slid the two open halves up over her shoulders.

In the real world, her bra was worn and frayed, but here, the lacey undergarment was new, though still thin and sheer. She watched Lloyd's face as his gaze dipped down. His jaw flexed, and something like reverence shone in his eyes.

"Green light?"

"Yes."

Immediately, he guided her back to the wall beside the window. She found herself sliding his suspenders down his shoulders. Once they were off, she reached for the buttons of his shirt, but then stopped and asked, "Is this all—"

"*Green.*"

She choked out a laugh, and he smiled too, though his eyes were burning. She kissed him and undid the buttons, and he helped her pull his shirt off. He wasn't wearing an undershirt, and for a moment, she was startled to be in the presence of so much bare male skin. But then Lloyd kissed her again, and she reached up and ran her hands down his back.

Over his smooth, scar-free skin.

She paused, and Lloyd did too, guessing what she was thinking.

"Yeah," he said, clearing his throat. "In the real world, it . . . feels different."

She didn't remove her fingers as she thought about the pain he must have once felt there, of all the terrible things his uncle had done to him. And yet, here he was—brave enough to be vulnerable with her. She looked into his eyes. They were wary, as if waiting for some kind of judgement.

She raised her hands to his face.

"Flawless skin doesn't do much for me. I wanted you the first day I met you, and your lip was busted open."

She'd thought he would laugh, but he bit his lip and looked her over, that awed, reverent look back in his eyes.

"What are you thinking?" she asked.

"I'm thinkin' that desk over there is a mighty inviting flat surface."

The next thing she knew, they were both scattering papers onto the floor. Stella lay back on the desk, and Lloyd poised himself above her, but then she saw their reflection in the glass of a painting of buffalo on the wall across from them. Lloyd looked so at ease, his movements confident and practiced; she realized something she'd never bothered to wonder about before.

"Is somethin' wrong?" he asked, pushing himself up.

"No," she said, jerking her gaze back to his. "Well . . . not *wrong.* I just realized you must have a lot of . . . experience."

He wrinkled his brow. "Experience?"

"Yes. With . . . this sort of thing. And I don't, if you couldn't tell. Have any experience, that is."

Her insecurity must have shown on her face, because he cupped her cheek and said, "Sugar, that don't make no difference to me. Unless it bothers you that I've—"

"No," she said truthfully, and then, since he'd had the courage to be vulnerable with her, she added, "I just feel sort of . . . I don't know. Maybe, I don't like it when anyone knows more about something than me."

A smiled ghosted over his lips. "That's probably 'cause it don't happen often. But I don't know all that much. Out on the road . . . people just try to find comfort wherever they can. There are girls out there, too, ridin' the rails and following the harvests, and they're as lonely and hungry as everyone else. And when you find someone, and find a moment where you can forget about all of that—"

"You don't have to explain yourself," Stella said, pushing herself up on her elbows. "It's none of my business."

"No," he insisted. "I want to explain it. 'Cause, I want you to know that this—*us*. It ain't like that for me. It's more than just a distraction."

Her heart expanded, filling her chest, but then constricted again.

Tell him it can't be that way. That you're not that kind of girl. That you're leaving.

"I meant what I said last night," Lloyd continued. "I'm nuts about you. And I want to stay with you as long as I can. As long as you'll have me."

She looked at him, tenderness and desire at war with her pragmatism and dreams. But then something caught her eye over his shoulder, through the window.

"What in the world," she murmured. She stood from the desk and started buttoning her dress as she hurried to the window.

Down below, just across the lawn, Mattie was creeping toward the mansion, looking over her shoulder as if to make sure no one was watching.

"Why is she going to the mansion?" Stella asked. She turned to see Lloyd beside her, sliding his shirt back on.

"Do you think she's goin' to see that ghost again?" he asked.

Stella's chest tightened as she remembered what happened last time. She finished her buttons and strode to the door. "She'd better not be."

She dashed down to the ground floor and out into the sun, shielding her eyes. She'd forgotten that, though it was night, Archie's memory was of the day.

"Mattie," she called, hurrying over the lawn. "What are you doing?"

Mattie stopped near the side of the mansion. She looked at Stella and then at Lloyd, who was trailing behind her and pulling his suspenders up over his shoulders. Mattie cocked her head to the side.

"What were *you two* doing?"

Stella's jaw flexed, but she ignored her. "Are you going back into that mansion?" she asked when she reached her.

"I need to. I have to see the ghost again."

"Are you nuts? Don't you remember what happened last time?"

"I need to see if I can make out the shape of her face—her features."

"Why?"

"Just something that occurred to me. A theory."

"What are the three of you doing?"

Stella, Lloyd, and Mattie turned to see Archie hurrying toward them, Lavinia on his heels.

"I thought we agreed you shouldn't go near the mansion," Archie huffed as he came to a stop. "Because of the ghost."

"Although now that we know she's your daughter, perhaps she isn't a danger to us," Lavinia said, joining his side.

"She screamed the word 'vengeance,'" Stella said flatly. "She's a danger."

"She wants vengeance against Ruin. He isn't here, so what do the rest of us have to fear?" Lavinia argued.

"Ruin may have taken her, but Archie is the reason she was taken," Stella reminded her, swinging a hand in his direction. "And if she wants vengeance against Archie, it only makes sense she would want it against us, since we've been dancing at his parties without a care."

Lavinia's face hardened. "She can't want to hurt Archie. He's her *father*."

"A father she never knew who got her murdered by the *Devil*," Stella cried.

Lavinia stared at her as if she'd just screamed a curse word in church. Then she turned to Archie. "I'm so sorry. Stella must have had too much to drink tonight. I don't know why else she would say something so rude."

"I must have *what*?" Stella shrieked, her eyes bulging. "How dare you say that, and how dare you *apologize* for me?"

Mattie sprang between them. "We should go. We're all exhausted."

"Yes, that might be best," Archie agreed. Then he turned to Lavinia. "It's all right. Stella didn't say anything that wasn't true. I'm not offended."

Lavinia smiled and gazed at Archie, as if he were a merciful god who'd stooped to bestow his forgiveness upon them. She raised her hand to touch his shoulder but then jerked it away. Stella narrowed her eyes. Lavinia's expression wasn't embarrassed, like she'd forgotten Archie was intangible, but almost . . . *guilty*. Like she'd made a mistake.

Like she'd revealed a secret.

As they headed toward the creek, Stella trailed behind Archie, thinking about the night she'd thought she imagined seeing a leaf land on his shoulder. Though the idea that flashed through her head next was unreasonable, perhaps even crazy, she dug her foot into the grass, cried out, and pretended to trip and fall—directly into Archie.

Where, of course, she tumbled right through him and hit the ground with a *thud*.

Archie gasped, Mattie shouted her name, and Lloyd cried, "Are you all right?"

Embarrassed, Stella pushed herself up but then winced and looked down at her hand. It had slammed into a rock, which had sliced the center of her palm. But then, before her eyes, her skin knitted itself back together. Mattie, who was now crouched beside her, murmured, "Oh my goodness," and Lloyd, standing above her, gave a low whistle of disbelief. Stella poked at the skin. The pain was gone, as if nothing had happened. She looked up at Archie and saw him slowly smile.

"I suppose that answers any lingering questions about whether or not my healing properties extend to the rest of you."

Lloyd helped Stella to her feet. She looked down at her hand again and then raised her gaze to Lavinia. She was standing near the creek, staring at Stella, her shoulders stiff.

"I guess so," Mattie said to Archie. "Thank goodness for that."

She and Lloyd bid Archie goodbye, but Stella and Lavinia were silent as they crept into the water. Once they had all passed through and were back in the dark and dusty creek bed, Lloyd and Mattie climbed out and headed toward the truck. Stella looked down at her hand. It was still healed, as if nothing had happened. Lavinia's and Lloyd's scars returned in the real world, but it seemed any injuries received while in Archie's world stayed healed on the outside. Stella turned to walk to the truck, but before she could, Lavinia gripped her arm and tugged her back.

"Why did you do that?" she whispered.

"Do what?"

"You tried to knock Archie over."

Stella forced out a laugh. "What? I can't knock him over. He's intangible, remember?"

Lavinia glared at her. She opened her mouth, closed it, and then said, "Why don't you like him?"

Stella rolled her eyes. "I do. He's a peach."

"I'm serious, Stella," Lavinia said, hauling her back when she tried to go. "It's obvious you're biased against him."

"It's obvious you are biased *toward* him," Stella cried. "Apologizing for me because I spoke the truth? Implying I was *drunk*? You threw dirt on me to keep from hurting his feelings. You *turned* on me."

Pain and shame flashed across Lavinia's face, but then she lifted her chin. "I didn't turn on you. I simply thought you could have put it more—"

"No. You've been spending too much time with him. Strolling through the orchard, picking out songs to sing, talking beside the creek. You're getting too attached to him."

"Too attached?"

"Yes. He's not our father."

Lavinia gaped at her, her face reddening, but then she lifted her chin. "He's acted as good as any father. He cares for us and provides for us, without any regard for himself. He lost his family, and we are his second chance."

"But we're *not* his family, Lavinia. We *have* a father."

"And he isn't here!"

They looked at each other, the grimy wind rippling their clothes, but it didn't blow away the truth of what Lavinia said. Stella straightened her shoulders.

"It's not Daddy's fault—"

"No, it's not. Daddy is doing what he must for our family, and that's what Archie did for his. I will not let you insult him or try to trick him. Besides, you have no room to judge what I do with my spare time."

"What is that supposed to mean?"

"It means your buttons are uneven."

She stormed away, and Stella looked down to see she had indeed missed the first button on her dress, mismatching all the others and leaving the whole top half lopsided. She didn't have time to fix them, so she crossed her arms in front of her chest, marched to the truck, and jumped in the driver's seat without a word.

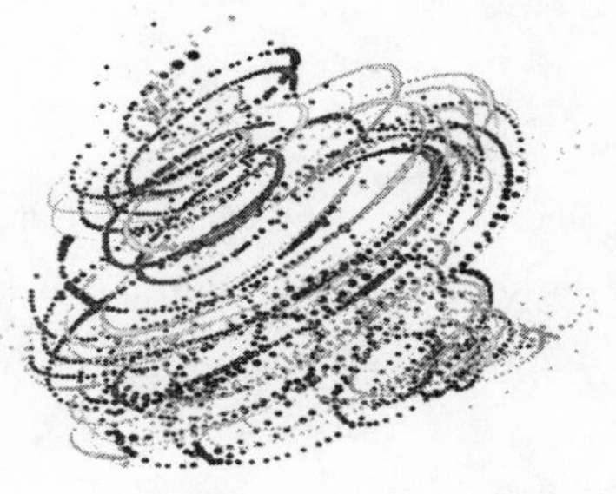

CHAPTER 14

"Ouch! Watch where you're going!"

Lavinia didn't respond, crossing the room and descending the ladder, as if she hadn't just kicked Stella's foot while passing the mattress where she was lying. She hadn't said a word to Stella since they'd arrived home the previous evening. Though, to be fair, Stella hadn't said much to her either. Rubbing her eyes, Stella pushed herself up. The excitement and energy that had pervaded her body the previous morning were gone, replaced by the weary exhaustion that always followed a night at Archie's. Only now, it was worse since she wasn't merely depleted, she was miserable.

"We didn't say it last night."

Stella twisted around to see Mattie sitting against the wall, a book in her hands. She wasn't looking at the pages, but staring out through the window. Stella knew what she meant. The three of them hadn't joined hands and murmured "*jekhipe*" before falling asleep last night. They hadn't failed to recite the Romani word for unity before bed since . . . Stella couldn't remember.

"It's not a big deal," she assured Mattie, attempting to mask the fact that it unsettled her as well. "Lavinia and I have fought and made up before. So have you and she and you and me. It will be fine."

Mattie didn't reply but continued to stare out the window. Stella's uneasiness grew, and she climbed to her feet and squinted at the book in Mattie's hands.

"What are you reading?"

Mattie blinked and then glanced at the book, as if she'd forgotten it. "Oh. *The Little Mermaid and Other Fairy Tales* by Hans Christian Anderson."

"Have you found anything useful in it?"

"Not so far," Mattie said. "There aren't many stories about people becoming trapped. 'The Little Mermaid' does involve the heroine making a deal with an otherworldly creature much like Archie did, however."

"What deal did she make?"

"The Little Mermaid falls in love with a human prince, and she also wants a human, immortal soul since mermaids don't have them. She goes to a sea witch who gives her legs in exchange for her voice. However, the Little Mermaid must make the prince fall in love with her. If not, she will die the morning after he marries someone else. Unfortunately, she fails, and he does marry someone else, but on the night of the wedding, her sisters bring her a dagger the sea witch gave them in exchange for their hair. They tell the Little Mermaid if she kills the prince and lets his blood drop onto her feet, she will escape death and become a mermaid again. But the Little Mermaid can't bring herself to kill the prince, so she throws herself and the dagger into the sea and dies with the dawn."

Stella screwed up her face. "And that's how it ends?"

"No. Because of her selflessness and self-sacrifice, she turns into an ethereal spirit, sort of like an angel. She doesn't get the prince, but she gets the immortal soul."

"And all she had to do was *not* murder someone," Stella said dryly. Then she blew out a breath and rose to her feet. "We'd better get dressed."

They did, but just as Stella snapped the last strap of her overalls over her shoulder, she heard Mattie say from the other side of the room, "Lloyd cares about you."

Stella turned to her. "What?"

"He cares about you," Mattie repeated, tugging on her boots.

"Not that it's any of your business," Stella said, crossing her arms, "but I know."

"Do you care about him?" Mattie asked, looking up, and Stella's eyes narrowed.

"Once again, not that it's any of your business, but I do."

Mattie held her gaze as she climbed to her feet. "I just . . ." She wet her lips. "I just notice the way he looks at you. It's more than attraction. It's adoration. The same way you look at Greta Garbo."

She gestured at the photograph on the wall, and heat crept up Stella's neck.

"So?"

"So, the only person you look at like that is . . . well, Greta Garbo."

"What are you saying?"

Mattie sighed and glanced at the floor. "I'm saying you're Lloyd's number one. His first priority. And I know you care about him, but he . . . well, he isn't yours. Hollywood is. And I don't want you to . . ." She looked at Stella, who slammed her hands on her hips.

"Don't want me to what?"

"I don't want you to . . . break him."

"*Break* him?" Stella repeated, stunned. "What is he? A vase?"

"He's a person. He has feelings—insecurities, fears."

Stella laughed. "Fears? Lloyd thinks the whole world is an ice cream sundae, Mattie. And trust me, he's plenty secure."

"He doesn't look at the world the way he does because he's only ever seen sunshine. It's because he's known real darkness. You think his outlook comes from ignorance, but it's really from understanding."

Anger stirred in Stella's veins. "Look, I know Lloyd better than you do. I don't care if you can hear that ghost and I can't. You can't read minds."

"I'm not claiming I can. I just—"

"What kind of a person do you think I am, anyway? That I would want to 'break' anyone? That I'd even be capable of it?"

Mattie swallowed and lifted her chin. "You've never given yourself enough credit, Stella. You don't think you matter enough to make a difference in anyone's life—either to bring them real joy or to truly hurt them. But you do."

The certainty, self-importance, and even outright superiority in her eyes flipped a switch inside Stella. "I've had enough of this 'village wise woman' bullshit, Mattie," she spat, stepping closer. "You may be smart, but you're a sixteen-year-old girl. You aren't blessed or clairvoyant. All you are is insufferable."

She turned around, marched to the ladder, and climbed down without looking back, trying not to think about the hurt on Mattie's face, the weariness in her own bones, or the tether she could feel fraying between her and both her sisters.

EVEN WITH THE LACK of conversation, the three sisters, plus Lloyd, managed to make their way to Archie's that night. Both Mattie and Lavinia had a look of determination about them. Stella didn't know why, though she doubted they were eager to accomplish the same task, as they had ignored each other as thoroughly as they ignored Stella. Lloyd's cautious, passive expression told Stella the tension was obvious, but that he was smart enough not to say anything about it.

Stella told herself she didn't care.

She had plans of her own that night, and they didn't involve her sisters. After finishing her chores that evening, she'd checked her Folger's can and found only two, crumpled dollars inside. Panic constricted her throat as she realized how much she'd been spending on gas, and Mattie's words about Hollywood being her first priority rang in her head.

She'd let her priorities slip.

Dancing in Archie's world and getting close to Lloyd had clouded her vision. Her dream was evaporating, and when she remembered Lloyd on top of her on the desk the other day, she realized she wasn't only ill-prepared financially. All her favorite stars, as well as the characters they played, were poised, experienced women who took lovers whenever they wanted with confidence, skill, and ease. With time, Stella could earn back the money, but there was only one way to educate herself and become like those women now, and she knew Lloyd would be more than willing to help her get that experience.

She hadn't told Lloyd what she'd been plotting yet, though she'd already taken precautions. As they walked from the truck to the creek, the tin she'd concealed in her pocket bounced soundlessly against her leg. She'd traded it with the hairdresser boarder who was also sometimes her customer for half a pint of moonshine. Stella had seen the small, round containers with names like "Spartans," "Stags," and "Romeos" at the town drug store. Though, of course, she would never have dared to buy one herself. In truth, she was surprised the clerk had sold it to the hairdresser, as prophylactics were considered unsuitable for women to purchase.

Her heart began to pound when Archie closed his eyes and brought out the moon and a blanket of stars. The revelers appeared, and when Lavinia joined the dance and Mattie slipped into the crowd, Lloyd turned to Stella and smiled.

"Wanna dance?"

"Actually, I have other ideas in mind," she said, her pulse racing. Lloyd's eyebrows shot up, and his smile broadened.

"Lead the way, then."

She did, taking his hand and guiding him up to the empty mill. They climbed the stairs to the office and slipped inside like the previous night. Since Archie's memory was of the evening and there was no sun streaming through the windows, Stella turned a knob and filled the room with flickering gaslight. She pulled Lloyd into the glow, smiled, and slid her hands up his chest.

"What's goin' on with you and your sisters?"

Her own chest deflated. "Nothing. It's just normal, sister stuff."

"Really? I haven't seen y'all like that since I been here. Though, I guess that ain't been too long."

"It happens sometimes," she insisted, guilt twisting her stomach. She'd never been anything but honest with Lloyd, but then she reminded herself she had every right to keep her and her sisters' business private.

"It feels like you've been here longer than you have though," she said truthfully. "Like I've known you for years."

He smiled. "I feel the same way."

She returned the smile, took his face in her hands, and pulled him down into a kiss. He returned it, and her heart revved back to life. She pulled away, stepped back, and slipped her hand inside her pocket.

"I . . . I brought something," she said, her throat tight. She kept her eyes down as she pulled out the tin, her cheeks already flaming.

She held it out and looked up to see Lloyd's eyes roam over the crimson letters that spelled out "Romeos," followed by the tagline, "a product of genuine, hygienic latex."

"I traded it for moonshine," Stella explained when he didn't speak. "The good ol' barter system, you know."

She tried to laugh, but the sound felt choked, and Lloyd continued to stare. Then, finally, he met her gaze.

"Are you sure about this, sugar?"

"Yes. Of course. And you know how I feel about . . . things. The Romani apple stories that scared me as a child. And my mother. I suppose I never told you this, but Lavinia was born only eight months after my father and mother married. They told people she was premature, but my grandmother suspected my father had gotten my mother pregnant before the wedding. But he didn't marry her because he *had* to—he adored her, and she him. Which is probably why they couldn't wait to—well, the point is . . ." Stella squeezed her eyes shut. She couldn't have sounded *less* like a seductress if she tried. "The point is," she said, opening her eyes. "*I* want to be prepared."

He studied her face; so carefully her chest began to cave in.

"What's wrong?" she asked. "Do you . . . not want to?"

"No, no." He laughed. "Jesus, of course I do. I'm just . . . surprised."

"Why?"

"I thought you'd want to wait a while. Since . . . you know."

"Since what?"

"Since you've never done it before."

Stella's cheeks burned even more. "No, but that's part of the reason I want to now."

"What's part of the reason?"

"To learn. To gain experience. I want to know everything you know. I don't want to be some . . ." She bit her cheek. "Some dumb, little virgin."

"Sugar, there ain't nothin' dumb about you—"

"You know what I mean." She closed her eyes, thinking her face might actually burst into flames. "In Hollywood—"

"Hollywood?"

"Yes," she replied, forcing her eyes back open. "Women there have experience. They're confident and . . . skilled. They know what they're doing."

He looked at her, a crease forming between his brows. "What are you saying?"

She fought the urge to scream. Why was he being so difficult? "I thought this made it clear," she replied, holding up the tin.

"I know *what* you want to do. I'm askin' *why*."

"Come on, Lloyd," she pleaded. "We're wasting time."

She cupped his cheek with her free hand and tried to kiss him, but he turned his face away.

"No. We need to talk."

"I don't want to talk," she murmured, her voice a near-perfect match to Greta Garbo's seductive alto. She could do this—she could convince him to give in and teach her. She smoothed her palm down his chest, over his torso, and then lower. "I know you want to."

"Stop," he snapped, slapping her hand away. "I told you *no*."

She stumbled backward, stung. "Why?"

"Because I want to talk."

"About what?"

"About exactly why you want to do this with me."

She barked out a frustrated laugh. "What does it matter? What do you care?"

"What do I *care*?"

"Yes! Why are you making this so hard? You'd think you'd be grateful."

His entire body went still. "*Grateful*?"

"No—well, I mean . . ." She swallowed. His eyes were so cold, she felt the chill in her bones. "You know what I mean."

"That I'm nothin' more than some dog chasin' after a piece of ass? That I should tell you 'thank you' for letting you use me to get your first time over with?"

Her stomach dropped. "No. That's not—"

"'Cause that's what it sounds like, Stella," he said, and for once, the sound of her name on his tongue sounded cool, distant, and harsh. "It sounds like you want to go out to Hollywood with a few notches on your belt, and I'm the first one."

"No, I don't—" Her voice died in her throat. It wasn't entirely true, but . . .

"So, that's what I am to you?" he asked. "Someone to get you ready for someone better? To give you some wear?"

"Lloyd, stop! That's disgusting."

"Damn right, it is." He flexed his jaw. "I am not a trial run, Stella. I won't be your 'experience stud.'"

He turned his back on her and strode to the door.

"Lloyd, wait," she called, running after him. "I don't think of you that way. When I got this, I wasn't thinking—"

She wasn't thinking about him at all.

As if he'd read her mind, he turned around.

"That's the problem."

He clenched his fists and looked down at his shoes, his jaw flexing again. But when he met her gaze, she didn't see anger in his eyes—only pain. Sharp, raw pain, like a gaping wound.

"I thought . . ." He clenched his teeth and closed his eyes. When he opened them again, he bit out, "I thought you liked me."

Her chest splintered. "Lloyd, I do—"

"And maybe I was a fool to think you could, that anyone could, but—"

"Lloyd, *stop*."

He laughed, closed his eyes, and raked his hands back through his hair. Then, he shook his head and muttered, "I gotta get out of here."

He was gone before Stella could suck in a breath to stop him. For a moment, she didn't move, didn't even realize she still clutched the tin in her hand. Once she saw it, she threw it across the room, tears stinging her eyes.

What just happened?

She tried to tell herself Lloyd was overreacting, but the heavy, churning sickness in her gut told her otherwise. She'd never seen him look so hurt and undone.

So utterly . . . broken.

He's a person. He has feelings—insecurities, fears, Mattie had said.

Stella hadn't been thinking about that, because she hadn't been thinking about him at all. She'd only thought of herself, of what *she* wanted. She'd treated Lloyd like a means to an end, an instrument to help her accomplish her goal, not a person with thoughts, opinions, and desires.

She'd treated him the way most men had treated her all her life.

Because he was a man, she'd assumed it wouldn't mean anything to him. And maybe Mattie was right—she hadn't thought *she* could mean much either. That she could possibly matter enough to someone to cause them pain.

She covered her face, pressing her thumbs to her temples. Never in her life had she wanted so badly to go back in time. Archie could remember scenes from a hundred years ago, but he couldn't reverse what she'd done. And his magical, healing world couldn't mend an injured heart.

But maybe she could. If she found Lloyd and apologized. She dashed down the stairs, out of the mill, and across the busy lawn. She didn't spot him in the crowd, so she scanned the buffet table, the band, the orchard, and the creek. But then, something else caught her eye. Mattie was hurrying toward Archie, who was standing by Lavinia on the northern edge of the dance floor.

And she was coming from the direction of the mansion.

Oh no, Stella thought. *She went back inside to see the ghost.* Mattie looked fine, however. Not frightened or running away like before. In fact, her eyes were blazing with that steely look she got when on the cusp of discovery.

"Archie," she called, "can you send the party away? We need to talk."

He stared at her but then closed his eyes, and the crowd and band disappeared. Only then did Stella spot Lloyd, crouched on the steps of the mansion's back porch, his head in his hands. He looked up at Mattie, Archie, and Lavinia, and caught Stella's eye beyond them. She started toward him.

"I think I've figured out how to free you," Mattie told Archie.

Stella stopped, Lloyd froze, Lavinia jolted, and Archie's mouth dropped open.

"How?" Archie asked.

"First, I need to see something," Mattie said. "Can you conjure the woman again? Your child's mother?"

Though perplexed, Archie did as she asked. The woman appeared a few feet away, sitting on a sofa Stella recognized from the mansion's parlor, a steaming mug in her hands. The memory must have been of when she and Archie shared that hot chocolate.

"This is delicious," she told Archie after a sip. "I've never tasted anything so sweet."

As she continued to drink, Mattie moved closer, studying her.

"Yes, I think," she murmured. "Her hair is blond, not quite as pale, but close. She's older, of course, and light hair darkens with age. Their eyes aren't identical, but a similar shade of blue. She has a smallish nose and high cheekbones . . . and attached earlobes. I think I'm right!"

"Right about what?" Stella asked.

"You can come and sit beside me if you want," the woman told Archie, and Mattie turned to him as well.

"That's enough. Thank you."

Archie banished the woman and looked at Mattie, his brows drawn tight. "What was that for?"

"I needed to see her again to test my theory," Mattie said.

"Your theory about *what*?" Stella demanded, and Mattie turned to all of them.

"I went back to the mansion to get a closer look at the ghost's face."

Archie paled, and Stella stiffened.

"I couldn't though," Mattie continued. "She was just as obscure as before. But it doesn't matter. After seeing this woman again, I'm fairly certain I'm right." She focused on Archie. "The ghost isn't your daughter."

Archie stilled, as if holding his breath. "Then who is she?"

"She's the woman you were with. Your daughter's *mother*."

Archie gaped at her, and Lavinia looked at him and then at Mattie.

"Her mother? But how—"

"It's always some kind of talisman that traps people," Mattie explained. "In every story. When someone loses the power to come and go as they please, it's because of a valuable object. Something precious to them has been stolen or lost, and the key to their freedom is reuniting them with that object. I've been thinking about it for a long time, though it always seemed impossible, since your possessions are all here, Archie. But then I thought, what could be more precious than a child?"

"But Ruin took—" Lavinia started.

"We assumed that," Mattie interrupted, "but we were wrong. His child is still out there somewhere. Alive."

Archie grasped the front of his shirt. The rest of them stared at Mattie, who continued, her eyes bright and certain.

"Because of the deal, Ruin was able to sense when Archie's child came of age, but because of that same deal, his connection is only with Archie. He can only know what Archie knows, and Archie didn't know who his child was, which kept the child safe. It's like in the tale of "The Maiden Without Hands" from the Brothers Grimm—the Devil can't take what he can't touch. Ruin trapped Archie as punishment for evading him, but he still didn't get the child. The mother, whoever she was, died—perhaps of natural causes, perhaps even in childbirth. Either way, she now haunts the place where she and Archie created their child, whom she was likely forced to have in secret or to give up for adoption. She's probably been here for years, but Archie didn't know until we arrived. Maybe the reason she brought us here was to reunite Archie with his child, which would be the ultimate vengeance against Ruin—the vengeance she craves." She stepped closer to Archie, breathing hard. "I think, if we bring your child here, it will break the enchantment that binds you."

"Wait," Lloyd said, rising from his steps. "If Archie's child comes here, won't Ruin show up and take her?"

"No," Mattie replied with an emphatic shake of her head. "She is the key that unlocks the truth, the means to restoring balance. That's how all the stories go. The demon is vanquished when his plan is undone by the magical missing link, when whatever initial wrong is made right again. She won't only free Archie—she will break his deal and banish Ruin for good, perhaps even destroy him."

"You keep saying 'she,'" Stella said. "How do you know the child is a girl?"

Mattie looked at Stella pointedly, as if trying to nudge her mind. Stella didn't understand, but when Mattie leveled the same look at Lavinia, Lavinia pressed her fingertips to her lips, downing a gasp. Archie looked at her and then at Mattie, his eyes expanding.

"Are you saying you . . . *know* her? You know who my daughter is?"

"I have a theory," Mattie confirmed.

"Well, then who is it?" Stella demanded.

Mattie started to speak, but Lavinia leapt in front of Archie, standing almost close enough to pass through him.

"We'll check everything out and then get back to you tomorrow, once we know for certain."

She stared into his face, a look of fierce meaning in her eyes, and he held her gaze and nodded, as if they'd just had a conversation.

"Tomorrow," she repeated. Then, she turned to the rest of them. "Come on. It's time to go home."

Stella furrowed her brow and turned to Mattie, assuming she'd argue. But Mattie studied Lavinia's face and followed her to the creek. Stella looked at Lloyd who avoided her gaze and hurried after her sisters without a word. Her chest cracking, Stella ran after the three of them and into the creek. Once they were back in the real world, she turned to Lloyd and opened her mouth, but he scrambled out of the creek bed and up to the truck before she could speak.

"Why did you want to leave before I could tell him?" Mattie asked.

Stella turned to see Lavinia meet Mattie's glare with a raised chin. "Why did you agree?"

"I wanted to talk to you alone, to find out why. But I think I know."

"What's going on?" Stella asked, approaching them.

"We—we can't be certain," Lavinia argued, setting her shoulders and keeping her gaze on Mattie. "Not that she's his daughter or that bringing her here will free him."

"But you don't want to try, do you?" Mattie retorted, stepping closer. "Because you don't *want* to free Archie. You don't want to risk losing a world where you don't have your scars."

A *smack* sounded in the air, and Stella leapt back. For a moment, she didn't believe Lavinia had actually slapped Mattie, even as she watched Mattie stumble back, her hand pressed to her cheek. But Lavinia *had* slapped Mattie, and her dark, fiery eyes contained no hint of apology.

"Everything all right?"

Stella spun around to see Lloyd peering down from beside the truck.

"Yes," Mattie replied, glaring at Lavinia. "We're coming."

"This is crazy," Stella cried. "Lavinia, what's gotten into you? And will one of you *please* tell me who the hell Archie's daughter is?"

Lavinia strode past her and to the truck without a word. Mattie watched her go, her hand still pressed to her cheek. Then she lowered her hand, swallowed, and turned to Stella.

"Think about it, Stella. Who do we know who is twenty-two, has a small nose, high cheek bones, that woman's blond hair, blue eyes, and was left on a stranger's doorstep as a baby?"

The air in Stella's lungs *whooshed* out as understanding swept in.

"That's right," Mattie said, starting toward the truck. "His daughter is Jane."

CHAPTER 15

It all made sense, once Stella thought about it. If Archie's dilemma was a fairy tale, then of course a girl like Jane would be the solution. Stella didn't read as much as Mattie, but she knew enough to know the sweet-natured, fair-haired maiden was always the one to break the curse.

But how could they tell Jane she was the key to releasing her long-lost father from a magical cage he was trapped in because of a deal he made with the Devil almost a hundred years ago? As daunting as the task seemed, Mattie insisted it be done. Stella agreed it was the right thing to do, not so much for Archie's sake, but for Jane's. She deserved to know her father hadn't abandoned her, that he was still alive and nearby.

In a roundabout way.

Lavinia, however, would have nothing to do with the plan to talk to Jane. She wouldn't have anything to do with either of her sisters, period. Not only had the three of them not murmured "*jekhipe*" for the second night in a row, Lavinia had chosen to sleep downstairs on the parlor sofa. While cooking breakfast and washing the dishes the following morning, she ignored Stella and Mattie with almost impressive dedication. Stella wasn't sure how but Mattie managed to swallow her hurt and pride from Lavinia's slap the night before and try to mend things, but she might as well have tried to talk to the chickens in the backyard. The effort moved something in Stella, who already felt sorry for what she'd told Mattie the previous morning, and as soon as they were alone, she apologized—even admitting Mattie had been right about her and Lloyd. Mattie forgave her, and it finally seemed as if something was starting to heal in the Fischer house. But there was still Lavinia to deal with.

And, of course, Lloyd.

Stella had lain awake half the night planning what to say to him. She'd hoped to pull him aside during breakfast, but he'd taken his plate to the sleeping porch and started work before the boarders arrived downstairs. He continued working all day, and if he took a break, Stella had missed it. She knew he was not only avoiding her but trying to get the job done as fast as he could.

So he could leave. The thought made Stella's chest tight, and with every *smack* of his hammer against the wood, tears stung her eyes. She moved through the day, doing her chores and trying to find the courage to approach him, but every time she worked up the nerve, her shame rushed back and won out. Her brain kept replaying the way she'd tried to touch him without his permission, the way he'd slapped her hand away, the pain and disgust in his eyes. At dinner, however, when he once again took his meal to the sleeping porch, Stella decided she had to talk to him while she had the chance. She managed to serve the boarders quickly without sloshing their stew all over the table, but when she finally reached the sleeping porch, she heard Mattie's voice inside.

"We're going as soon as we finish the dishes, and I'd like it if you came too," she was saying. "You see . . . Lavinia isn't coming, and with all the unbelievable things we're going to tell Jane . . . I think the more people we have to confirm the truth, the more likely it is she'll believe us."

There was silence for a moment, then Lloyd murmured, "Sure, I'll come. If you think it will help. She deserves to know the truth."

"Thank you, so much," Mattie said. "Stella and I will come get you once we've finished."

Stella heard her approach the doorway, and she jumped back to avoid a collision. Mattie leapt back as well when she saw Stella in the shadows. She looked up into her eyes, glanced back through the doorway, looked back, and nodded. Stella's apprehension must have been obvious, because Mattie reached out and gave her hand a squeeze before moving on. Once she was gone, Stella sucked in a breath and walked out to the sleeping porch.

Lloyd was leaning back against the arm of the wicker settee, a bowl of stew in one hand and a loaded spoon in the other. When he looked up and saw Stella, he froze, his stew dripping into his bowl.

"I won't take up too much of your time," she said, her heart in her throat. "I just wanted to say I'm sorry."

He held her gaze and placed the spoon back in the bowl.

"I know—I know there's not much I can do to make up for it," she stammered. "And I know you want to leave now, as soon as you can. And I don't blame you. But before you go, I just wanted you to know, I know what I did was wrong. It was selfish, thoughtless, and stupid." She took another deep breath. "*I* was selfish, thoughtless, and stupid. I often am, really, if you didn't already know, and that's one of the differences between us." She clenched her jaw, closed her eyes, and then forced them back open. "I treated you like your feelings didn't matter, like you were nothing, but I . . . I don't want you to leave here thinking for one second that it's true. Because, Lloyd, you . . ."

A lump rose in her throat, and she closed her eyes again, fighting tears.

"You're not nothing," she said, her voice breaking. "You're one of the best people I've ever known. You're brave, honest, thoughtful, and kind . . ."

Her lungs clamped shut, and the tears leaked from her eyes. She sucked in a breath and opened them to find Lloyd a watery blur.

"You're better than me, that's for sure, and I'm just glad—" She sucked back a sob. "I'm just glad I got to know you, and I'm sorry I mucked it all up."

She started to leave, but after one step, she felt a hand on her shoulder. She spun around to see a still-blurry Lloyd standing in front of her. Before she could blink, his arms were around her, pressing her head to his chest. Her mind scattered in confusion, but the comforting strength of his arms kept her from asking any questions, from doing anything but squeezing him back.

"You know what your mistake was?" he asked, his chest rumbling under her cheek. She shook her head against him. There were so many.

"Your mistake was not startin' off with the crying. I can't stand to see a woman cry. If you'd done that first, you wouldn't have had to say a word. I'd have already forgiven you, and my stew wouldn't be gettin' cold."

A wet laugh escaped her, and she sniffed against his shirt. "You really forgive me?"

He pulled back and lifted her chin. She wiped her eyes and nose with her forearm, not caring how childlike it looked.

"We all make mistakes," he said. "I'd be a goddamned hypocrite not to. And if I stick around, you should know I'll be makin' plenty myself. Just to give you fair warning, so you can plan on forgivin' me too."

She stared at him, barely breathing. "You . . . want to stay?"

"You did somethin' thoughtless and hurt me, but that don't make you a bad person. All it does is make you a *person*, and you're still one of my favorites." He inclined his head, meeting her gaze. "You still want me to stay?"

"Yes," she said without hesitation. "I want you here, Lloyd. I was afraid of falling for you, of what that would mean for what I thought I wanted, and I pushed you away because of it, but I'm not afraid anymore. I don't know about Hollywood or what else the future holds, but I know I want you here with me, right now. If you'll still have me."

He smiled. "If that's the case, sugar, I will stay 'till kingdom come."

Her heart swelled, filling her chest, and a smile brighter than film in a darkened theater lit her face. "Have I ever told you how much I love it when you call me that?"

"No," he said, his smile growing. "Why don't you show me how much?"

She kissed him, and when he kissed her back, she felt as if something thrown out of alignment was back in place. Then, she heard a throat clearing. She pulled away and turned to see Mattie smiling in the doorway.

"We need to eat," she said to Stella, "so, we can clean up and get to Jane's."

Stella nodded, gave Lloyd a smile, and followed Mattie to the kitchen. Just before they entered, however, Lavinia walked out, hurrying through the dining room and heading for the stairs.

"Did you even eat?" Stella demanded as she passed, but she didn't reply. "Lavinia," she called, loudly enough that the table of boarders would hear and so would Aunt Elsa, who was filling their water glasses. She knew Lavinia couldn't ignore her in front of all of them, and she was right. Lavinia paused on the stairs and turned back around.

"I'm sorry . . . I'm not feeling well," she said to everyone. "I'm going to go lie down for a bit. I'll be back down to help with the dishes."

LAVINIA DID NOT RETURN to help with the dishes. Aunt Elsa insisted they let her rest when Stella offered to wake her up, so Stella and Mattie cleaned up on their own.

"It's just as well," Mattie said, drying her hands once they'd finished. "She isn't coming anyway."

"What's wrong with her?" Stella asked, craning her neck to make sure Aunt Elsa was still in the dining room. "She's never acted this way before. She's never hit anyone in her life."

Mattie touched her cheek absently, pain glinting in her eyes. Then she dropped her hand, her jaw tightening.

"It's just what I said. She doesn't want to free Archie. She's afraid his world will disappear or be altered, and she'll no longer have a place where her scars don't exist. She's probably right, and I understand why she feels the way she does, but—"

"I understand that too, but it also doesn't make sense for her to want to keep Archie trapped. She thinks of him like a father," Stella said, her heart clenching as she remembered their fight about it.

"But we're not his family, Lavinia. We have a father."

"And he isn't here!"

"I know," Mattie agreed, "but maybe that's part of her problem. She cares about Archie and wants to free him, but she can't free him without losing his world, which she also wants."

Stella supposed she understood the dilemma. She'd been troubled by conflicting desires, though obviously not the magical ones that plagued Lavinia. But she still didn't know exactly what she wanted for her future—to stay in Dodge with Lloyd, to go to Hollywood, to take him with her, or something else entirely she'd never imagined before. Lloyd had been right when he'd said she loved running things and had a good head for business. What if there were other goals to pursue she'd never dreamed of?

What if the movies weren't the only way for her to be *someone*?

She turned the thought over in her mind as they drove to Jane's house. The setting sun shifted the sky from a hazy, festering yellow to dirty, blood red. Stella glanced at Lloyd beside her. In the eerie glow, his hand on the open window looked as crimson as in Mattie's pictures. She shook the image from her mind. No point in thinking about that now.

She pulled the truck into Jane's drive and parked behind her old Chevrolet. The wind ripped through her curls when she climbed out, more violently than usual, and Mrs. Woodrow's wind chimes screamed at them from her porch. Instead of irritating Stella the way they used to, the sound made her sick to her stomach. But then she noticed the red Cadillac in Mrs. Woodrow's drive, and the sickness threatened to rise up into her throat.

"What is Mr. Donaldson doing here?" Mattie called out over the chimes and whistling wind.

Stella met Lloyd's gaze. He glanced at the car and flexed his jaw.

"I'll tell you later," Stella said. "But don't be surprised if Jane is watching Mrs. Woodrow's twins."

They climbed up Jane's front porch, and Stella knocked, but no one answered. She tried a few more times but received no reply.

"I don't understand," she called back to Mattie and Lloyd. "Her car is in the drive."

"Maybe she's in the kitchen and can't hear us over the wind and the chimes," Mattie said. "Let's try the back door."

Stella and Lloyd followed Mattie up the patch of brown lawn that separated Jane's and Mrs. Woodrow's houses. Despite the roaring wind and clanging chimes, the evening seemed quiet. Or maybe just eerily still, as if abandoned by all signs of life. But when they passed Mrs. Woodrow's sleeping porch, a sudden, shattering *crash* from inside the house tore through the screens. Stella froze, and the three of them turned to look. At first, Stella saw nothing, but then Mrs. Woodrow backed through the doorway and onto the sleeping porch. She was holding a broken Coke bottle and pointing the jagged end at the doorway.

"I mean it," she gasped. "It's over. I'll get by another way."

Mr. Donaldson stepped through the doorway, his posture calm, but his eyes impatient. "Put that down, Priscilla."

Mrs. Woodrow lunged with the bottle, but Mr. Donaldson caught her wrist, and the bottle *clanked* to the floor. She started to speak, but he backhanded her across the face, his hand so deft and quick, Stella didn't register the blow until Mrs. Woodrow flew to her knees.

"Why did you have to make me hurt you?" he asked, standing over her. "This could have been nice and easy, but you had to go and make it hard."

He picked her up by the hair and shoved her face-first against the wall. Suddenly, his head jerked back and slammed into the wall above her.

Stella hadn't realized Lloyd was no longer standing beside her.

He was moving so fast, he was almost a blur as he wrenched Mr. Donaldson back from the wall and drove his fist into his face. Mr. Donaldson staggered backward, and then they were both inside the house. Mrs. Woodrow turned around but stayed pinned to the wall, shaking. Stella dashed up the steps and through the screen door, her pulse in her ears. She passed Mrs. Woodrow and stumbled through the door and into the house.

She'd seen Lloyd be violent before. The first time she'd ever laid eyes on him, he'd broken a man's nose. But that was nothing compared to what she saw him doing now. The boy pounding his fists into Mr. Donaldson's face looked nothing like Lloyd. He was more animal than human—grunting, panting, and wheezing as his fists flung strings of beaded blood over his head again and again. Stella couldn't move, couldn't see anything but the blood, couldn't hear anything but the *squelch* and *crunch* of skin on skin, bone on bone. But then she became aware of Mr. Donaldson's drooping arms, his lifeless legs. He wasn't conscious, but Lloyd wasn't stopping.

He was going to kill him.

"Lloyd," she croaked. She picked up her feet and ran to him. "Lloyd, *stop*!"

It was as though he couldn't hear her. He brought his fist down again, and Mr. Donaldson's bloody face lolled to the side, limp as a doll's.

"Stop!" Stella cried again. "You're going to kill him!"

She grabbed the back of his shirt, but he didn't let up, so she crawled onto his back and wrapped her arms around his neck.

"You have to *stop*!"

She dug her knees into the carpet and heaved back as hard as she could. Lloyd released a strangled sound and fell backward on top of her. She scrambled out from beneath him, ready to stop him from lunging again, but once she was on her feet, she saw he hadn't moved from the floor.

Instead, he rolled over, released a guttural moan . . .

And started to cry.

Not soft, sniffling tears, but abandoned, heaving sobs. As piercing as an animal's and as unrestrained as a child's. The sound frightened Stella even more than the blood and his flying fists. She watched him, her limbs encased in stone, unable to move or think.

"Oh my God."

Stella turned to see Mattie guiding Mrs. Woodrow through the door. They were gaping at Mr. Donaldson on the floor.

"Mattie," Stella rasped, her throat bone dry. "Go see if he's dead."

She didn't explain why she couldn't, that her body refused to move, but Mattie helped Mrs. Woodrow into a chair and dashed toward him. She bent down beside him, and Stella now saw that blood was seeping out and staining the carpet beneath his head.

He's dead, she thought. *Lloyd killed him. He's dead.*

"He's alive," Mattie said, and Stella blinked and looked up at her.

"He is?"

"Yes. He's breathing. But he needs a doctor, now."

"No."

They both turned to Mrs. Woodrow, whose protest had been so sharp it cut through Lloyd's sobs.

"If we call a doctor, they'll call the police," she explained. "And I'll have to tell them why Mr. Donaldson . . . the reason he . . ." Her gaze darted between Stella and Mattie and then down at Lloyd, still curled on the floor. "And this boy—he saved me. I can't let him go to jail."

"But we can't let Mr. Donaldson die," Mattie argued. "He probably deserves it, but Lloyd—" She looked at Stella. "We can't let him become a murderer."

"Oh my God!"

The three women turned to see Jane standing in the doorway. Mrs. Woodrow leapt to her feet.

"Jane! Where are my girls?"

"They're with Jasper, up in my attic," she replied, staring down at Mr. Donaldson. "I took them up there to show them some of my old dolls, and when I came back down to the kitchen and heard crying from your house, I thought . . ." Her gaze shot to Lloyd and then back to Mr. Donaldson. "Is he . . . dead?"

"No," Mattie said. "But he needs a doctor."

"No," Mrs. Woodrow repeated.

"Mrs. Woodrow, we have to be practical—"

Stella raised her hand. The gesture must have been imbued with authority, because Mattie stopped speaking and Jane and Mrs. Woodrow turned toward her. She lowered her hand, a steady calm pervading her veins.

Practical.

Stella was practical.

And she knew what to do.

"I'm going to take Lloyd to that place of ours," she said to Mattie, meeting her gaze to make certain she understood. "He can lie low there until it's safe."

Mattie nodded in agreement, and Stella turned to Mrs. Woodrow. "You will call the doctor and the police."

"No, they—"

"Just listen. You'll tell them Mr. Donaldson was here to discuss your mortgage. You were out on the porch, when suddenly a desperate, passing vagrant burst through the screen door and tried to rob you. He probably saw the Cadillac out front and figured there would be good money inside."

Stella walked up to Mr. Donaldson, steeled herself, and thrust her hand inside his pocket. Once she found his wallet, she drew it out, and slid it inside her own pocket.

"He beat Mr. Donaldson up and took his wallet, but eventually your screams scared him off. You," she said to Jane, "heard the screams from your house and ran to help. You," she said, turning to Mattie, "were here visiting when it happened. But both of you saw a nondescript hobo run out of the house. They won't question the word of three people, especially not a young girl and two mothers."

"But what if they come to my house and find the . . . you know?" Jane asked, meeting Stella's gaze. Stella knew what she meant—the whiskey still.

"They shouldn't have any reason to go to your house, especially the basement. The crime scene is here." She glanced back at Mr. Donaldson, her stomach turning. "And I doubt he got a good look at Lloyd, if he remembers what happened at all." With a breath, she walked around his body and took Mattie's hand in her own. Then, she leaned close and whispered, "When everything's over, tell Jane what we came to tell her and join us out at the mill. You can take Jane's car, and Mrs. Woodrow can watch Jasper."

Mattie nodded again. Stella released her hand and turned to the other two women.

"Is the plan clear?"

Jane and Mrs. Woodrow nodded as well, and Stella looked back down at Lloyd. He was still sobbing like a child, lost in a world she couldn't see. For a moment, her steady calm faltered, but only a moment.

"Let's get him out to the truck. Once we're gone, then make the call."

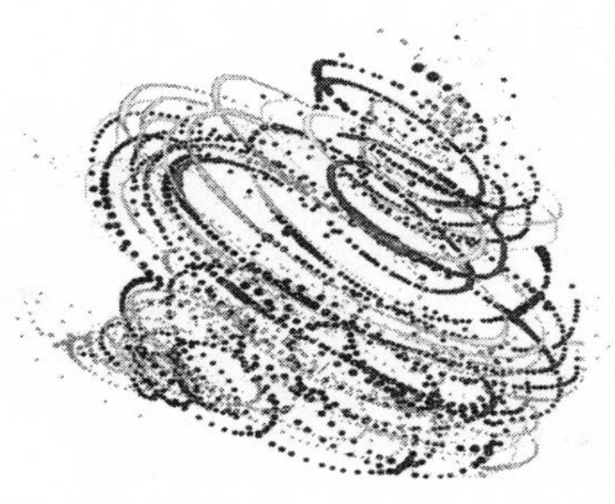

CHAPTER 16

The sun had set by the time the bent, iron archway came into view. Instead of continuing up the hill to the property, Stella parked beneath the archway and turned to Lloyd in the passenger seat. He hadn't stopped crying or spoken a word the entire drive, and she couldn't go one more inch without trying to bring him back to himself.

"Lloyd," she said softly, but he didn't look at her. He'd drawn up his knees and buried his face against them, hugging his legs while his shoulders shook. "Lloyd," she said again, because she didn't know what else to say. She'd never been much good at comforting people, not like her mother or Aunt Elsa. She reached for Lloyd's shoulder, but when her finger brushed his shirt, he flinched. She jerked her hand back, but then downed her fear and laid her palm on his back. He shuddered, but didn't recoil, so she said what she thought he needed to hear the most.

"I'm here. You're safe."

The last words had an effect on him, though not the one she'd hoped for. His shoulders collapsed, and a deep, strangled whine escaped his throat. Stella swallowed the panic that threatened to rise and kept her hand firm against his back. Then she placed her other hand on his arm.

"You're safe," she assured him again, and again, he whimpered. "You're safe."

She repeated the words for a minute, maybe longer, holding him tight. Then, finally, she felt and heard his breathing become more even.

"You're safe," she continued. "We both are. Everyone is. You saved Mrs. Woodrow."

At that, Lloyd's shoulders stiffened. He sucked in a rattling breath and said, "I killed him."

"No, no, you didn't," Stella insisted. She scooted back to look into his eyes, but he kept his head pressed to his knees. "He was still breathing—Mattie checked. They called a doctor. He'll be okay."

"No." He sucked in another jagged breath. "My uncle."

Stella's mouth dried. She stared at the back of his head. "You . . . killed your uncle?"

He nodded against his knees. "I beat him to death. Two years ago."

Words and breath deserted Stella. She had no idea what to say, so instead of saying anything, she tightened her grip on his arm and his back, assuring him of her presence. His muscles flexed under her hands, and he bit out another sob.

"I burned his place afterward," he said. "He brewed moonshine—like I said, my mamma's family had for decades—so I made it look like the still exploded. As far as I know, the law never suspected, but I left Pampa anyway. Started riding the rails, just in case. I thought it was all in the past, that I could forget it ever happened. But then today, when that son of a bitch—"

His shoulders hunched, and Stella smoothed her palm down his back. "Mr. Donaldson? He reminded you of your uncle?"

Lloyd gripped his knees tighter, then forced his next words out like vomit. "It was . . . what he said. 'Why did you have to make me hurt you?' That's what my uncle always said. Every time he raised his fists or grabbed whatever object was near, he'd stand over me and say, 'Why do you make me hurt you, Lloyd?'"

He bent down further, as if trying to vanish inside himself. Stella held on, refusing to tremble.

"When you saw that man and me, down by the station," Lloyd continued. "He was after me 'cause I'd pulled him off his son, just this six-year-old kid. He'd been whaling on him for spilling all the water they'd just boiled. I fought him so his kid could get clear of him, and also 'cause he deserved it, but that was nothin' like what happened just now. I was in control that day, but today—when I heard that bastard say that—it was like I was back there in Pampa. I was that helpless, scared-shitless kid again, and I lost my mind."

Another string of sobs ripped through him, and Stella tightened her grip. He still hadn't looked at her, but he seemed determined to finish, to get all the poison out at once. So she stayed silent as he went on.

"I should've run away long before. I don't know why I didn't, except that he was the only blood I had left. He had my mamma's eyes, and I just missed her so damn much." His shoulders quaked, and he cried like the child Stella had almost forgotten he'd been when he lost both his parents. "I told him if he came at me again, I'd do more than fight—I'd kill him. He didn't listen. When he grabbed me the next time, I grabbed the frying pan. I beat him 'til I had no strength left, 'til long after he stopped moving. And today . . . I almost did it again." He slid his hands through his hair. "I was that kid—that killer—again."

Stella stared at his blood-caked fingers, curled in his sweat-matted hair. She wanted to vomit or maybe to murder Lloyd's uncle again herself, but instead, she wrenched Lloyd up, embraced him, and buried her face in his neck. He jolted against her, his chest going rigid.

Then, in a hoarse whisper, he said, "How can you stand to do that?"

"Do what?" she murmured, tears stinging her eyes. His Adam's apple bobbed against her cheek.

"Touch me."

She pulled back and stared up at him. "What on earth are you talking about?"

He blinked his wet eyes at her, his brows drawn together. "After everything I just told you . . . after knowin' all I done . . . I *killed* someone, Stella. I almost did it again today."

"Your uncle deserved to die," she said fiercely, without a scrap of shame or doubt. "So did Mr. Donaldson. But he won't. I took care of everything. He'll live, and no one will know it was you. Mrs. Woodrow is safe now. Because of *you*."

"But how can you look at me and—"

"Lloyd, after seeing what I saw today and hearing what you just told me, I think more of you than ever. You're braver, stronger, and nobler than I imagined. Mrs. Woodrow is lucky. *I* am lucky. But I already knew that." She took his face in her hands. "I will never look at you and see anything but the best person I've ever known."

He closed his eyes, then covered her hand with his. "I don't deserve—"

"Yes, you do. I'm practical, remember? I don't go throwing around compliments like I don't go throwing around money. It's a waste. So, if you get one, you deserve it."

The faintest hint of a smile tugged at his lips, but when he opened his eyes, his gaze was serious. "I meant you. I don't deserve *you*."

"Me?"

"Yes. Look at what you did today. Saved my ass when I was useless. Kept your head when the world went nuts. Stayed here and comforted me instead of drivin' away like you could've. And now, knowin' everything you know, you're still here. Lookin' at me like it's worth it. Like *I'm* worth it."

She raised an eyebrow. "Well, that's because you are, you stupid ass. Haven't you been listening?"

His hint of a smile became a full one. "No. Why don't you tell me again?"

She returned the smile and smoothed her thumbs over his cheeks, wiping the tears. When she lowered her hands, he ran his sleeve under his nose.

"Aren't we the pair?" he said. "Both cryin' the same day."

Laughter escaped Stella's throat, but it faded when she glanced at Lloyd's knuckles. "Let's go to Archie's," she said, taking his hand and studying the torn skin. "At least you'll be healed there, until we can bandage these at home. I told Mattie to come here with Jane once everything's over. Then, who knows if we'll heal there anymore. Once Archie's free."

She started to release his hand, but then stopped, staring at the blood.

"What is it?"

She continued to stare, numbness coating her skin. "The pictures Mattie developed of Archie's world . . . I'm sorry I never told you this, Lloyd, but they were . . . strange."

"Strange? How?"

"The apples, Lavinia's hair, the stones in that cave, and the highest window in the back of the mansion were red. In every picture."

"Red?"

She bit her lip, looking back up at him. "Yes. And so were two other things. Archie's hands . . . and yours."

Lloyd looked at his hand, which Stella released.

"My hands showed up red in the pictures?" he asked.

"Yes. And what if . . . well, what if your hands were red because you've . . ."

She didn't say *killed someone*, but Lloyd's gaze told her she didn't need to.

"And if that's the reason," she continued, "then Archie—"

"We don't know that," he said. "The whole thing could be a fluke."

"But what if it's not? Archie has lied to us before. What if he lied about something else?"

Lloyd glanced up at the hill. "Should we . . . ask him?"

Stella bit her thumbnail. "I don't know. Maybe, we should drive up to the creek and wait for Mattie and Jane. Then, we can tell Mattie—if you don't mind. She'll know what to do."

Lloyd thought about it and then agreed, so Stella turned the ignition and drove up the hill to the ruined buildings. When they reached the creek, however, an empty Ford appeared in her headlights.

"What the . . ." Stella murmured, parking the truck. "No one else ever comes here."

Lloyd leaned forward, narrowing his eyes. "Wait. I know that car. Isn't that—"

"Yes," Stella gasped. The Ford belonged to Mr. Snider, one of their boarders. "But why would Mr. Snider come here?"

The answer was, he wouldn't.

But someone else in Stella's house would.

"Oh God," she breathed. "It's Lavinia. She took his car and came here alone."

Lloyd's eyes widened. "Why would she do that?"

Stella flung the door open. She didn't know why, but she knew Lavinia hadn't been acting like herself, and right now, she was alone with a man who—intangible or not—had lied to them and might be a killer.

"I don't know, but I'm going to go find out."

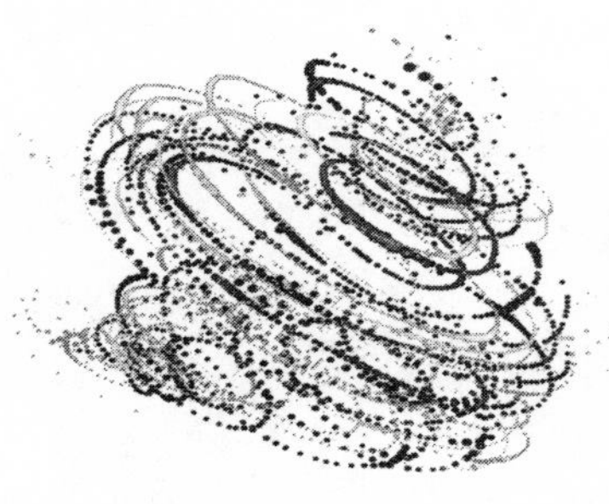

CHAPTER 17

Archie didn't come running like he usually did when Stella and Lloyd climbed out of the creek, which was the first thing that felt wrong. It was a mild, bright afternoon in his world, but the peaceful setting did nothing to calm Stella's nerves.

"Lavinia," she cried, hurrying over the lawn. "Are you here?"

"Archie?" Lloyd called out beside her.

They received no response. Stella glanced up at the mansion, to the window that had been red in all the pictures. "Let's look inside."

"Really?" Lloyd asked. "Even with—"

"I'm scared of the ghost, too, but all this time, we've been wondering how to help Archie—what about her? Maybe, if we talk to her, we can help her, and she can help us. Or at least we can find some answers."

"All right. I been kind of curious to see her up close anyway."

Stella looked at him. A small, brave smile was on his lips. Her heart swelled, and she glanced at his knuckles, still bloody but no longer torn.

She took his hand, and the two of them walked to the mansion. Lloyd gave a low whistle when they entered the front parlor. Stella had almost forgotten how beautiful it was, the way the polished floors, ornate furniture, chandelier, and fireplace gleamed. It had been night when she'd been there before, and the interior had been lit by candelabras and old-fashioned gaslights.

Now, however, the afternoon sun streamed through the immaculate windows. Stella approached the one nearest to the front door, searching for the ghost. But then Lloyd, who had made his way to the staircase, murmured, "Hey, sugar?"

"Yes?" Stella asked, studying the pane.

"I think I found her."

Stella's head shot up. Lloyd was staring into the staircase window where she'd first seen the ghost. She ran up beside him and saw the swirling, indecipherable face staring out from the glass. Like before, the ghost simply stared, and Mattie wasn't there to let them know if she was saying anything. Stella inched closer, holding her breath. Though she had no idea if the ghost would be able to hear or understand her, she wet her lips and asked, "Are you . . . the mother of Archie's child?"

The ghost's translucent gaze shifted to Stella. She nodded, and Stella's heart sped up. It had to be the woman Archie had shown them, the one from Old Clara's.

"Have you seen my sister, Lavinia, today? She has red hair, curly and cut like this."

She tugged at her own hair, but the ghost shook her head in continued, unearthly silence.

"Why are you trapped here?" Stella asked. "Can we . . . help you?"

The ghost stared at her for a moment. Then, with a wraithlike twist, her figure glided out of the window. Stella turned to the right and saw her appear in another window atop the stairs on the second floor.

"Do you think she wants us to follow her?" Lloyd asked.

Stella nodded, keeping her eyes on the ghost. "Yes, I do."

They climbed the stairs, and when they reached the window, the ghost disappeared again. After a moment, Lloyd spotted her in the window a flight above. They followed again, and again, when they reached the window, she disappeared. Stella looked around, searching for the next pane she would appear in, but now they were in a dark hallway, and there wasn't a window in sight. There was, however, a door at the end of the hall.

"Should we go inside?" she asked Lloyd. He nodded, and they walked to the door. He clutched the knob and tried to turn it, but nothing happened.

"It's locked?" Stella asked.

"Yeah."

Stella backed up, tensing like a cat on high alert. She'd never come across a locked door in Archie's world. A gust of wind *creaked* through the walls, and she jumped, looking around as if the ghost might leap out at them from the shadows.

"That makes me think we need to go inside even more," she said, lurching forward and gripping the knob with a hammering heart. The metal was cold, but her trembling palm was slick and sweaty against it. She backed up again, bumped into a side table, and yelped as if someone had grabbed her from behind.

"Hey, it's just a table," Lloyd said, though he looked as bloodless as she felt.

"I think we need to get inside," she said. "There's got to be something important and secret behind that door, or it wouldn't be locked."

"I agree. Remember when Archie offered to conjure up tents when he asked us to spend the night? Like he didn't want us snooping around inside."

"Yes," Stella realized. "And the first time he offered to take us back to the 1800s? It was right after Lavinia suggested we go to the mansion. He was trying to distract us, and it worked." She turned to Lloyd. "Have you ever broken down a door?"

"No," he said, the barest trace of a smile on his lips. "Have you?"

"No, of course not. But they do it all the time in the movies." She approached the door. "You aim right there, by the knob. And then, you kick. Hard."

Lloyd shrugged, took a few steps back, and did as she said.

It was not like the movies.

Nothing happened. Not the first time or the next ten. Soon, Lloyd was sweating, and Stella was afraid he was going to break his ankle. But just as she was about to tell him to forget it, a splintering *crack* rent the air. The door flapped open, and sunlight spilled from the room out into the hall. Stella's eyes followed its streams to a window inside, on the opposite wall. Beyond the glass, a few yards away, was the creek.

She knew where they were.

This was the room with the window that showed up red in Mattie's pictures.

She murmured her realization to Lloyd as he pushed the door the rest of the way open. The room looked like an office, with a large desk, a comfortable chair, two smaller chairs, and a coffee table. Stella and Lloyd crept inside. Stella searched for the ghost in the window, but then, something else caught her eye. A purse on one of the smaller chairs.

A purse she recognized.

She crept toward it, her lungs tightening, but something below caught her eye. She looked down. On the floor beside the coffee table, was the motionless, sprawled-out body of a woman.

"Oh God," she cried, backing up and crashing into the desk behind her. Lloyd followed her gaze and then jumped back as well. Stella narrowed her eyes, and the spinning world ground to a halt. She knew those suede, camel oxfords and that organza, apricot dress. A buzzing filled her ears as she stood up from the desk and moved closer. The woman was on her side, her face turned, but Stella had seen that bob of curly, butterscotch hair before, as well as the opal ring that gleamed on the soft, pale hand she knew as well as her own.

"Stella?"

Lloyd's voice was distant and watery, as if Stella were sinking inside a well. She kept walking, the dark water rising around her, blocking out all light and sound. When she knelt beside the woman, she felt no impact against her knees. She didn't realize her hands were shaking until she laid them against the woman's shoulders. Lloyd said something about stopping as she turned the woman over, but she couldn't, not when she saw the pearl earring winking in her earlobe. The flash of an emerald necklace shot through her blurring vision as she laid the woman on her back. She struggled for breath, each inhale a blade twisting between her ribs. A tear splashed onto the woman's cheek.

"Stella, do you know . . ."

Lloyd's voice trailed off as a sob broke through Stella's throat.

"This is my *mother*."

Another sob ripped through her as she touched her mother's face. It was cold and stiff as marble. She looked as she had the last day Stella saw her four years ago, but with her coffee brown eyes closed, her skin too pale, and no breath stirring her body.

"That's your . . . *mother*?" Lloyd repeated.

"Why is she here?" Stella gasped. "Why, and how . . ."

Firm, warm arms surrounded her, and she realized Lloyd was kneeling beside her, pulling her to his chest.

"It's all right," he whispered. "You found her. She's with you now. That's where she should be."

Stella squeezed her eyes shut, her heart swelling and breaking at once. "But that's just it—she *shouldn't* be," she said, wiping her eyes. Lloyd loosened his embrace and sat back. "This is what she was wearing," Stella explained. "She looked *exactly* like this the day she died in the dust storm."

"I'm sorry, sugar, but she didn't die in that storm."

"What?"

"Your mamma died here."

Stella blinked her tears away and followed Lloyd's pointing hand. Black-red blood had pooled beneath the side of her mother's head, fed by a deep gash in her right temple.

"She must have hit her head here," Lloyd said, and Stella looked up to see him touching the sharp, wooden edge of the coffee table, stained red as well. She flinched, imaging her mother's head making impact there. Pain cleaved her in two, and she squeezed her eyes shut.

"Thing is," Lloyd said, his voice rough, like he was trying to keep it even, "her blood is dry, but still sort of fresh. Not like it was spilled four years ago."

"Yes, and her . . . her *body* . . ." Stella choked on the word, her stomach turning. "It's like that, too. Cold, but not decayed. Not . . . bones." She forced her eyes open and looked at the wound on her mother's head but then knit her brow. "Her hat. The one we saw at the dry goods store—"

"The one some tramp claimed he found, with blood on it?"

"Yes. It isn't here, but how did it get *there*? And why are her clothes as pressed and clean as if they'd just been laundered? Her hair in place and styled? It's like she walked in this room this morning."

Lloyd stood up and surveyed the room, and Stella followed suit. It was clean and tidy. Like the rest of Archie's world, it contained no dust or wear.

"Archie's world is frozen in time," Stella realized. "Nothing here has changed since he became trapped. Which happened—"

"Four years ago," Lloyd finished, meeting her gaze in understanding. "The same year your mamma went missing."

Stella nodded, a hard frost prickling over her skin. "She was here when it happened. *Dead* when it happened. Which means . . ."

They stared at each other, neither of them needing to finish the sentence.

Her mother had been in this room, lying in her own blood, for the last four years.

Stella's stomach lurched, and she stumbled into the corner and vomited into a potted plant. Soon, Lloyd was behind her, rubbing her shoulders and telling her to breathe. She wiped her mouth and tried to obey, but another sob seized her throat.

"We were *dancing*," she cried, stumbling back from the plant. "This whole time. We were dancing and eating and drinking and laughing and . . . and you and I were—" She looked at Lloyd, who dropped his gaze. "And she was *here*," Stella screamed, gesturing at her mother. "How could we—how could we do that when—"

"We didn't know," Lloyd said, moving toward her. "None of us did."

"No. *Archie* did."

Lloyd stopped, and Stella covered her face, trembling with rage. How could Archie do this? How could he let them dance the night away while a woman lay dead upstairs? Did he know she was their mother? Stella lowered her hands and turned back to ask Lloyd what he thought, but he was on knees beside her mother, his hand reaching under her side.

"What are you doing?"

"I think she fell on something." He pulled out a crisp, white sheet of paper, rose, and read it. "Holy Moses."

Stella ran to him, and he held out the paper, the color drained from his face. She snatched it and peered at the midnight black typeface. It was a legal document, dated July 12, 1930. The words wavered before her as her hands began to shake.

"This is dated to the day my mother went missing."

"Keep reading," he said, his voice thin.

Stella did. The document concerned Archie's property and finances, the ownership of the mansion, orchard, and mill. Stella skipped to a blank space at the bottom with Archie's name printed beneath it, the place for his signature should he agree to the document's terms. Stella jerked her gaze back up and continued reading until she found the terms—a fifty-fifty share of Archie's holdings and finances and ownership of all of it once he died. Then she read the name of the person he was to share it with.

Lavinia Dorothy Fischer.

The floor dropped out from beneath Stella's feet. She stumbled backward, like she were on the edge of a crumbling cliff.

"Lavinia," she whispered, as if saying the name out loud would make it make sense, would make the earth solid again.

"It looks like your mamma came here to get him to sign this, to give half of what he owned to Lavinia."

"But why?" Stella asked, ripping her eyes from the paper to stare at Lloyd. "My father had lost his dealership, and we'd exhausted all our savings, but why would my mother come to *Archie* for help? And why ask him to give it to Lavinia? Our mother didn't even like Archie. She never let us go to his parties . . ."

The pieces clicked into place in Stella's mind with a jarring *snap*.

"Oh my God."

"What?" Lloyd asked.

"Our mother never wanted us near Archie or the mill, particularly Lavinia. She gave birth to Lavinia too soon after she and my father were married. And no one else in our family has red hair—on either side—but Lavinia's hair is red as—"

"As Archie's apples," Lloyd finished, his eyes expanding. "Are you saying what I think you are? That Archie might be Lavinia's—"

"Biological father," Stella said. "It's crazy, but it's possible. Lavinia is twenty-two, just like Jane. And Jane may have similar features to the woman Archie showed us, but lots of people have small noses, blond hair, and blue eyes. My mother being here proves he knew her, and this paper proves he knew Lavinia, which means he was lying when he pretended not to know who she was when we told him our names that first day."

Lloyd nodded, breathing harder. "He's always been partial to her. The way he watched her when she danced and sang, and he spent most of the nights we came here talking with her."

Stella thought of her fight with Lavinia, how Stella had accused Lavinia of spending too much time with Archie, and how Lavinia had defended Archie for being a father figure. Did Lavinia know the truth? Was that what she meant?

No. Stella couldn't believe it. No matter how angry she was with them, Lavinia would have told Stella and Mattie something so life-altering. But even if Lavinia didn't know, the idea of her being Archie's daughter seemed less crazy the more Stella thought about it.

"If my mother and Archie . . ." Stella closed her eyes, fighting the image that threatened. "If he got her in trouble," she said, opening her eyes, "and she married my father to keep it a secret—because she really did love my father, and he loved her—it explains why she never wanted us near Archie's mill. It also explains why she went to Archie with this document when we lost everything. She was only willing to risk the truth coming out to save us. How could she not when we couldn't pay our bills and Archie was sitting on acres of thriving land and piles of money? She wanted Lavinia to have what she deserved . . . and while she was here, asking Archie to sign the document, maybe she fell and hit her head or maybe . . ."

"Maybe he killed her."

Stella looked at Lloyd. She'd been thinking the same thing, but hearing him say it out loud flooded her mouth with metallic fear. She turned to her mother and then out the window. The ghost—her mother's ghost—wasn't in the reflection, but Archie was somewhere out there, beyond the glass.

With Lavinia.

Stella thought of the way Lavinia had looked at Archie the previous night, how she'd promised, "tomorrow," and he'd nodded, as if he they'd made some kind of arrangement.

She turned to Lloyd, the poisonous taste in her mouth spreading through her veins.

"We need to find Lavinia. Now."

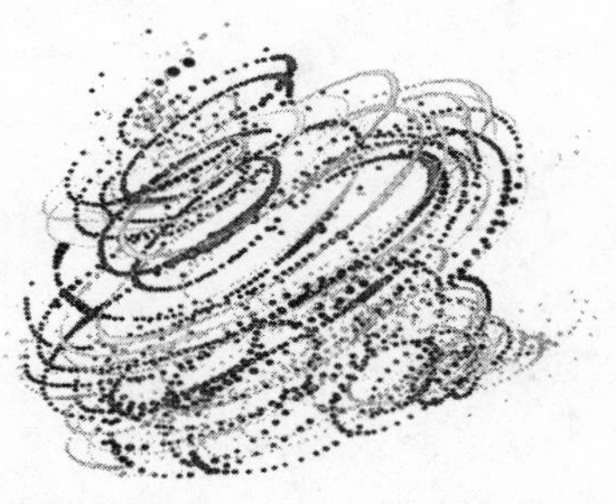

CHAPTER

18

Stella folded the document and tucked it into the pocket of her dress. Then, she and Lloyd rushed out of the room, down the stairs, and onto the porch. Once outside, they started toward the orchard, the branches of its lush trees swaying lazily in the breeze, as if Stella's mother weren't lying dead a few yards away.

"Where do you think they are?" Lloyd asked.

"I don't know. Maybe we should try the other places that were red in the photos."

"You said it was the window to that room, the apples, my hands, Archie's hands, Lavinia's hair, and . . . what else?"

Stella halted. "The stones in that cave." She turned to Lloyd. "Do you remember where it is?"

Understanding flashed in his eyes as he paled. "Yeah. This way."

He turned and dashed toward the hill beyond the mill, and Stella followed.

"Lavinia must be okay, right?" she gasped as they ran. "Archie can't touch her. He can't touch anything. We've seen that."

"You can hurt someone without touchin' 'em, sugar," Lloyd said, but then he glanced over and saw she'd stopped running, her face tight with panic. "But it don't matter. We'll find her first. She'll be all right."

"I wish I hadn't told Mattie to come here or to bring Jane with her." She looked at Lloyd. "If we're right, that means Mattie was . . . *wrong*." The dread inside her ballooned, untethering her from the earth. "If Archie's daughter is the key to freeing him, he would have been free the first night we came here. But Mattie knows everything about this sort of thing, and she was so certain—"

"If she was wrong, it's because we've never had the true story," Lloyd assured her. "Maybe it's good she's coming. She'll know what to do."

"Is someone up there? Lavinia? Stella? Mattie?"

Lloyd and Stella froze. Archie emerged from the other side of the hill, jogging in their direction.

"Hello," he called with a smile. "Where are Lavinia and Mattie?"

Lloyd glanced at Stella, who wet her lips. If she accused Archie of lying immediately, he would probably only lie more. If she wanted to find out where Lavinia was, she needed to keep him calm and catch him off guard. She forced a smile.

"Mattie will be here soon. She's bringing your daughter."

Archie's eyes widened as he neared them and came to a stop.

"You know who she is? You found her?"

"Yes," Stella said. She pretended to glance around. "Where is Lavinia?"

"What do you mean? She's not with you or Mattie?"

"There's a car up there, in our world," Lloyd said. "It belongs to one of the Fischers' boarders."

"We figured Lavinia borrowed it and came to give you the news," Stella finished.

Archie pursed his lips. "That's strange. She isn't here."

Liar, Stella thought, her mother's lifeless body flashing before her eyes. She flexed her fingers, blew out a breath, and said, "Were you just down by that cave? The one Lloyd told me about?"

Archie glanced behind him and then turned back. "Oh, yes. I've been strolling over the grounds."

"I've always wanted to see it. I think I'll have a look while we wait for Mattie."

She started toward the hill, but Archie stepped in front of her.

"No, please . . ."

Stella's blood cooled. "What do you mean, 'no'?"

"I . . . I'd rather you not go down there just now."

"Why?"

Archie wet his lips and then sighed. "I'm sorry. Lavinia *is* there, at the cave. She wanted some time alone. Away from you and Mattie. She said the three of you haven't been getting along lately and asked me to keep you away."

Stella was silent. She believed Lavinia—at least the Lavinia she'd known lately—would ask Archie to do that. But then she remembered her mother's body.

"I understand, but I need to see her. Come on, Lloyd."

She marched forward again, and Lloyd followed, but then Archie leapt into her path once more.

"Please. She's . . . she's very upset."

Stella squared her shoulders. "Archie, she's my sister, and I need to speak with her."

She took another step, but he didn't move out of the way. Her muscles stiffened. Up this close, she could see he was sweating. She couldn't remember him ever sweating before.

"I'm serious, Archie. I'll walk through you if I have to."

Archie held up his hands, his face anguished. "Please, Stella. I'm begging you."

"You can't stop me."

She steeled herself to walk through him, but then she felt a hand close around her wrist. She looked down, her mind reeling, and then back up, her heart in her throat. Archie's fingers dug into her skin.

"I'm sorry, Stella, but I can."

She tried to jerk away, but he held firm.

"How?" she gasped. "You can't touch—"

"Let her go," Lloyd shouted.

Archie released Stella's wrist and stepped back. "I'm sorry. I told you not—"

"How?" Stella repeated, touching the flesh where his fingers had been. His touch had felt hot, and his sweat was still damp on her skin.

"Please, leave," he begged, his voice rising. "For your own sakes, leave here. *Now*."

"I'm not leaving without my sister."

"Please, believe me—"

"Believe you?" Stella exploded. "How can I believe you when my mother is lying dead inside your mansion?"

Archie froze. The breeze ruffled his denim shirt, but he didn't blink or breathe. He shifted his gaze to Lloyd and then back to Stella.

"You got into the room? You saw—"

"I saw my mother lying dead on your floor. Looking like she did when she left our house four years ago."

"We know she's been here since then," Lloyd said. "That she was here when you became trapped."

Stella dug the document out of her pocket and held it up before Archie. "And we know she came here to ask you to give half of what you own to Lavinia. And we think we know why. Because . . . because she's—"

"Because she's my daughter."

Stella and Lloyd gaped at Archie. He looked at the ground, misery flooding his eyes. Stella lowered the paper, her mouth dry.

"So . . . it's true?"

"Yes. The woman from Old Clara's I showed you was just one of my workers. We never shared more than hot chocolate.

"Does—does Lavinia know?"

Archie gritted his teeth and turned away. "I told her today."

A hundred questions gathered in Stella's mouth, but before she could give voice to one, Archie turned back and continued.

"The story I told you about meeting a lonely young woman was true. Sadie and I shared a summer in 1912."

Stella jolted at hearing her mother's name on Archie's lips, but when he waved his hand, she cried out and stumbled backward. Her mother was standing before her. No—not her mother. Archie's memory of her mother.

She was younger than Stella had known her, maybe twenty, her butterscotch curls long and tumbling down her back. Still, Stella found herself wanting to run to her, to fall into her arms and sob like a child. Her body urged her forward, but then Archie conjured his memory self, and she froze, her muscles rigid. Her mother took memory Archie's hand and beamed up at him. Stella gaped as he smiled back, interlacing their fingers.

"I was lonely, like I said," Archie explained, "and Sadie was lost and heartbroken. She was in love with Robert Fischer, your father, but he'd begun courting another girl. We sort of . . . crashed together. Or maybe sought refuge in each other. Either way, for a time, I found the comfort I'd been missing since Eliza and William died."

Stella watched, unable to move, as her mother turned to memory Archie and pressed their foreheads together, her smile falling.

Ignore this and get to Lavinia, she thought, but she couldn't tear her gaze from her mother's face.

"At the end of the summer," Archie continued, "she and Robert reconciled, and he proposed. I was happy for her. We could never have stayed together, and being with her was a risk I should never have let myself take. When I heard she'd had a daughter, I assumed the child was Robert's. I understood why she avoided me in town, and I never sought her out either. She wanted to move on with her life, and I wanted to forget how reckless I'd been.

"But then, the crash happened, and in 1930 it became clear the drought was more serious than a mere dry spell. Everyone was suffering but me, and I knew I needed to move on to avoid suspicion. But the day before I was to leave, Sadie showed up at my door."

The scene before them faded, and with another wave of his hand, Archie conjured his mansion's office. Stella's stomach rolled when her mother walked through the door, wearing the clothes she'd worn the day she died—the clothes she still wore.

When memory Archie joined her and closed the door, the real Archie turned away.

"Archie," Stella whispered, "is this—"

"You wanted the truth," he bit out, as if Stella were the one causing *him* pain by asking for it. "Now, you can see it."

"Sadie, what brings you—" memory Archie began.

"Archie, my daughter . . ." she began, blinking her eyes rapidly against tears. "My oldest daughter, Lavinia. She's yours."

Stella jolted at her mother's voice, the rich, ringing sound she'd thought she'd never hear again. Then her words sank in, and the truth was as real to Stella as never before. Lavinia *was* Archie's daughter. Memory Archie's face went white.

"No. You can't be certain she's—"

"I'm so sorry," Sadie said, stepping closer. "I never wanted you to know, never wanted *anyone* to know. But yes, I'm certain. And I'm desperate now, Archie . . ."

Memory Archie turned from her. His hands were shaking, but her mother didn't seem to notice.

"I thought I was cursed for being with you," she admitted. The tears slipped down her cheeks, and Stella's heart clenched. "After Lavinia, I gave birth to four stillborn girls. I was sure I was being punished. But then I had two more beautiful, perfect daughters, and I knew I wasn't cursed. I was *blessed.*"

She pulled a handkerchief from her purse and wiped her cheeks, and Stella realized tears were falling down her own face. Lloyd touched her shoulder, and she sucked in a sob.

"I don't care what people will say anymore," Stella's mother continued, tucking the handkerchief into her purse. "Nothing scares me now except my children starving to death."

With a shuddering breath, she pulled a piece of paper from her purse. Stella glanced at the document in her own hand, knowing it was the same.

Her mother sat her purse on the chair where Stella had first seen it, smoothed out the paper's creases, and lifted her chin.

"Robert has lost his business," she continued to Archie's back. "I know this must all be a shock, but I need you to take responsibility for Lavinia. She needs you. We have nothing, and you have so much."

A low, frightening laugh rumbled from memory Archie. "Responsibility?" he repeated. Stella's mother stiffened.

"Yes. I brought a document with me. If you sign it, it will—"

"You know nothing of responsibility," he roared, spinning to face her. She jolted and took a step back.

"Like I said, I know it's a shock—"

"You bore my child—"

"I'm sorry—"

Stella shrieked as he grabbed her mother's shoulders, shaking her like a rag doll.

"I can't have children! You don't know what you've done to me!"

"I couldn't lose another child," the real Archie told Stella, his back still to the scene. "And I knew if Ruin found her, he would use her to hurt me somehow."

"Archie," her mother yelped. "Please—"

"I can't go through that again!" memory Archie cried.

Before Stella could process what was about to happen, he threw her mother down. Stella screamed and covered her eyes but still saw her mother's head *smack* the coffee table, spurting blood. The unmistakable rumble of a dust storm filled her ears, and she opened her eyes to see dust and wind blasting into the office. Memory Archie crouched on the floor, covering his face, and her mother's bloodstained hat sailed off her head and flew out the window.

"Archibald Bright."

Though she knew it was only a memory, Stella shuddered at Ruin's voice. He materialized in the office, his black coat flapping. Stella held her breath, waiting, but the scene before them vanished. She turned to Archie, who jammed his fists into his eyes, sobs wracking his frame. Rather than softening her, his tears flooded her with rage. She lurched toward him, but Lloyd grabbed her shoulder.

"Why did you stop the memory?" he asked. "What did Ruin say?"

Archie lowered his fists. "It doesn't matter."

"No—it *does* matter," Stella realized, understanding why Lloyd had asked. She looked at him, and he released her shoulder. "Why did Ruin trap you? It wasn't because your child turned eighteen because Lavinia would have turned eighteen that March."

"Please, you must leave," Archie said, spinning back to them. "I'm begging you."

"You think we're leaving here *now*? After I watched you *kill my mother*?"

"You saw for yourself. It was an acci—"

"Where is my sister? What did you do to her?"

Archie stared back at Stella, sweating again, and his silence sliced through her.

"What did you do to her?" Lloyd repeated, but Stella wasn't waiting for a response.

She stuffed the document into her pocket and bolted toward the cave. Archie caught her wrist, and she stumbled, but then Lloyd slammed his palms into his chest. Archie's grip slipped from her wrist, and he staggered backward.

"That's another reason not to trust you," Stella yelled. "Have you been corporeal this whole time?"

"No," Archie said, panting. "It wasn't a lie at first. The first night you came here, as you were leaving, I felt my hand become solid again, but only for a moment. After the next night, I was able to will myself into tangibility for minutes at a time, then half an hour, then an hour. Each night you came, my strength grew."

Stella thought about how depleted she and her sisters had been after every evening at Archie's, how their bodies, and even their clothes, had been drained of energy and substance.

"That's why we've been so tired, why my shoes wore out so quickly," she murmured. "You *took* something from us."

"No, I didn't take it. Your life force fed me. My blood runs through Lavinia's veins, and her blood runs through yours, so all three of you restored me bit by bit. You shared your vitality with me, your beating, breathing essence. You just didn't know."

Stella looked at Lloyd, remembering how he'd never been as affected by Archie's world as the rest of them, and then turned back.

"Why didn't you tell us?"

"I needed you to keep coming back, and I was afraid you wouldn't."

"Why? Was Mattie right? Did Lavinia's blood free you?"

Archie pressed his lips together. "No. I'm corporeal, but still trapped. I just needed to be corporeal to . . ."

"To *what?*"

"Please, you must leave now. And don't let Mattie or the girl you thought was my daughter come here."

"No power on earth will make me leave here without Lavinia."

"Stella, *please.*"

Stella charged forward, ready to shove him out of the way, but before she could, he reached behind his back.

And pulled out a gun.

Stella stopped. Archie cocked the gun, tears filling his eyes.

"Please. Leave now."

"Archie," Lloyd said gently, "you don't want to use—"

"Of course, I don't," Archie snapped. "That's why I've been begging you to leave. In a few hours, the enchantment binding me here will break, and I will leave this place forever. You'll never have to see me again, but you need to leave here. *Now.*"

Dread washed through Stella's veins. "Where is Lavinia? What have you done with her that will break the enchantment?"

Archie shook his head, and the tears slipped down his cheeks. "Trust me, it's better this way. Walk away and live your lives. The grief will always stay with you, but you will carry on. Let her go."

Let her go. The words echoed in Stella's head. They were ludicrous words, impossible words, words she would not accept in a million years.

And they also told her Lavinia was either dying or dead.

The world fell away. The gun in Archie's hand no longer mattered. Stella lunged at him. A shot rang out as they fell to the ground, and she jolted but felt no pain. Then Lloyd was beside her, thrusting his forearm into Archie's throat. Stella clawed at Archie's hand, trying to pry the gun from his fingers, but he twisted his arm away, reached back, and swung it up at her face. Metal collided with her cheek, and she flew backward onto the grass. She pushed herself up, and saw Archie shove the gun against Lloyd's stomach.

"No!"

The deafening blast swallowed the sound of her voice. Lloyd doubled over and rolled to his side. Archie scrambled to his feet, and before Stella could suck in another breath, fired again. Lloyd flopped onto his back, his body limp.

And a hole in his forehead.

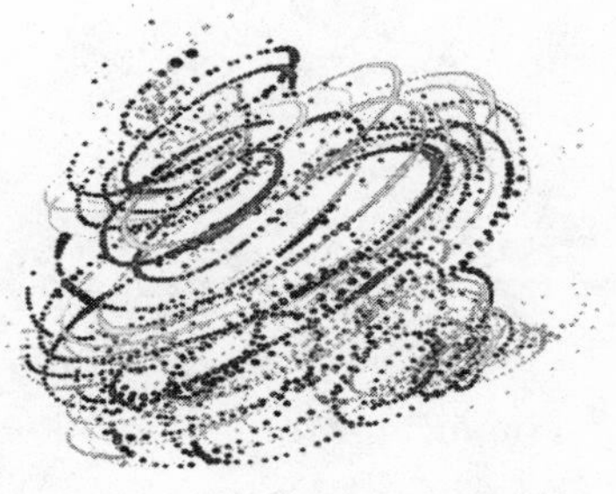

CHAPTER 19

Stella felt like her vocal cords were shredding. She couldn't stop screaming.

"Lloyd!"

She couldn't see anything but the hole in his forehead, couldn't hear anything but the echoing blast of the gun. She didn't even notice when Archie grabbed her arm and pulled her up.

"Please, Stella. I don't want to hurt you, too."

She wrenched her arm back and spat in his face. He stumbled backward, losing his grip, and she fell to the ground. She started to climb to her feet, but then a powerful blow to the back of her thigh knocked her flat on her face. She didn't even register the sound of the gunshot at first. Not until her leg began to burn from the inside out.

"*Stop* making me hurt you," Archie cried. Stella's head spun. It was what Mr. Donaldson had said to Mrs. Woodrow, the same words that had flipped a switch inside Lloyd. Archie's hand closed around her wrist, and then she was on her back, and he was dragging her up the hill. She looked down and saw blood staining her dress and leaving a trail through the grass. She searched for Lloyd. He was still on his back, growing farther and farther away. But then, as she and Archie reached the top of the hill, the fire in her thigh crept from the center toward the surface. The next moment, a piece of metal rolled down her leg and onto the grass, and the pain disappeared.

Her leg had healed and expelled the bullet.

Stella had almost forgotten injuries healed in Archie's world. Her heart swelled with hope and she bit back a shriek as tears of joy filled her eyes. Lloyd wasn't dead after all—he was just healing. Maybe Lavinia would be all right too.

She pretended to still be too hurt to fight as Archie dragged her down the other side of the hill. Then, when he glanced away, she twisted free, leapt to her feet, and lunged for the gun. He swung it out of her reach and pointed it at her.

"Please, Stella. Don't make me shoot you again."

"It doesn't matter if you do. I'll heal again. And so will Lloyd. He'll be here any minute."

Archie shook his head, tears filling his eyes. "A blow to the brain isn't the same as a shot to the leg or a scrape on your palm."

Stella tensed. No. She wouldn't believe it. If she could heal so could Lloyd. Maybe it would be more complicated or take longer than her leg, but it would happen. He wouldn't die.

"Besides," Archie continued. "Once the enchantment breaks, my healing power will no longer extend to the rest of you. If he hasn't healed by then, he'll—well, he'll . . ." He squeezed the gun tighter, the tears slipping down his cheeks. "This is why I told you to leave! Why couldn't you listen?"

Stella drew in a breath and tried to make her voice even. "Please, Archie. What will break the enchantment? What did you do with my sister?"

Archie hesitated but then gestured with the gun.

"Go in there. I'll show you."

He kept the gun trained on her as he directed her to the sloping entrance of the cave. Stella crept inside, blinking in the dim light and searching for Lavinia. The wall of stones from the pictures appeared a few feet to their left. Loose rocks littered the ground below a window-sized gap in the middle, and as they passed it, Stella spied a mound of freshly turned earth inside, like a recent grave. The cold, damp air in the cave dissolved.

"Archie, is that . . ."

She turned to him, and he lowered his gaze in shame.

"No," she whispered, and then she screamed. "No!"

"Stella—"

"You killed her! You killed my sister—"

"No. She isn't dead. But . . ."

Stella stared at Archie, his unspoken words ripping through her like fire.

But she will be soon.

Stella turned back to the mound of earth. Archie had buried Lavinia alive. He'd said the enchantment would break within hours.

When Lavinia died.

Stella could heal from a gunshot wound, but no amount of healing could put air in Lavinia's lungs once she suffocated.

Stella bolted toward the gap in the wall, but Archie was ready. He seized the back of her dress and yanked her backward so hard, her rear end slammed onto the ground. She scrambled to get back up, but then a shot echoed through the cave, and her right foot exploded with pain. She rolled onto her side and screamed. The sensation was more than a burning this time. She was certain the bones in her foot were nothing but shards inside her shoe. The pain was so intense, she thought she might lose consciousness. She *wanted* to lose consciousness.

No. Lavinia. I have to save her.

But she could do nothing but writhe as Archie tucked the gun into his jacket and retrieved a knife from his boot. With it, he cut a length of rope that lay coiled on the ground. Then he slid the knife back into his boot, walked to Stella, and bound her wrists behind her back.

"Please, Stella, let me explain."

"Explain? You're going to kill my sister. Your own *daughter*."

Archie finished tying the rope and knelt in front of her. "Stella—"

"You bastard," she moaned, gritting her teeth as the bones in her foot reformed. "Why didn't you just shoot me in the head, like Lloyd?"

"I can't risk spilling your blood in death. Like Lavinia, you have your mother's blood, and ending her life by spilling it above the earth is how I became trapped."

Stella stilled and stared at him. "What?"

"Everything I told you about my family in Ohio was true. I was dying, Ruin saved me, and seven years later, he demanded my son as payment. But what I didn't tell you was when Eliza and I begged Ruin to take anyone but William, he agreed."

With a jerk of his hand, Archie conjured his wife, his memory self, and William as a young man. Ruin appeared as well, stalking toward them. Stella's wrists twitched against the rope, and she tried to remember to breathe. William lurched back as his parents leapt in front of him protectively.

"I will grant your request," Ruin rasped at memory Archie, his stone-on-stone voice scraping Stella's bones. "But on one condition. You must bury another alive on your property before night falls. When they die, they will give their life force to your land, satisfying our deal and keeping you healthy and prosperous. Otherwise, I return for your son tonight."

"So, you killed someone else," Stella said, realizing. "To save your son."

Archie wiped himself, Eliza, and William away, his shoulders bunching.

"Yes. I went to town and found a traveler willing to work for food and a place to stay. I brought him to my farm and . . . and then I did it.

I tied him up and buried him. A few hours later, Ruin appeared again. He told me I'd done well, that William was safe, and I thought the ordeal was over. But then he said I'd have to commit the same crime every seven years to keep William safe, to keep my immortality, and to keep my land flourishing."

Stella stared at the memory of Ruin, still smoldering before them. A breeze whistled through the cave as she realized what Archie's words meant.

"You've killed someone every *seven years*? For the last century? Archie, that's almost *fifteen people*—"

"I know," he cried, pushing himself up from the ground and turning his back. "And it didn't even matter."

"What do you mean?"

"Because William died anyway," he roared, spinning back around. "Two years later, of swamp fever. He might have been safe from Ruin, but he wasn't safe from the world. I'd taken a life to save him, and I still lost him."

Stella furrowed her brow. "But then why continue to . . . if William was gone—"

"I couldn't break the deal! William might have been gone, but if I didn't keep up my end of the bargain, *I* would die. I'd made a deal with a devil and committed murder—I'd be sure to face eternal damnation, even if my life was hell without William and Eliza. She did take her own life, just as I told you. Not only was she unable to bear the loss of our son, but the weight of the sins I'd committed. So, I moved around the country, maintaining my orchards and burying people who wouldn't be missed. But then I met your mother and did the worst thing I could have done."

"Why? If the deal didn't involve a child you fathered reaching eighteen—"

"I couldn't lose a child again," he cried, stretching out his hands. "The loss of Eliza wounded me, but William . . ." He pressed the heels of his palms to his eyes. "You don't know what it's like to lose a child. There is no greater suffering. I couldn't bear it again. That's why I lost my mind when your mother . . ."

He turned his back as Ruin stepped forward, the filth and wind of a dust storm now swirling around him. Stella held her breath, knowing this must the memory from just after her mother died, the one Archie had refused to show them earlier.

"Archibald Bright," Ruin droned. "You have broken our deal by spilling blood above the earth, rather than putting it inside as I commanded. Though this is a breach, it is not enough cause to take your life. That will come when you miss your seven-year deadline. And you *will*."

"That's why he trapped me and stole my corporeality," Archie said, sweeping Ruin away and turning to Stella. "So I couldn't make my next offering. Then he could he drag me to hell for good."

Stella's mind spun. Her first thought was that Archie must have buried at least three other people on this property to have kept the deal as long as he'd been in Dodge, which explained why the stones were red in the pictures—the people he'd killed were here, with Lavinia. Then Stella remembered how upset Archie had been when they first told him what year it was. When he realized how much time had passed.

"My last seven years is up two weeks from today," Archie continued. "I don't want to kill Lavinia, but I don't have a choice. She carries her mother's blood, the blood I spilled above the ground. Putting her in the earth is the only thing that will make that right again."

"But Mattie and I have the same—"

"But Lavinia also carries *my* blood—what Ruin wanted in the first place. My child. Sacrificing her is only way to satisfy him and mend the broken deal. Yesterday, when I was certain I had become fully corporeal, I asked her to come here alone. I told her I'd found a way to erase her scars for good. It was torture to tell her the truth once she got here, to tie her up and put her in that grave—" A sob punched through his last word, and he fisted his hands in his hair and turned to where Lavinia lay. "But the only alternative is eternal damnation." He dropped his hands and turned back to Stella. "You understand now, don't you? At least, when this is over, Lavinia will be in paradise."

Rage swooped through Stella's body so hot and fierce, she thought it might burn through ropes. "Is that what you tell yourself? How you live with what you've done? The innocent people you've killed and now your own *daughter*—"

"Stop!" Archie shouted. "You never had to learn all of this. I wouldn't have had to hurt Lloyd or tell you any of this if you had just *listened.* Why couldn't you have left when I told you to?"

Stella stopped fighting the rope. It was useless. Her words could not convince Archie to dig Lavinia out of that grave, and even if she managed to free her wrists, she couldn't overpower him. She couldn't do anything but sit there as Lloyd and Lavinia slowly died. She pictured Lavinia, helpless beneath the earth, and Lloyd, bleeding out in the grass, but then an idea took shape in her mind. Maybe there *was* something she could do, but she'd only have one chance.

"You're right," she said, dropping her voice to a numb, defeated tone. "I should have left. Lloyd and I should have listened to you." She met Archie's gaze, her eyes filling with tears that came easily. "But would you trust me to leave now? If I promised to keep Mattie away from here and never tell?"

"I'm sorry, Stella. It's too late now. But once the enchantment breaks, I'll let you go. I'll leave in your truck, and you can take the car Lavinia brought. You'll be all right. And you'll move past this one day, you'll see."

Stella downed her rage and forced her breathing to remain slow. "Can you at least tie my hands in front of me? This hurts."

"No, I'm sorry—"

"Please," Stella begged, blinking and sending the tears down her cheeks. "I'm sitting here watching my sister die. Can't you do *one* kindness for me?"

Archie's face scrunched up in shame. Then he glanced through the gap in the wall and back at Stella.

"All right. Roll onto on your stomach."

Stella murmured "thank you" and obeyed. Archie knelt beside her and tugged at the rope. Once her hands were free, she fought the urge to claw his eyes out and followed his instructions to put her hands above her head. Though her body cried out against it, she allowed him to retie her wrists. Then he rolled her onto her back and helped her to sit up, facing him. She closed her eyes, took a breath, and opened her eyes.

"There," Archie said. "Now you—"

Stella seized his hair and rammed her knee into his face, just as she'd seen Lloyd do to the man at the station the first time she saw him. She felt and heard the *crunch* as Archie's blood splattered on her knee. He reared back, roaring in pain, and she thrust her hands into his jacket. Even with her wrists bound, she managed to pull out the gun. He sat up, one hand on his nose and the other outstretched to stop her, but she pointed the gun at his face and pulled the trigger. Her arms flew back, blood sprayed her face, and Archie slumped to the ground. She pushed herself to her feet, aimed the gun at his head again, and squeezed the trigger, but nothing happened. She must have used the last bullet. She still didn't know if Lloyd would heal from his gunshot, but she had a feeling Archie would. He was the one who'd made the deal, the one who didn't age. The rest of their healing had always been a mere extension of his.

She had to work fast.

She dropped the gun and used her teeth to loosen the rope around her wrists. Once her hands were free, she ran to the gap in the stone wall and clambered through. A shovel lay next to the mound of earth, so she snatched it and started digging. She had no idea how deep Archie had buried Lavinia, and with each strike, she feared both not plowing far enough in time and hitting her sister with the blade.

The following minutes were the longest of her life. With every swing of the shovel, every shallow, labored breath, she pictured Lavinia dead or Archie popping up behind her. She knew her muscles must be aching, but she couldn't feel them. Sweat and tears streamed down her face, but the only thought in her head was *my sister, my sister, my sister.*

She was over three feet deep in the earth when she spotted a flash of white. A still, curled finger.

She tossed the shovel aside and flew to the ground, clawing at the dirt.

"Lavinia!"

She found the back of her neck and wrenched her up. Dirt fell from her face. Her eyes were closed, and her body was limp, but her face was still unscarred. If the enchantment hadn't been broken, that meant she had to still be alive.

"Lavinia," Stella screamed again. When she didn't respond, she hooked her elbows beneath her underarms, pulled her out of the pit, and laid her on the flat ground. "Wake up!"

Lavinia still didn't respond. Stella clutched her shoulders and shook her. When that didn't work, she gripped the sides of her face and forced her mouth open. There was dirt inside, so Stella pulled her into a sitting position and smacked her upper back with the base of her palm.

"Breathe. Breathe!"

Lavinia's sagging head swung with each blow, but she didn't wake. Stella began to sob as she continued to pound her back. Maybe, it *was* too late. The scars may not have returned, but her sister wasn't breathing. But then, Lavinia's shoulders shook, and a cough echoed through the cave. Stella's heart stopped.

And Lavinia opened her eyes.

"Oh thank God. You're alive!" Stella cried.

She threw her arms around her, fresh sobs overtaking her body. Lavinia coughed again and then croaked, "Stella?"

"Yes," Stella gasped, pulling back and wiping her eyes. "I'm here. You're safe."

"Oh God," Lavinia rasped, seizing Stella and pulling her into an embrace. Sobs racked her chest as she squeezed Stella harder, sucking in gulps of air. "I'm alive. I'm *alive*!" A howl broke loose in her throat. "Stella, you *saved* me."

"Shh. It's okay," Stella said.

Lavinia pulled back, clumps of dirt falling from her lashes. "Archie," she cried, "he's corporeal. He tied me up and buried me—"

"I know," Stella said, cupping her face. "He told me everything." She glanced back through the hole in the wall. "He's unconscious, but we need to leave before he wakes up."

She untied Lavinia's wrists and started to rise, but Lavinia didn't move. Instead, she closed her eyes and sobbed. "I was so stupid, Stella."

"Don't you dare say that. This wasn't your fault."

"Yes, it was. I trusted him and came here alone. I wanted so badly . . . to stay, to *be*—"

"Lavinia, stop it," Stella said, taking her face in her hands. "There is nothing wrong with wanting what you wanted or doing what you did."

Lavinia's shoulders slumped as another sob ripped through her. "You came for me. After everything, you still risked your life to save me."

"Of course I did. You'd do the same for me, and so would Mattie. We're sisters, Lavinia. I love you, and nothing will change that. Ever."

Lavinia lowered her head, sobbing again, but Stella gripped her chin and forced it back up.

"Trust me, I can't wait to hold it over your head forever, but I'll never get the chance if we don't get out of here."

Lavinia choked out a laugh, wiped her nose, and the two of them climbed to their feet.

"You're okay!"

Stella turned and squinted through the gap in the wall. Mattie stood silhouetted against the sunlight at the cave's entrance.

"I followed a trail of blood," Mattie said, running toward her, but she stopped when she saw Archie. "Oh my—"

"Did you see Lloyd?" Stella demanded, dashing to the opening. "Is he all right?"

Mattie wrenched her gaze away from Archie. "I spotted him first. He's unconscious. I tried to wake him but couldn't. I didn't see any wounds, but his head and stomach are splattered with blood." She narrowed her eyes at Stella. "Like your face." She shifted her gaze to Lavinia, who'd joined Stella beside the gap, still covered in dirt. "What happened? Archie—" She gestured back at him. "He's corporeal? He's *dead?*"

"Where is Jane?" Stella demanded.

"Still at the police station," Mattie replied. "They finished questioning me first, and I wanted to check on Lloyd. Now, please tell me what—"

"Archie's my father," Lavinia announced, at the same time Stella blurted, "Archie killed our mother." Mattie stared at each of them.

"*What?*"

As quickly as they could while climbing through the gap, they filled Mattie in on the basics.

"Oh my God. Lavinia," Mattie cried, throwing her arms around her.

"I'm so sorry about how I've been acting," Lavinia said, squeezing her back. "I can't believe I *hit* you—"

"Don't give it another thought." Mattie pulled back and looked at Stella. "And Stella, you saved Lavinia's—"

A scream echoed through the cave, and Mattie flew backward. Archie clutched her by the hair, the blade of his knife pressed to her throat. Stella's chest hollowed out. In her rush to save Lavinia, she'd forgotten about the knife in Archie's boot. She should have taken it. She should have tied him up. She'd been so *stupid*.

"I won't kill her," Archie said. "Not if Lavinia gets in that grave."

Though he'd healed, his face was still covered with blood. His eyes were wild, and his tears made pale rivulets through the crimson gore.

"You can't kill her," Stella yelled. "She'll heal and—"

"Do you think you should take that chance? If I sever her windpipe, how long will she last without breathing before it heals?"

Mattie took a wobbly breath. "Archie, you don't have to do this."

"If I don't, I will die and enter the gates of Hell."

"You belong there!" Stella shouted, unable to stop herself, but Lavinia seized her shoulder.

"There is such a thing as forgiveness," she told Archie, her jaw tight and eyes pleading. "You've done terrible things, but you're not a bad man. You never wanted any of this to happen."

Stella opened her mouth to argue but snapped it shut when Archie relaxed the blade against Mattie's neck.

"Sacrifices," he said, his voice breaking. "I was willing to sacrifice everything to keep my family alive. Ruin wanted me to sacrifice William, but I couldn't, so I sacrificed the others, and in doing so, lost my soul. You're right, Lavinia." He fixed his gaze on her, misery twisting his face. "I don't want to make you get back in that grave, but there's no other way for me. You are my blood, like William, and a good woman any father would be proud of, but . . ." A sob rattled his body. "It's too late now."

"Sacrifice."

They all looked at Mattie, who had a familiar light dancing in her eyes.

"That's the answer." She gazed at Stella. "A sacrifice, like the Little Mermaid. When she discovered she could only save herself by killing the person she loved, she chose to give herself up to the sea instead. She gained a soul by sacrificing herself."

Archie narrowed his eyes. "What do you mean?"

"You've had the power to end the deal all along," Mattie told him, glancing at the blade and then up at him. "Ruin made the deal with you. *You're* the one he really wants. If you spare Lavinia and give him yourself, you can atone for your sins."

"No. I can't risk it," Archie said, but there was the slightest hitch of hesitation in his voice, and Stella seized her chance.

"How would he do it?" she asked Mattie. "Could he call Ruin here right now?"

"No," Archie yelled, but Mattie shouted over him.

"Lavinia, *you* can call him. Use your—"

"No," Archie cried, thrusting the blade against Mattie's neck. Blood trickled down her throat, but she didn't stop.

"You can call him with your—"

"Shut up!" Archie roared. "You don't know what powers you're playing with."

But apparently, Lavinia didn't need Mattie to finish her sentence. She swiped a rock from the cave floor and dug it into her palm. Bright, red blood bloomed on her dirt-caked skin.

"No," Archie screamed, but Lavinia bent down and pressed her palm to the ground.

"I call you, Ruin," she shouted. "With the blood of my slain mother and the blood of Archibald Bright, I summon you to modify the bargain you struck with him."

A low moan *creaked* through the earth, and the walls around them shook. Lavinia stood and wrapped her arms around herself as a cold, biting wind swept into the cave. Stella shivered and clutched herself, too, as another groaning tremor knocked dirt from the ceiling. Then a plume of smoke bloomed in the corner, as tall as a man and as dark as coal. Sulfur stung Stella's nose as it moved toward them, opening up like a giant, rotting flower.

Ruin stepped out from inside the smoke, the whites of his eyes black as tar and his irises like living fire.

This was no memory.

Archie released Mattie and plastered himself against the wall, his knife *pinging* to the ground. Mattie ran to Lavinia and Stella, and the three of them held each other as Ruin approached, his smoldering coat billowing and the moss beneath his boots darting away like frightened fish.

"Brave girl," he rasped in his stone-scraping voice, his eyes on Lavinia. "Your blood should be in the ground, feeding my deal with Archibald. And yet, you summon me here, where I can take you for myself."

Lavinia shrank back, and Stella gripped her tighter, but Mattie stepped forward, chin raised.

"You can't take anyone unless they go willingly. Or make a deal with you. Otherwise, you'd never have to make deals at all, and you could have taken Archie from the beginning. It works that way in every story and fable I've ever read."

Ruin inclined his head. "Clever girl. Then why was I summoned here?"

"To take Archie to Hell, where you *both* belong," Stella spat.

Ruin looked at her, his fiery eyes flaring. "Impudent girl."

Stella blanched but then lifted an eyebrow in pride. Impudent was actually the perfect word.

Ruin turned to Archie, who was staring at him, his back still pressed to the wall. A wolf's smile lifted the corners of Ruin's mouth, revealing his pointed teeth.

"Is that what you wish, Archibald? To conclude our business by offering me the ultimate sacrifice?"

"No," Archie shouted, pushing himself up from the wall.

"Then you know what you have to do."

Archie looked at Lavinia and started toward her. Stella leapt in front of her, but then something seized her middle and yanked her backward. Her back hit stone, and she looked down to see a ring of smoke encircling her waist, pinning her to the wall. When she looked up, she saw Mattie bound to the opposite wall by the same winding chain of smoke and Ruin stretching his open palms toward them. Perhaps he couldn't take them against their will but he could keep them from interfering with his business. Archie continued toward Lavinia, but instead of running, she stood straight and tall, looking into his eyes. He paused, as if her gaze was a blow that had knocked him off balance.

"Giving Ruin yourself is the only way to end your torment," Mattie shouted at Archie. "What kind of an eternal life is worth the blood you've spilled to live it?"

Archie glanced at her and then back at Lavinia, not moving.

"And it isn't practical," Stella added, struggling against the smoke. "You can't go on feeding this deal forever. One day it has to end, and how do you think that will be? Save yourself the pain and suffering now."

Archie turned to her and then to Lavinia, still not moving.

"It's time to make your choice," Ruin grated.

Archie sobbed and bowed his head, covering his face. Stella writhed against the smoke but then froze when Lavinia reached out and took Archie's hands in her own. She lowered them from his face and looked into his eyes.

"You started this because you were a good man," she said. "I wish I could have known you before you were forced to make such terrible choices. You would have been a good father. You *were* a good father."

Archie's shoulders collapsed, and he pulled his hands from Lavinia's. For a moment, the only sounds in the cave were the breeze and his echoing sobs. Then he straightened, looked at Lavinia, and choked out "I'm so sorry." Stella's stomach dropped, and she closed her eyes, not wanting to see him drag Lavinia back into the grave. But Lavinia didn't cry out, and no sounds of a scuffle came. Stella opened her eyes and saw Archie cup Lavinia's cheek in his hand. Then he turned around and faced Ruin.

"I want to atone. Take me instead."

Stella's breath caught in her throat as she dropped to her feet, no longer trapped by Ruin's smoke. Ruin grinned and opened his arms, his rippling coat spreading out like the clouds of a gathering dust storm behind him.

"As you wish."

Archie turned around and looked at Stella, Mattie, and then Lavinia. "I'm sorry," he said again, and he walked toward Ruin. When he reached him, the coat of smoke and dust swirled around them both. Stella and Mattie dashed to Lavinia, and the three of them huddled together as the gritty, black tornado obscured Archie and Ruin from view. The girls squeezed their eyes shut and covered their mouths, the wind whipping through their hair and clothes. Then the cloud broke apart, the wind died, and they coughed and wiped their eyes. Only Ruin stood before them in the settling soot and ash. Archie had left no bones or bloody clothes like in the story he'd made up. He was gone, as if he'd never been there at all. The light in the cave shifted from buttery yellow to moonlight blue, and Stella remembered it was nighttime in the real world—the sunny afternoon had only existed in Archie's memory.

Now that he was gone, the enchantment was broken.

Stella looked at Lavinia. Her scars had returned. Lavinia met her gaze and then Mattie's, reading their expressions. Stella thought her face would fall, but she smiled and touched their shoulders.

"It's all right."

"Before I go, there is one more thing you should know."

They turned to Ruin, who glided toward them, his teeth glinting as he pulled his lips into a smile.

"I've been inside your heads, Lavinia, Stella, and Mattie Fischer. I know what each of you want and can give it to you." He fastened his gaze on Mattie. "How would you like a free ride to college, to enter any field you wish regardless of your sex?" He looked at Stella. "To escape this barren wasteland and shine like a star in Hollywood?" He grinned at Lavinia. "To erase the scars that mar your face and find romance with a good man?"

"Go to hell," Stella spat, but she jolted when she realized Mattie and Lavinia had shouted the exact same words in unison with her. A smile split her face, Lavinia laughed, and Mattie's eyes widened.

"Unity."

They grasped each other's hands and murmured another word in unison, the sacred refrain they hadn't said in days.

"Jekhipe."

Stella looked at Ruin, who sneered in disgust.

"Have it your way."

He burst into smoke, and the wind rose again, carrying his grainy, dissolving form through the mouth of the cave. Stella, Mattie, and Lavinia clung to each other until the gale died down, and then Stella squinted at the cave's entrance.

"Mattie. Lavinia," she whispered.

Mattie and Lavinia followed her gaze.

There, in the pocket of moonlight, the sisters saw flecks of sparkling dust gathering together. Stella stared as the whirling flecks formed a coherent shape, solidifying into the ghost of a woman.

The ghost of their mother.

She wasn't swirling dust anymore, but she wasn't flesh and blood either. An iridescent sheen radiated from her skin, and the breeze had no effect on her hair or clothes—the same ones she'd worn when she died.

She looked at her daughters, the love on her face so fierce, it seemed more tangible than her body.

"Mamma," Lavinia choked out.

They ran to her but stopped before getting too close, afraid doing so would blow her out like a candle. Their mother looked at each of them.

"My girls."

As one, they fell into sobs. Her voice echoed against the walls of the cave with a resonance that reminded Stella that she wasn't with them in the flesh. She was both in their world and the next.

"We miss you so much," she said, wiping her nose with the back of her hand.

"I miss you too," her mother replied. "And I will until I see you all again."

That promise—that *possibility*—broke Stella. She pressed her hands against her knees, sobbing harder.

"I'm so proud of you all," their mother continued. Then she looked at Lavinia. "I'm sorry I never told you the truth."

"It's all right," Lavinia said. "I understand."

"We'll give you a proper burial," Mattie promised, her voice raw.

Their mother smiled. She didn't cry—perhaps ghosts couldn't—but she might as well have been. Love, longing, regret, and finally, peace passed over her face.

Then, she faded into mist, drifting away with the breeze and melting into the silver-blue moonlight. Once she was gone, Stella realized someone was standing a few steps away from where she'd been at the cave's entrance.

Lloyd.

His head and stomach were coated with blood, but he was awake and alive. He stared at the spot where their mother's ghost had been.

"Holy Moses."

Stella laughed, ran to him, and threw her arms around him.

"You're okay," she cried, fresh sobs erupting.

He squeezed her back, breathing her in. "I'm okay." He pulled back and looked her over. "And you—"

"I'm okay. More than okay. Also, I love you."

He laughed and kissed her, hard and fast. "I love you too, sugar." Then he glanced at her sisters, the upended dirt, and the blood-splattered ground. "Now, can you tell me what the hell happened?"

CHAPTER 20

Excitedly and talking over each other, Stella, Mattie, and Lavinia explained what had happened to Lloyd. As they talked, Stella couldn't stop staring at his healed forehead. Now, the only wounded part of him was his knuckles, once again, cut and bruised from Mr. Donaldson's bones and teeth.

Lavinia noticed and asked about the injuries, so Mattie recounted the story.

"What happened after Lloyd and I left?" Stella asked Mattie once she'd finished.

"We called a doctor and the police," Mattie answered. "The doctor said Mr. Donaldson needed to go to the hospital, so he took him there while we went to the station with the police. We gave them the story you told us to, and I don't know about Jane and Mrs. Woodrow, but I could tell the officers I talked to believed me. Still," she added, nodding at Lloyd's knuckles, "it's probably best not to show those off around the police for a while."

Lloyd raised his palms. "No argument here."

"So, where do you think we are?" Lavinia asked, looking around. "I mean, if the enchantment is gone, is Archie's world gone too?"

"Let's find out," Stella replied.

They crept out of the cave and into the moonlight to climb the hill. When they reached the top, Stella gasped, and she wasn't alone.

It was different, but also the same.

Three cars were parked beside the creek—the Fischer's truck, Mr. Snider's Ford, and Jane's Chevrolet, which Mattie had borrowed. Since they'd been left behind in the real world, their presence implied that Archie's world was gone. However, in the real world, the creek had been dry, and now it was filled with running water reflecting the starlight. And the mansion and mill that had been rubble were now whole and standing, just like they were in Archie's world. However, while they'd been sleek and pristine in that world, they were now shabby and weather-beaten, as if they'd endured the last four dust-storm years, alone and neglected.

The same was true for the orchard. When they first found it, it had been dotted with gnarled, diseased-looking stumps. Now it was filled with trees again, but rather than lush, well-trimmed branches brimming with shining fruit, the trees had wild, uncared-for boughs dotted with ordinary apples.

"I don't understand," Lavinia said, voicing Stella's thoughts. "Is this the real world or not?"

"There's one way to find out," Mattie replied, and she took off down the hill.

After glancing at each other, the rest of them followed. When Mattie reached the edge of the creek, Stella realized what she was doing. They slowed to a stop as Mattie splashed into the water, heading to the apple-shaped mark in the dirt. She waded and searched, her head bent close to the surface. Then, finally, she looked up and declared, "The apple mark is gone."

"What does that mean?" Stella asked.

"It means Archie's world no longer exists, and this is the real world now."

Lavinia turned to stare at the buildings and trees as Mattie splashed back to the shore.

"But how?" she asked, turning to the rest of them. "The buildings were rubble in the real world, and the trees were dead."

"I think this land was only wreckage while Archie's world existed," Mattie answered. "It was, well, *ruined* when Archie broke his deal with Ruin. Now that Archie is gone, so is the deal and its consequences. Everything affected by the curse is as it would have been if Archie had simply abandoned it that day. It's not dead or destroyed, just rough and unkempt after four years of neglect."

Stella looked around. Like most of Mattie's explanations, it made sense.

The creek didn't sparkle with the immaculate, unearthly beauty of the creek in Archie's world, but it wasn't dry and useless as it had been in the world she'd known. The land and buildings had lost their unnatural perfection, but they were whole and presumably functional.

"Do you think," Lavinia said quietly, "Mamma's body is still in the mansion?"

Stella took her hand and then Mattie's. "Let's go see."

As they headed toward the mansion, Stella glanced at the mill, wondering if it contained all the old equipment. Then she stopped. "Do the rest of you see that?" she asked, pointing at the mill.

The others halted and followed her gesture. When Lloyd murmured "What the hell?" Stella knew they saw it too. Random boards were missing from different places in the mill's walls, leaving a handful of oddly-placed holes that hadn't been there before.

"Oh my goodness," Mattie giggled, covering her mouth. "Those are the boards *we* took. The ones that are now on the sleeping porch."

Stella continued to stare but laughed as well. "I suppose I'm glad they didn't return here when the enchantment broke."

"*You're* glad?" Lloyd asked, his tone serious. "You're not the one who would've had to explain to your aunt how you did all that work with nothin' to show for it."

They continued up to the mansion. When they reached the front door, it creaked with age, but it opened. The gaslights no longer worked, so Mattie found a box of matches, lit a candelabra, and handed it to Lloyd, since he was the tallest.

He started toward the stairs, and the rest of them followed. As she walked through the parlor, Stella noticed that, though dust-coated and moth-eaten, the interior was still grand. With cleaning and repair, it could be comfortable again.

They ascended the staircase, but it wasn't the cobwebs and flickering candlelight that tightened Stella's stomach. She knew her mother's spirit was gone and at peace, but she wasn't sure what would remain of the body she'd left behind.

Once they reached the second floor, they edged by the kicked-in door and into the office. Their mother was still there in the same place, but she looked the way Stella would have expected a body to look after four years.

Only her bones were left, her clothes were dusty and faded, and the blood on the floor was a dry, discolored stain. Mattie and Lavinia let out breaths, and the three girls leaned in together.

"We'll bury her, just like you said," Lavinia told Mattie. "She's been in Archie's mansion long enough."

"Although," Lloyd said, "since he's gone now, this mansion ain't really *his* no more."

Stella's eyes widened. "You're right. It's not." She dug her hand in her pocket, drew out the paper, and turned to Lavinia. "It's *yours*. The land, the orchard, the mill. Everything. Archie left it to you."

Lavinia took the paper from Stella and read it over. Then she raised her head, her brow furrowed. "But Archie didn't sign this."

"That doesn't matter. I'll forge his name."

"Stella," Mattie said, peering at her, "even if it's been a few years since anyone has seen Archie's signature, how can you be certain we'd get away with that?"

Stella took the paper, turned it over, and pointed to the stamp on the back so everyone could see. It was the name and address of the lawyer who had drawn up the legal document—Mr. Charles A. Coberly, Esquire.

"Mr. Coberly happens to have a particular fondness for moonshine. He's a loyal customer who wouldn't dream of questioning the girl who provides what he needs." She grinned at Lloyd, who grinned back, and then lifted her chin and smirked at her sisters. "Who said crime doesn't pay?"

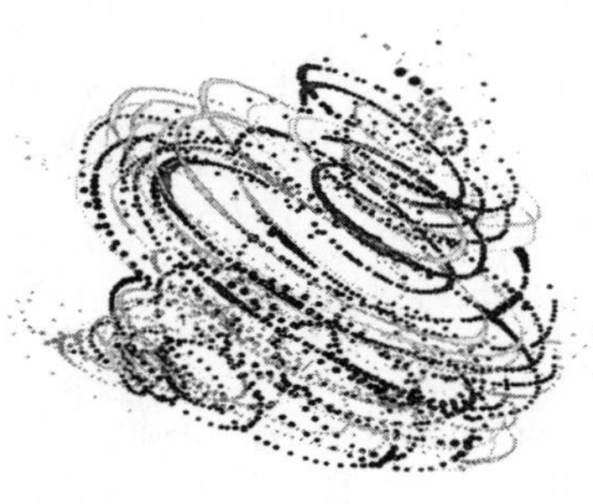

EPILOGUE

The crisp, September breeze blew through the gaps from the missing boards on the mill's ground floor. Perhaps when winter came, Stella would buy more wood and replace them. For now, she enjoyed the scent of ripening apples and newly turned leaves on the wind. It paired nicely with the thick, yeasty warmth of the still beside her. Jane had just finished the latest batch of applejack—a liquor distilled from concentrated cider rather than corn and sugar, like moonshine—and Stella was counting and labeling the jars. Mattie had been the one to come up with the idea.

"It was especially popular during the colonial period," she'd told Stella. "I bet I can find some books about it at the library. George Washington distilled his own at Mount Vernon."

At that, Stella had rolled her eyes and pretended to shove a pair of invisible glasses up Mattie's nose. But she'd been right. Now that they had access to apples, applejack was cheaper to make than moonshine, though Jane still made that as well, as the demand remained. But applejack tasted better and mixed with more drinks, so they were able to charge more for it, and no one else was making it, so they had no competition.

"You 'bout done? Everyone's here."

Stella looked up to see Lloyd smiling and leaning against the doorframe. His knuckles had healed since the incident with Mr. Donaldson, who had been released from the hospital with no memory of his attack. Stella doubted even a beating like that would change his ways, but at least Mrs. Woodrow was safe. When Stella and her sisters moved to the mill, they knew Aunt Elsa would need help at the boarding house, so they suggested Mrs. Woodrow. Aunt Elsa offered her room and board in exchange for help cooking and cleaning, and she jumped at the chance.

"Just finishing the last jar," Stella said, marking the lid. Then she rose and brushed her hands off on her skirt. "Where are Mattie and Lavinia?"

"Gettin' ready. Apparently, they both bought new dresses for the occasion. I'm kinda curious. I've never seen Mattie in a dress."

Stella set her hands on her hips and raised an eyebrow. "Oh really? *Mattie's* the one you're looking forward to seeing tonight?"

Lloyd's smile broadened. "She'll be in a dress. That's a rare sight."

Stella picked up the lid from an empty jar and chucked it at him. He dodged it, laughing.

"You *have* seen her in a dress," Stella snapped. "At Archie's old-time parties, remember? All three of us had to wear those corseted nightmares to fit in."

"Ah," Lloyd said, shoving his hands into his pockets and sauntering toward her. "That explains it. I only remember one girl in a dress those nights."

Stella's lips quirked as he approached her. He smelled like Ivory soap and freshly-laundered cotton. But then her face fell. She shouldn't have mentioned Archie. The mill and the orchard were theirs now. Lavinia made apple juice and apple cider vinegar, which she and Mattie sold in town, along with the apples. Stella kept the books for that business and her sideline and also helped Jane with her bi-weekly brewing visits. Lloyd made deliveries for both enterprises, and all of them tended the orchard, which—thanks to Mattie's research on apple tree husbandry, "blessed touch," and plant-speak—was thriving as well as it could amid the dust storms and dry spells. It was hard work, and they were far from rich, but they made enough to get by, which—while a miracle in itself—had allowed for the greatest miracle of all.

Stella's father had come home.

Since arriving, he'd taken Lavinia's place at the juice press, giving her more time to clean and renovate the mansion, where they all lived. There were four bedrooms, but they currently used only three, as Stella and her sisters still preferred to sleep together in the largest room. Their father slept in the second largest, and Lloyd stayed in the third. Most of them avoided the office where their mother had died, but Lavinia purchased a rug to cover the bloodstain and was determined to remodel it into a sewing room—which their mother would have liked—or maybe one day, a nursery. After everything they'd been through, she'd discovered she possessed more strength and courage than she'd known, which had made her brave enough to reach out for her dreams. When she'd decided to accompany Mattie to sell their products in town, she'd said "I'll never meet anyone without showing my face," flashing a smile that told Stella she wasn't afraid to anymore.

As they'd promised, the three of them had buried their mother. Now she rested beside their late grandmother in the cemetery, and their father brought her flowers every Sunday. Though they'd omitted the magic parts, Stella and her sisters had told him and Aunt Elsa how they'd found their mother's body and the legal document in the abandoned mansion, as well as their "theory" about why she'd been there, how she died, and why Archie would have left everything to Lavinia. They'd prepared themselves for their father to be offended by the suggestion that Lavinia had been fathered by someone else, but he revealed he'd always known, though he hadn't known who the man was. When their mother told him she was pregnant after they became engaged, he told her he didn't care and didn't need any explanation. He loved her, and he would protect her. She would be his wife, and her child would be his.

"And you were," he had told Lavinia, tears in his eyes. "You *are*, and always will be."

Lavinia had smiled, cried as well, and thrown her arms around him, because—as she'd already told Stella and Mattie—a father by blood was nothing compared to a father by love.

Which was why mentioning Archie dirtied everything up for Stella. His memory was a shadow that came and went, and she knew it might never fade completely. She touched her mother's emerald necklace at her throat. Like everything they had gained, it remained a recovered treasure and a sad reminder at once.

"Hey," Lloyd said, reading her expression and lifting her chin. "Tonight's party will be better than any of those. I'm gonna teach you the Texas two-step."

"It's not as if we'll really have a *band*," Stella said, though she couldn't help but smile. "It's just Mr. Snider and Mr. Price playing the guitar and fiddle."

"It won't matter. You and I are always at our best when we're on the dance floor."

Stella's lips twitched. "I don't know that I necessarily agree with that."

"Oh yeah?" Lloyd asked, inclining his head, and Stella rose up and kissed him. He returned it, and she trailed her fingertips down his back, tracing the places where both smooth skin and scars lay beneath his shirt. She'd seen them by now, kissed them too, loving them the way she loved all of Lloyd, inside and out.

He cupped the back of her neck and brushed his thumb up over her throat. He knew she loved that, that it always gave her goosebumps.

She parted her lips, and he sighed against her mouth but then pulled back.

"Oh, sugar," he breathed, closing his eyes and pressing his forehead to hers. "If we keep this up, we won't make it to the party."

Stella knew he was right but pouted anyway. When he opened his eyes and saw her frown, he chuckled.

"Don't worry. Meet me here tonight after everyone's gone to sleep, and I'll make it up to you."

Stella fought the smile that tugged at her lips. "You promise?"

"Cross my heart."

His Coca-Cola eyes twinkled, and she allowed her smile to unfurl. Then she took his hand, and they walked outside. As they headed toward the mansion, she glanced at the hill above the cave. They'd repaired the hole in the cave wall and placed honeysuckle blossoms between the stones in honor of Archie's victims—both those inside and those in unmarked graves all over the country.

The sun was beginning to set when Stella and Lloyd reached the back of the mansion, but Jane and Mrs. Woodrow had already hung the paper lanterns. Currently, the two of them, along with Aunt Elsa and Stella's father, were carrying plates of food from inside the house to the buffet table for their Labor Day evening picnic. The scents of fried chicken, corn, and apple pie made Stella's mouth water.

"Coal! Come back here, boy!"

One of Mrs. Woodrow's twins—Stella wasn't sure if it was Amy or Amelia—dashed past Lloyd, chasing the big, black mutt they'd taken in. The other twin, who was playing with Jasper on a quilt, called out, "Amy, if you'd stop chasing him, he'd stop running away from you."

"Coal," Amy yelled again as the dog splashed into the creek. She sighed and turned to her sister, waving a piece of checkered cloth. "I thought he'd look smart in this bandana."

Lloyd smiled and strolled over to her. "You want me to help you catch him?"

She beamed and nodded, and they ran toward the creek.

"I bet Lloyd jumps in."

Stella turned to see Lavinia walking down the porch steps. She was wearing a bright pink dress that looked stunning with her hair, as well as their mother's pearl earrings.

"He won't jump in," Mattie said, hopping down the porch steps behind her. She looked almost like a woman in her navy-blue dress and their mother's opal ring, which she no longer had to wear on her thumb as it finally fit her fingers.

Lavinia rolled her eyes. "Thank goodness you're starting school tomorrow. Then we'll only have to put up with your clairvoyance in the evenings."

Stella raised her eyebrows, impressed by the jibe, but Mattie sighed and shook her head.

"I'm leaving detailed instructions for you two about caring for the trees. If you don't want to talk to them, fine. I can do that after school. But you need to remember—"

"We'll be fine," Stella assured her. "We've been caring for them alongside you all this time. We know what to do, and so do Lloyd and Daddy."

Mattie bunched her lips to the side. "Okay. But I'm leaving the list. Just in case."

"Can I sing to the trees?" Lavinia asked.

"I know you're joking, but that would actually be even better," Mattie replied, raising her chin.

"I plan on talking dirty to them," Stella said. "Turn those apples really red."

Lavinia snorted with laughter while Mattie tried—and failed—to hide her smile.

Next year, she would leave for college, but Stella knew the three of them would always be close, no matter where they went. And for now, Stella was already doing what she loved—running a business. She was still saving money, sometimes dreaming of expanding the mill, sometimes still dreaming of leaving. But for now, she was happy where she was.

"Looks like the band's settin' up."

All three of them turned to see Lloyd jogging toward them. Apparently, Mattie had been right, as he wasn't sopping wet. Beyond him, Stella saw Mr. Snider and Mr. Price, two of Aunt Elsa's boarders, tuning their instruments, a few of the other boarders gathered around them.

"I'll be right back," Lavinia said, trotting in their direction.

"Told you he wouldn't jump in," Mattie called after her. Then, she turned to Stella and Lloyd. "I'm going to see if Daddy needs help with the punch."

"Did you catch the dog?" Stella asked Lloyd as Mattie scampered off.

"Yeah. Turns out Coal is *not* fond of the bandana. I convinced Amy to leave it alone, for now."

Stella laughed. "Well, now you've seen Mattie in her dress."

"Did I? Again, I seem to see only one girl tonight."

He grinned and looked her over, and Stella's heart sped up. She'd recently bought a new dress. It hadn't been expensive, just a checkered-green, daytime dress. New shoes had been more important to her, and she'd decided to splurge on sleek, black pumps with stylish, Spanish heels. Unfortunately, those heels were currently sinking into the lawn.

"Blue night and you, alone with me
My heart has never known such ecstasy
Am I on earth, am I in heaven?"

Stella's lips parted at the sound of Lavinia's voice, and she turned to see her standing beside Mr. Snider and Mr. Price, who'd begun playing.

"Can it be the trees that fill the breeze
With rare and magic perfume?
Oh no, it isn't the trees, it's love in bloom"

She winked at Stella on the last line and then smiled at everyone else who'd stopped to listen. Stella's throat tightened as she watched Aunt Elsa and her father put their arms around each other and beam at Lavinia. Especially when her father reached up to brush away a tear from his eye.

"Wanna dance?"

Stella turned back to Lloyd, who'd extended his hand. Her chest expanded as she took it, but when he guided her onto the open lawn, her heels sank deeper into the earth. Maybe, once she'd saved enough, she would buy a proper, wooden dance floor. For now, the heels were impractical, and Stella was not. She reached down and slipped them off, curling her toes in the cool, damp grass.

"Can it be the spring that seems

To bring the stars right into this room?

Oh no, it isn't the spring, it's love in bloom"

Stella breathed Lloyd in as he took her waist and pulled her close. Then they moved to the music and to Lavinia's proud, soaring voice.

"Is it all a dream, the joy supreme

That came to us in the gloom?

You know it isn't a dream, it's love in bloom"

Stella smiled. It wasn't a dream or magic.

It was better.

ACKNOWLEDGMENTS

The first person I have to thank is my agent, Elizabeth Copps. When I say she never gave up on this book, I mean she *never* gave up on this book. She believed in it ever since I signed with her, and it exists today because of her determination to see it out in the world.

It also wouldn't be in the amazing shape it's in without my fantastic editor, Elana Gibson, who saw *Dust Spells*'s potential and took it to the next level.

I also couldn't be more grateful to Sue Arroyo and CamCat Books for their unbelievable support, breathtaking cover, and invaluable input from Rue Dickey, my sensitivity reader. *Dust Spells* truly found the perfect home.

I also have to thank my immediate and extended family, as this book wouldn't exist without them. My sons, Max and Leo, for inspiring me (and giving me the space to write when I needed it). My parents, Scott and Vicki, for supporting my storytelling even before I could read and write. My brother-in-law, Chaz, for his legal expertise, and my brother, David, for relaxation and soul rejuvenation. And of course, my sister, Megan, to whom this book about sisters is dedicated. As the song goes, my life would suck without you.

There are so many other people and places that made writing this book possible. The state of Kansas, my home for four decades now; my past and present high school students; my college creative writing teacher, Darcy Anne, who first told me I could do this; the public libraries in every town I've ever lived in; my uncle, James Bryan Smith, who always made me feel like I could be in the "author club;" my coffeemaker and tea kettle; my coworkers, particularly my English teacher comrades; and the music of The Civil Wars, Hozier, The Lumineers, and Taylor Swift.

Finally, thank you to *you* for reading. You're who all this is for, after all.

ABOUT THE AUTHOR

Andrea Lynn grew up performing on the stage but now directs behind the scenes as a high school English and drama teacher. She lives in Winfield, Kansas, with her two sons and loves tea, comfy hoodies, Broadway musicals, and of course, books.

If you enjoyed
Andrea Lynn's *Dust Spells*,
please consider leaving a review
to help our authors.

And check out
Inevitable Fate by Lindsay K. Bandy.

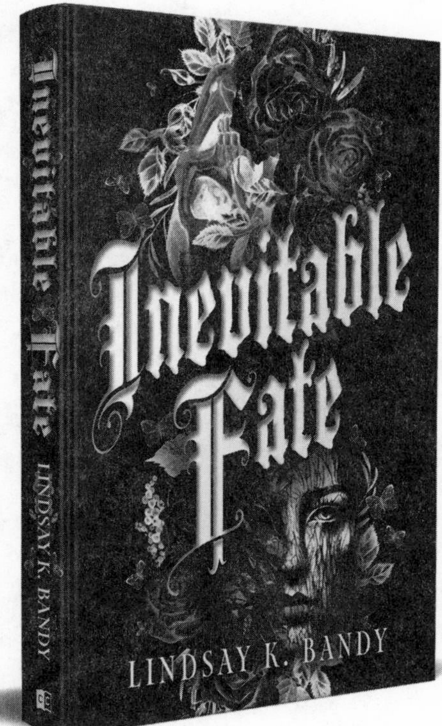

CHAPTER

I

If life was a highway, Evan Kiernan's consisted of riding shotgun while his mother inched along in the right lane of I-95, looking for an exit so his little sister could pee.

This time, they were headed to Manhattan. It should have only been a two and a half hour drive from Lancaster, Pennsylvania, but in Evan's experience, what *should be* rarely translated to reality. For example, kids *should* know who their fathers are. Diamond rings (plural) *should* lead to weddings (preferably singular), instead of pawn shops and moving trucks (plural). Five-year-olds *should* have a greater bladder capacity, and seventeen-year-olds *should* still be in high school—not riding shotgun while their mothers drive them to freshman move-in day at NYU.

But maybe, for once, Evan Kiernan was about to be exactly where he should be. According to his mother, the Promising Young Artist program was his destiny, as if the sparkle-winged gods of the arts had arranged for his early college acceptance. Really, it was her, conspiring with his art teacher, Mr. Burns, to fill out the application behind his back. Evan had been sure he had no shot in hell at getting into the elite program, which accepted one upcoming senior. *One.* But somehow, against all odds, they'd chosen him. He was still convinced it was some sort of mistake, due to his mother's exaggerated belief that her son was exceptional and Mr. Burns' flair for the dramatic.

But the written application wasn't the main criteria. His portfolio had gotten him into the program, and he couldn't deny being proud of that, even if he wasn't sure he was really Greenwich Village material. And as Hailey kicked the back of his seat in time with "Look What You Made Me Do" on the radio and wailed about needing to pee for the thousandth time, he couldn't deny his that it would be amazing to have a little time to himself for once.

"Rest stop ahead!" his mom exclaimed, removing her hands from the steering wheel to applaud as she read the sign. "One more mile, okay, Hails? Envision the desert. *Be* the camel, baby." She brought her thumbs and forefingers together as if meditating before taking hold of the wheel again.

Evan glanced at the speedometer. They were crawling along at six miles per hour. He ran a hand through the dark curls flopping into his eyes, then pressed his palm against the freshly trimmed sides, trying to ignore the small feet pounding his back. The song switched to "God is a Woman," and when his mother started singing along with Ariana Grande, he cringed and tried to go somewhere else—anywhere else—in his mind. He could have envisioned the desert, or been the camel, but instead, he went back to Advanced Drawing class.

To the day he drew *her*.

The drawing that changed everything.

It was the first day at Pennwood High School. They'd just moved out of their mother's ex-fiancée Dave's house and into a little Cape Cod with peeling white paint and a picket fence missing a few teeth. That morning, he'd pulled rumpled jeans and a black-and-red flannel shirt from the box at the foot of his bed, wishing for another ten years of sleep. Hailey had woken him multiple times through the night, scared and disoriented in her new room. His mom was downstairs already, in her bathrobe and slippers, cooking the traditional fresh-start breakfast/peace offering. He wondered, sometimes, if she'd chosen the realty profession just to have the inside scoop on immediately available rental properties.

"You want me to iron your shirt?" she'd asked over her shoulder while flipping a pancake.

"Nah." He gave her a sideways hug with one arm and reached for the coffee pot with the other.

She rubbed her cheek where his had brushed against it. "You should shave."

"I can't find the razors," he said, even though he hadn't really looked. "It's fine."

"Come on." She cracked an egg into sizzling butter. "Don't you want to make a good first impression?" She said it a little too brightly, and even without his contacts in, he could see from the puffiness of her eyes that she'd been crying already this morning. He wanted to throttle Dave.

First impressions had lost their charm years ago, but transferring to Pennwood had been easy enough. After reviewing his portfolio the previous week, the head of the art department had agreed to place him in Advanced Drawing, Ceramics, and Advanced Painting Techniques.

"Honestly," Mr. Burns had said during Evan's registration appointment, glancing between his sketchbook and his mother. "He's probably more advanced than the staff here. Have you considered art school?"

"He's always been exceptional," his mom had gushed, while Evan looked at his shoes. She'd insisted he be tested for the gifted program in kindergarten, and ever since, she'd been using that word. *Exceptional.* She might as well have called him an alien. Exceptional was just another word for different. He'd read somewhere that all great artists and writers feel that they experience the world fundamentally differently from everyone else, and he assumed that's why so many great artists became alcoholics and vagrants and mental patients. But Evan liked Mr. Burns, whose easy smile didn't seem to be covering up psychotic tendencies. And best of all, he was gay, which meant his mom wouldn't be trying to line up any dates with another one of his art teachers.

His first assignment in Advanced Drawing class was to draw a face entirely from memory, so Evan closed his eyes and tried to picture Hailey. He couldn't believe how hard it was to conjure up a detailed image of his own sister's face. She had brown eyes like his, but how far apart were they in relation to the corners of her mouth? Her nose was . . . kid-sized, but what was the exact shape?

Glancing around at his classmates' work, they seemed to be having the same problem, laughing at each other's attempts to draw friends or teachers from other classes. People they recognized, but who were all strangers to him.

Mr. Burns went behind his desk to pop a CD into an ancient-looking stereo system, and suddenly the deep thrum of electronic trance music transformed the atmosphere of the room. The rhythm became hypnotic as the beats per minute steadily increased, and the notes blurred, like a dream. Evan stared at the backs of his eyelids, feeling like he was lost in some sort of European dance club. He tipped his chin toward the ceiling, and flashes of red flared through the darkness. Splotchy afterimages danced like flames, like the time they went camping with Dave and Hailey wouldn't quit shining a flashlight in his face and gave him a migraine.

But then slowly, like a Polaroid picture, a pair of eyes began to develop. Not brown and familiar. Not his mom's or his sister's or anyone's from his old school. These eyes were a startling jade green, peering at him around a huge, heavy black door.

A girl.

Her nose and the apples of her cheeks were sprinkled with freckles, and her mouth was open in a tiny gasp of surprise, revealing a small space between her two front teeth. She was frozen in this expression, as if he'd knocked on her door and snapped a photograph as she opened it, shocked to find a stranger there.

He was afraid that if he opened his eyes, he'd lose the image, so he fumbled for a pencil and began drawing furiously without looking at the paper.

Who was she? Why was she opening the door? Would she invite him in? He didn't want to be a stranger to this girl.

But as soon as he finished the last wavy strand of her soft, black hair, it was as if the door closed.

The sound of murmuring and stools scraping the floor brought him back. When he opened his eyes, the whole class was gathered around his table, staring in silence.

It was only pencil, but the luminosity of the eyes was apparent even without color. He'd captured the girl's surprise, and there was something so perfectly adorable about it.

"Who is she?" someone whispered.

Evan opened his mouth, then closed it again. He couldn't tell an entire classroom full of seniors that he had no idea who she was. Not on his first day at a new school. Probably not ever.

"Just . . . a girl I used to know," he said with a shrug, and looked into her pencil-drawn eyes again, overcome with a sense of wonder.

She was beautiful, but not in a magazine cover way.

She was beautiful because she was so . . . so . . . real.

And that, he knew, was ridiculous, because she was absolutely not real. He was sure he'd never seen that girl before in his life.

He would have remembered.

Ten months later, here he was, pulling into a rest stop in New Jersey with his mom and sister on his way to NYU because of her. *The Green-Eyed Girl*, painted life-sized in oil, became the centerpiece of his portfolio. The piece that earned the attention of his program mentor, Dr. Vanessa Mortakis.

Absolutely luminous, she'd called it in the acceptance letter. *Intensely realistic and gorgeously sensitive. I can't wait to work with you in New York.*

When Dr. Mortakis strode into the admissions office later that afternoon, Evan exchanged a surprised glance with his mom: Hourglass figure in a tight black dress, glossy ebony hair to her waist, and blood-red heels that defined her calves beyond professional levels. None of that had shown up in her headshot.

"Evan Kiernan!" she exclaimed warmly, as if greeting an old friend. "Welcome to NYU!"

"Thank you so much." He shook her cool, slender hand, and her delicate bracelets jangled. "This is my mom, Melissa. And my sister, Hailey."

"You must be so proud," Dr. Mortakis said, clasping hands with Evan's mother, then bending down to shake with Hailey, too. "And you must be really proud of your big brother."

Hailey bounced up on her toes and nodded, and Evan felt a twinge in his chest. Ever since the acceptance letter arrived, his mom had been waving off his concerns about the cost of after-school care for Hailey and who would drive her to ballet or tuck her in when their mom had to work late. *You're her brother, not her dad*, she kept insisting. *It's your job to grow up and live your life. It's my job to take care of the two of you. Okay?*

"You are cute as button!" Dr. Mortakis exclaimed, booping Hailey's nose, and she giggled. Clearly, the professor hadn't been along for the car ride.

"He's so good with her," his mom bragged as they took their seats in the admissions office. "He even illustrates little stories for her."

Dr. Mortakis' eyes brightened. "Really? Well, we have an excellent illustration department. That could be a great option for you."

Evan smiled politely, but kicked his mom under the table, hoping she wouldn't pull out any doodled-on receipts or grocery lists from her purse to display The Adventures of Kitty-Corn. Whenever they were sitting in the waiting room at the doctor's office or waiting for their food at a restaurant, Kitty-Corn embarked upon another zany adventure. It kept Hailey occupied, but it wasn't exactly Promising Young Artist material.

"Let's take a look at your course load for this semester," Dr. Mortakis continued, and Melissa Kiernan's purse remained mercifully on the floor. "I'll answer any questions you have, give you a little tour, and then let you settle in before classes start up on Monday. Okay?"

She donned a pair of red reading glasses and opened his welcome packet on the desk. Evan's heart raced with anticipation, making his face tingle a little. He was really here. Really going to college early. Really a promising young artist.

"So, all of our incoming freshman take Freshman Composition and World History first semester. You'll get a science Gen-Ed out of the way with Bio, and then Fundamentals of 2-D is a prerequisite for upper-level studio art classes. However, I thought I'd sign off on one upper-level art history class, so you're enrolled in Mythology in Modern Art, as well. I teach that one, and I'm here any time you need me, okay? If you're ever feeling concerned or overwhelmed or even just homesick, I'm only a text, email, or two-block walk away. Melissa," she said, covering his mom's hand with hers. "I'm going to take great care of your son."

"I know you will," his mom said, smiling, but Evan could see the tears in her eyes already.

A few hours later, his clothes were unpacked and his desk was set up, and she and Hailey were all-out weeping in the doorway.

"This was your idea, remember?" he said, trying to make her laugh, and it worked. "If you don't want me stay, I can just tell Dr. Mortakis what a forger you really are—"

"You'll do no such thing," she laughed, and kissed his cheek. "And I'm not repentant."

After they left, he sat alone on the twin XL mattress, waiting for his roommate to arrive. Waiting for his new life to begin. He was used to fresh starts and new schools, but this was different. As long as he kept his scholarship, New York would be his home for the next four years. He'd never lived anywhere for four whole years. And after graduation, if he liked it here, he could stay.

For seventeen years, his life had felt like painting by someone else's numbers, waiting for grown-ups to tell him where to color next.

Watching the sun go down over New York City, he let it sink in: He wasn't someone else's canvas anymore. Now, he was the hand, holding the brush.